P9-DNY-364

DAKOTA

Also by Gwen Florio

Montana

DAKOTA

GWEN FLORIO

The Permanent Press
Sag Harbor, NY 11963

For information, address:
The Permanent Press
4170 Noyac Road
Sag Harbor, NY 11963
www.thepermanentpress.com

Library of Congress Cataloging-in-Publication Data

Florio, Gwen—
Dakota / Gwen Florio.
pages cm
ISBN 978-1-57962-362-3
1. Women journalists—Fiction. 2. Drug traffic—Fiction. 3. Missing persons—Fiction. 4. Sihasapa Indians—North Dakota—Fiction. 5. Indian women—Fiction. 6. Murder—Investigation—Fiction. I. Title.

PS3606.L664D35 2014
813'.6—dc23 2013043538

Printed in the United States of America

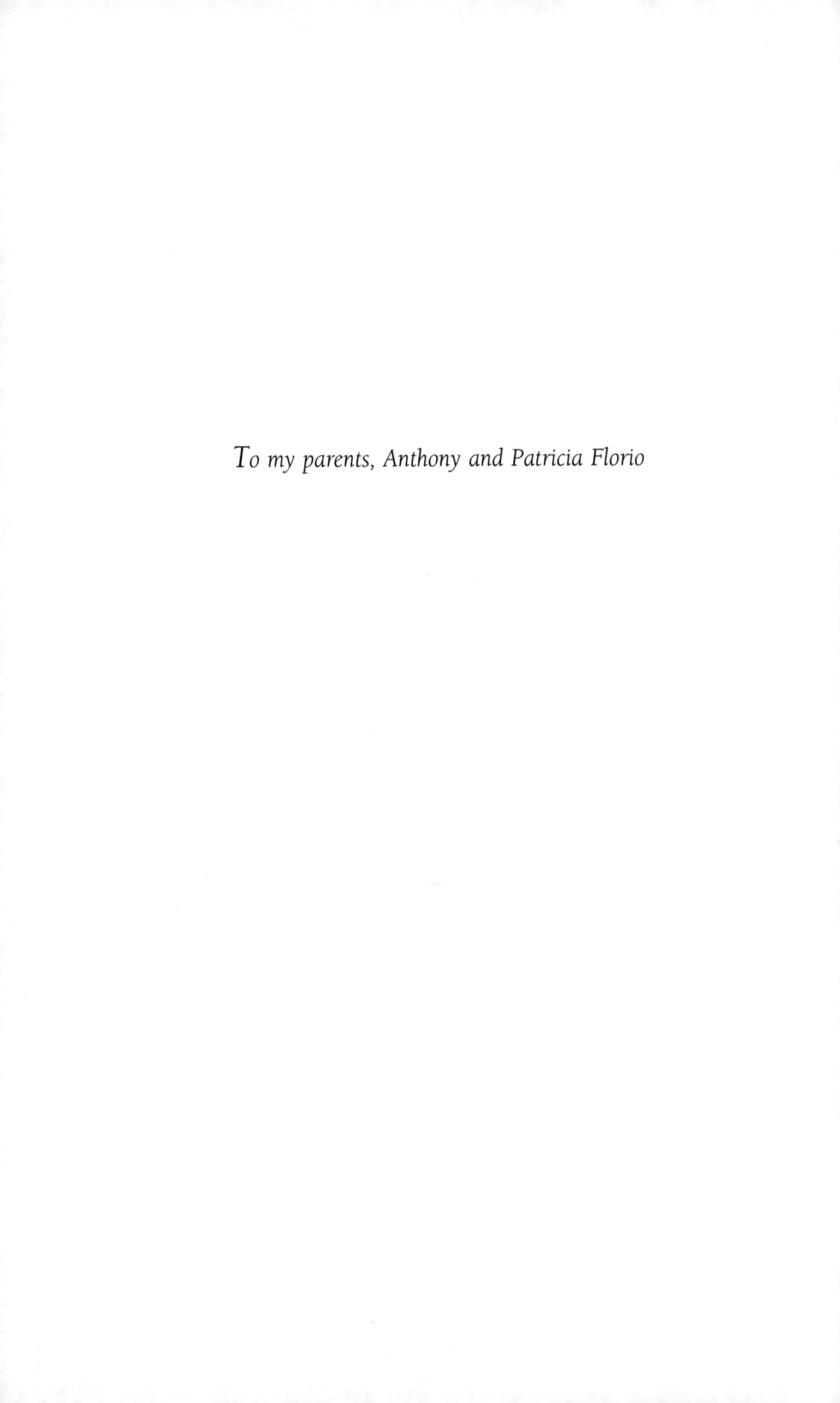

To my parents, Anthony and Patricia Florio

ACKNOWLEDGMENTS

I'm so grateful for the support and expertise of Permanent Press publishers Martin and Judith Shepard, agent Barbara Braun, editor Judy Sternlight, and copy editor Barbara Anderson. Lon Kirschner designed another terrific cover and Shaila Abudullah is the best of website gurus.

This book benefited immensely from the input of the following:

The Creel crew at the Guthrie cabin on the Rocky Mountain Front, the best place in the world to write and to talk about writing: Alex Sakariassen, Bill Oram, Jamie Rogers, Camilla Mortensen, Matthew LaPlante, Aaron Falk and Stephen Dark.

Journalist Amy Sisk for her guidance on life in the very heart of the oil patch, and Jerry and Maryellen Navratil for their stark accounts of life on the edge of the patch.

On the Blackfeet Nation, Jessica Racine and Pat Cross Guns for pointing a clueless writer who walked into their workplace in the right direction, which in turn led me to Marvin Weatherwax and Boss Racine, who generously provided much-needed cultural information.

A young woman calling herself Chloe who detailed the workaday world of exotic dancers. And yes, I freely embroidered upon it.

Along those lines, although many locations in the book are real, others—such as St. Anthony's Church—are fictional. However, a similarly unnerving statue of Saint Lucy stood in the stairwell of my childhood church in Dover, Delaware.

Love and gratitude to Scott Crichton, who deftly piloted a Subaru among the towering truck traffic in the patch as I scribbled notes; and to my parents, Pat and Tony Florio, and my children, Sean and Kate Breslin, all fine writers and downright carnivorous readers.

PROLOGUE

The truck driver hunched and swore, peering through the slanting assault of snow. The steering wheel dug into his potato-sack gut. The teenager beside him looked away. She was small and breakable-looking and the sex between them, in the confines of the cab, had been problematic.

"I can't see a goddamn thing," he said. "I never seen it snow like this."

"It's not snowing." Her voice was hoarse, as though despite her cries of feigned pleasure, she hadn't used it much recently. "It's just a ground blizzard."

"Say what?"

"It's when the wind picks up the snow and blows it around." As if to prove her point, the curtain of white draping the windshield briefly parted. Beyond, all was black.

"I never heard of any such thing. I worked on a refinery down in Louisiana where we had snakes by the bushel. But it beats this cold and snow you all got up here. At least you can kill a snake. But there's no getting away from this. Speaking of which—" He straightened and looked in the rearview mirror, then hit a button. The side window slid down halfway. Cold blasted through the cab. The girl ducked away. The driver scraped at the sheet of ice dulling the side mirror. He yanked his arm back inside and raised the window and blew on his fingers. "Huh."

"Shouldn't you be watching the road? You just told me you're not used to driving in this kind of weather."

"I was checking on that guy behind us."

The girl turned her head so quickly that skeins of black hair lashed the dashboard. She'd been slouched against the passenger-side door, as far from the man as she could get, but now she sat up straight and hitched an inch toward him. "What guy?"

"Truck that's been on our ass ever since we stopped so's you could pee."

The girl checked her own side mirror. The wind quieted again and the swirling snow lay down. She saw a blur of light. "There are trucks all over this road," she protested. "Every day. Nothing but trucks." She reached into the pouch of her oversize sweatshirt and ran her fingertip along the vane of the spear-like feather there, imagining she could feel the place where its color changed from white to bronze. She forced her gaze away from the lights behind them and stared through the windshield as though somehow, despite the dark, she could see the mountains ahead that had sheltered her people since the beginning of time. They were close, she knew, their presence signaling safety.

The driver spoke in the querulous manner that afflicted some big men. "When was the last truck you saw tonight? Nobody's on the road but us and our friend back there. All those other drivers got more sense. Daddy always said my dick would get me in trouble. Trouble's one thing. Killed's another."

"What do you mean, killed?" The girl's voice jumped an octave. She moved closer to him still.

"I mean I could end up sliding right off this road, smash my fool head to pieces and your pretty one, too." He touched a meaty hand to her cheek.

She twisted and looked again at the mirrors. The lights winked behind them. "How do you know it's the same truck?"

"It's riding high. Most trucks coming out of the oil patch are full, traveling down lower to the ground. That, and the fact it stuck with me on this little detour we're taking to drop you off. Might be he's lost. If he's still with us when we stop, I'll talk to him. Tough night to be out here alone."

The girl's thin chest rose and fell. The other trucker wasn't lost. Her hands scrabbled at the seat. "Listen. I changed my mind. I'm getting out here."

The man gaped. "Girl, are you crazy? It's only four, five miles yet to the reservation. I'll drop you off there like you asked."

The lights behind them drew nearer. The girl stared into their reflected glare. "A big bend's coming up, and then the road goes uphill. I'll get out once we're around the curve. You've got to slow way down, but don't stop. If you do, you'll never get the truck up the hill."

"You don't even have a coat. You'll freeze to death. Let me drop you where there's people."

"I know a shortcut." Her lips thinned and tightened in a mirthless smile. There was no shortcut. But she'd take the storm over the menace creeping closer behind them. "Just let me out. Here's the curve." A yellow warning sign depicting a fishhook bend flashed past. The man worked at the shift. The gears ground down. The girl put her hand on the door. The truck crawled around the curve. The lights behind them disappeared.

"Tell a single soul you ever saw me," the girl said, "and I'll tell the world what a tiny, worthless dick you've got."

She pulled the feather from her sweatshirt, shoved open the door and flew into the night.

CHAPTER ONE

The dead girl in the snowbank could have been asleep, one hand curled beneath her cheek, hair feathered across the pillowy drift. Only the cruisers' blue-and-red lights, flashing across her face, disturbed her tranquility. Lola Wicks extracted a notebook from deep within her parka and edged into the circle of uniforms surrounding the body.

"What's going on?" Nobody replied. Lola stepped between two tribal policemen. "Good Christ. It's Judith Calf Looking."

One of the officers detached himself from the group. "What the hell are you doing here?" The tribal cops shifted their attention from the dead girl to a live face-off between sheriff and reporter.

"I heard it on the scanner. What are *you* doing here? Aren't we on the rez? This is their turf." She nodded toward the cops. They dipped their chins in return.

But for the difference in uniform, Charlie Laurendeau, the county's first Indian sheriff, could have been one of them, brown and broad, easy on his feet despite his heft. Lola floundered toward him through the snow, mentally cursing the impulse that had led her to move from Baltimore to Montana at the end of summer, just weeks before winter blew in. Charlie met her halfway, careless of his steps, steady nonetheless. "County automatically gets notified whenever there's a felony. There's no saying that's what this is. But just in case, the feds are on their way, too."

The tribal cops' faces went still and stern at his words. Even in her short time in Montana, Lola had learned that decades worth of turf negotiations between tribal and outside law enforcement had spun a web of local, state, federal and Indian nation regulations that seemed to hinder any single agency's ability to deal with crime involving the Blackfeet. Charlie's tightrope walk as both an Indian and the sheriff of the white county that largely surrounded the reservation served only to make each of those roles more difficult. Indignant Blackfeet mothers whose sons went astray off the reservation and ended up in Charlie's jail accused him of forgetting his roots; white townspeople groused that during Charlie's tenure as sheriff, Indian kids were getting away with everything short of murder. And then Lola had come along.

"I thought you weren't listening to the scanner anymore," Charlie said. "Hasn't Jan handled all the crime stories ever since—"

"Ever since you and I started sleeping together?"

The tribal cops looked up. Lola could only imagine the laughter that would burst forth in the retelling. Lola had met Charlie that summer, when she'd traveled to Montana to visit a friend who worked there as a reporter, only to find her dead—murdered—upon Lola's arrival. During the investigation into Mary Alice's death, Lola and Charlie had become close, so close that he'd been able to convince her to leave her newspaper job in Baltimore for one at the small daily paper in Magpie that covered the news for a county whose population wouldn't have comprised a single Baltimore neighborhood. At the time, with Lola still smarting from being downsized from an overseas posting to Kabul, it had seemed like a perfect kiss-off to the Baltimore paper. Now, especially as the reality of a Montana winter settled in, she wasn't so sure.

Charlie took Lola's arm and tugged her a few steps away. "Lola. For God's sake."

"Jan's out on another story," she said. "Besides, you know I cover the reservation. The scanner only said something about a body. It didn't say anything about a crime. Is this suspicious? Because if it is, I'll pull Jan off whatever she's working on." She tapped her pencil against her teeth—it hadn't taken her long to learn that ink froze when the temperature dove to single digits and below—and waited for his answer. The shapeless coat, its still-slick synthetic surface proclaiming recent purchase, hung halfway to her knees. She was almost as tall as the men, nearing six feet. But where they were thickset through shoulder and thigh, solid as the grain elevators that marked the surrounding High Plains towns, Lola's gangly frame swam within the outsize parka. A fresh blast of wind sent her staggering. The men moved not at all. Her breath caught and froze in the curls escaping her wool watch cap. Tiny icicles tinkled when she gave Charlie an encouraging nod. The sheriff was bareheaded, lips blueing in the subzero cold. Exhaustion knuckled bruises beneath his eyes, and dug cruel grooves from mouth to chin. He'd been up most of the night dealing with a fatal semitrailer crash, and now this. The wind wrapped his uniform pants around his legs. Lola had watched him dress that morning, holding the blankets tight beneath her chin as he pulled on a pair of silk long johns, then the traditional waffle weave, before finally stuffing his legs into pants and then starting the whole process again with sock liners and two pairs of socks. The radio announced twenty below. "They say some cowboys wear pantyhose under their jeans to keep warm," he'd said when he caught her looking. "Me, I never went that far. But on a day this cold, I'm tempted."

Judith was long past feeling the cold. Which was good, Lola thought, as she studied the men's pants Judith wore, rolled into sloppy cuffs around bare feet stuck into cheap sneakers. Lola's years as a foreign correspondent had featured war zones distinguishable mainly by the inventiveness of their butchery, experience recent enough to make her grateful for the mercifully intact corpses in her own country. One of the tribal cops pulled a camera from within his coat, aimed it at Judith's body, and clicked twice. The dime-size star tattoo on her neck, tucked just below her earlobe, shone newly distinct against skin gone waxen. He tucked the camera back inside his coat, walked a few steps for a different angle, took the camera out and clicked quickly before replacing it against the warmth of his body. Something thin and lacy fluttered beneath Judith's hooded sweatshirt. Lola stooped for a better view. "It almost looks like a nightie," she said to Charlie. "You never said whether you think someone killed her. What's that in her hand?"

"An eagle feather."

"That's odd. Isn't it?"

"Stop fishing, Lola. She probably died of exposure. We haven't turned her over yet, but there's no obvious injury. Maybe she was trying to hitchhike home from wherever she ran away to last year. If somebody dropped her off at the crossroads in the middle of the night, the cold would've gotten her before anyone else came along, given that storm last night. It's a shame. She didn't have much farther to go."

"If she was hitchhiking," Lola asked, "what's she doing all the way out here? Did an eagle drop her from the sky?" The tribal cops' heads swiveled as one, turning to take in the road a quarter mile away. Lola had bumped across the prairie's frozen ruts in her pickup, a ride that challenged the very fillings in her teeth.

Charlie didn't respond to her question. He dropped his mittens into the snow, snapped blue latex disposable gloves over his hands and stooped beside Judith's body. He hooked a fingertip in the sweatshirt's sleeve and drew it up to Judith's elbow. Checking to see if Judith had been using again, Lola thought. The girl's struggles with whatever drug was most easily available at any given moment were public knowledge. Lola leaned over Charlie and looked. "Hell," she said. Bruises with pinpoint centers laced the soft pale skin of Judith's inner arm. Something else, too. Charlie's breath caught. The tribal cops crowded close. Charlie ignored the track marks and ran a gloved finger over a tilted heart shape. The lines were raised and brown and shiny.

"That's new. Right?" Lola said.

"Yes." Charlie bit the word off.

"That is one messed-up tattoo."

"It's not a tattoo," Charlie said. "It's a brand."

Charlie's announcement occasioned an outbreak of subdued activity. A tribal officer turned his head and hawked and spat. Another walked a slow circle in the snow. A third took off his gloves, blew in them, and put them back on. Lola stood and bent backward from the waist, as though to ease the nonexistent crick in her back. Only Charlie remained motionless, kneeling beside Judith's body as though in prayer.

"I guess it's the latest trend," he said. "Tattoos and piercings weren't enough."

"But Judith didn't really go for those," Lola pointed out. "Other than the star. And earrings—everybody's got those. Everybody." She liked reminding Charlie of the faint dimple in his earlobe, a reminder of a youthful exuberance she could hardly imagine. As far as she could tell, Charlie had been born old.

Charlie stood and peeled off the gloves. He threw them into the snow and kicked at them. The sun hung pale and indistinct within the mottled sky, lowering over a line of mountains whose names bespoke their history as Blackfeet territory, despite the fact that the reservation's whiteman-drawn boundaries relegated the mountains to nearby Glacier National Park. Lola studied their shapes. Somewhere over there was Sinopah. As a way of filling the long winter evenings, she'd set herself the challenge of learning the names of the more imposing peaks, poring over atlases and online photos, and querying Charlie as to their Blackfeet names. Her most recent focus, Sinopah—a woman's name, the daughter of a chief—was known for the perfection of its shape, the snow-capped triangle of a child's drawing. But to Lola, a born flatlander, all the peaks looked distinctive. A gust shoved exhaust fumes into her face. The cruisers and Lola's pickup sat running nearby. Lola knew each vehicle's heater was blowing full blast. She stuck her hands under her arms and hopped on one foot, then the other. She wore padded arctic boots with layers of synthetic stuff between her feet and the snow, along with the requisite multiple pairs of socks, and still her toes were icy. "Does Joshua know yet? It's going to be tough on him, losing a twin."

"We called the tribal offices as soon as I saw who it was," one of the cops said. "They said they'd send somebody over to tell him. That was about an hour ago."

Lola groped at her sleeve until her watch emerged. She peered at it and pulled the cuff back down over the exposed skin. "So you all got here around three? Who found her?"

Charlie's boots squeaked across the snow. He opened the door of Lola's truck. A black and white dog peered out, then shrank back into the warmth. "Hey! You're letting all the heat out. Bub's going to freeze." Lola kicked her way through the snow and tried to wrest the door from his hands.

"Forget it, Lola. You're not doing this story. This isn't officially a death by natural causes until I say it is. And I'm nowhere near that point. You go back to the newspaper and do whatever you were doing before you started listening to the scanner. Have Jan give me a call. I'll give her what I've got."

The heat inside the truck enfolded Lola like a blanket. She was not entirely sorry when Charlie slammed the door behind her. Bub stood up and braced his forepaws against the dash and balanced expertly on his single hind leg as Lola steered between drifts and wind-scoured earth, hard as bare rock. The road was not much of an improvement. Wind buffeted the truck. Snow slid across the blacktop. Lola drove down the middle, pulling into her own lane whenever a tanker truck blew past. This happened frequently. Lola stopped at a crossroads. Arrows nailed to a fence post indicated the county seat of Magpie in one direction, the Blackfeet Nation in the other. Lola dialed her cellphone.

"*Magpie Daily Express*," a voice of indeterminate gender warbled in her ear.

"Hey, Finch."

The voice cooled considerably. "Lola. I'll switch you over to Jan."

Lola began without preamble when Jan picked up. "They found Judith Calf Looking in the snow just past Deadman's Curve. Charlie thinks she probably froze to death, but he can't say for sure. So I can't write the story." Jan's reply started loud and got louder. Lola held the phone away from her ear. "Yes. I know I never should have slept with him. Do we have to have this conversation again? Look, I'll grab your town council meeting tonight if you cover this. Thanks." She ended the call and looked at the phone. Its face had fogged in the heat of the truck. She rubbed it. It wasn't yet four. The council meeting wouldn't start until seven.

"An eagle feather?" she said.

The feathers were reserved for the most solemn occasions. Warriors received them upon returning from Afghanistan or Iraq. They might be presented to family members after the death of a person who had helped the tribe in significant ways. Or given to people for particularly significant graduations, or election to office. But not to a drugged-out teenager. Lola let herself wonder, for just a second, if Judith might have stolen the feather. Impossible, she knew. Feathers were so sacred that if one fell to the ground, only a veteran or someone specially designated could retrieve it.

She turned the truck toward the reservation. It was only right that she pay her respects to Judith's family, she reassured herself. And if she happened to glean some answers in the process, well, that would be just fine, too.

CHAPTER TWO

Lola parked a block away from the Calf Looking home. Not much more than a couple of hours had passed since Charlie called the tribal offices, but news traveled the reservation with a speed that put the Internet to shame. Pickups—some new, most far from it—and sprung-suspension cars were already double-parked along the street in a signal that the multiday process of a reservation funeral had already begun. Lola urged Bub from the truck. He took two steps, tilted onto his remaining hind leg to pee, then hopped back in.

"Back in awhile," she told him. When winter first set in, she'd worried about leaving Bub in the truck. Charlie had pointed out the scores of cattle and horses that overwintered outdoors, as well as the ranch dogs who seemed to spend their lives in the beds of pickups, no matter what the weather. "He won't freeze," he'd reassured her. "And you do him no favors by having him spend too much time indoors. He'll lose his winter coat. And he needs his just as much as you need yours."

Lola swung her legs wide in the best approximation of a jog she could manage in her swaddling gear and caught up with a knot of women entering the house. Inside, the air was tropical. By the time Lola had shucked out of her parka and kicked off her boots, adding both to the heaps by the front door, sweat slicked her face. The house, like all the reservation prefabs, was cramped at its best. On this evening, it had gone claustrophobic—at least to Lola, who had yet to grow accustomed to the crush of relatives at each and every occasion of note. At least as far as she could tell, everyone was related in some way to everyone else; it seemed as though the entire reservation turned out for each graduation, each military sendoff and each funeral.

"It's a pain," Charlie had told her once, the affection in his tone belying the words. "As a kid, I could never get away with anything. Aunties everywhere. They'd feed you, sure, but they had their eye on you all the time."

Lola, an only child of only-children parents, couldn't fathom such a total-immersion experience of family life. Would it feel protected, cocoon-like? Or smothering? "A little of both," Charlie had allowed. She blotted her forehead on her sleeve and stood on her toes and searched the crowd for Joshua.

"Over there." Josephine deRoche pointed with pursed lips. Lola knew Josephine from covering tribal council meetings. As treasurer, Josephine managed the budget as meticulously as she did her own appearance. But the twin assaults of heat and grief were too much for her, causing her normally shellacked beehive to list to one side. Mascara pooled atop plump cheeks.

People clustered around a pair of easy chairs in the corner of the room where Joshua, who appeared to be the only man in a roomful of women, sat beside Alice Kicking Woman. He clutched a framed graduation photo of himself and Judith, star quilts draping their shoulders, waist-length hair flowing free beneath their mortarboards. Lola put a hand to her head, self-conscious as always on the reservation about her thin, kinked curls. Every head around her was topped with hair so strong and shiny and straight that it could have been featured in a shampoo commercial. Every head except Joshua's, that is. His own hair, freshly shorn, stood up in clumps. Alice's twisted frame curled toward him like a question mark. Deep grooves seamed her face, disappearing into the hollows of her cheeks, reemerging as vertical stitching around her mouth.

Lola hesitated. Etiquette mandated that attention be paid first to an elder. But what happened when someone died? Would the bereaved then take precedence? She looked around for Alice's great-granddaughter, Tina, a high school senior who'd recently declared herself a reporter in training. Lola allowed Tina to follow her around on stories and in return, Tina helped Lola navigate the swirling complexities of tribal custom. Lacking Tina's guidance, Lola finally knelt between the chairs and took Alice's hand in one of her own and Joshua's in the other. "I'm so sorry about Ju—" A foot nudged her shin. She glanced up. Tina's familiar ponytail switched back and forth as she shook her head at Lola.

"No names now," Tina mouthed.

"—your sister," Lola finished.

Joshua gave no sign of having heard. Lola stood to make room for the next person, and followed Tina's bobbing ponytail into the kitchen, where a fry bread assembly line was in progress. "What happened to his hair?" she whispered as they moved to join it.

"He cut it as soon as he heard," Tina said. "It's a traditional sign of mourning. Give me your hands."

Tina dusted Lola's palms with flour and then slapped a ball of dough into her hands. Lola began rolling and shaping it, her movements awkward compared to the swift, sure work of the others, and waited for the feeling of strangeness she always felt, as the lone white person in the room, to subside.

"It's so sad," someone said. "First their parents and then their gran'mother. Those two practically raised themselves after she died."

Lola looked to see who'd spoken and put a finger through her disc of dough. It was Josephine's married granddaughter, Angela Kills At Night. Lola rolled the dough back into a ball and started over. "When was that?"

"Maybe five, six years. The twins were just starting high school," Angela said. "They were a couple of years behind me." She used a fork to flip a piece of fry bread from the pan and onto a stack of paper towels, which darkened instantly beneath it. She dropped her own circle of dough, paper-thin and sized perfectly to the pan, into the smoking lard. It puffed high and golden. "And half their relatives who are left, the men anyway, are working over in the oil patch. It's going to be a problem getting them here for this."

"Because of the weather?" Lola asked.

"Because they just started their three weeks."

Lola nodded, catching the reference to the fact that people commuted to jobs in western North Dakota's Bakken oil field in multiple-week shifts.

"I don't imagine those bosses let anything, even a funeral, mess with their production schedules," Angela said. "Bad enough we lose our men for weeks on end. Now they'll have to worry about losing their jobs if they want to do the right thing."

Even Lola felt the way the air leaked out of the room. Especially in winter, when the seasonal jobs catering to tourists on their way to Glacier dried up, unemployment on the reservation often soared toward 70, 80 percent. Still, funerals took precedence over jobs. Everybody—all the local employers, at least—knew that. But would bosses nearly five hundred miles away understand?

Josephine brought the subject back to Judith. "I hear she almost made it home," she said. Lola knew Josephine was past sixty, yet her skin remained unlined and her hair gleamed like obsidian. Lola, only in her mid-thirties, was acutely aware of the silver already threading her own tangled chestnut curls, the insistent etchings at the corners of her grey eyes. Josephine sat rounds of bread on a tray, beside a stack of the inevitable sandwiches of bologna and cheese on white bread. She wiped her hand on a dishtowel and dipped it into a plastic bag of powdered sugar. She sifted the sugar over the fry bread, toweled her hand again, lifted the tray and swung a hip against the kitchen door. The women waited until it closed behind her. "At least we know where Joshua's sister is now," Angela said. "Not like those other ones who ran away."

Beside Lola, Tina stiffened. But in a group of older women, it wasn't Tina's place to talk. Lola swiped her sleeve across her forehead again. "What other ones?" Sometimes there was an advantage being shaky on etiquette.

Angela counted on floury fingers. "Let's see. There was Maylinn Kiyo. She was the first. Carole Bear Shoe and Annie Lenoir, they ran away, too."

Jeannette Finley Heavy Runner dumped more flour into a bowl, added baking powder and salt, and rubbed in lard with her fingers. She was Salish, from the other side of the Continental Divide, but had married a Blackfeet man thirty years earlier and long since mastered the labyrinth of kinship and gossip. "And Nancy deRoche. Josephine's husband's nephew's daughter. Josephine raised her." The women looked toward the door.

"I don't know any of them," Lola said.

"They left last year. A few months after Judith, but before you got here. For a while there, it seemed like every time you turned around, another girl ran off."

"My sister didn't run away." Joshua stood in the doorway. The fat in the skillet hissed and popped, tiny explosions in the sudden silence.

"Nobody ever heard from her," Angela said finally.

"That's how I know she didn't run away. She never would have just up and disappeared on me. She was doing so well. Those other ones, they were—" He looked around the room at the women, and dropped his voice—"using."

Lola thought of the tracks on Judith's forearms, the angry brand. "I know that—" she caught herself just as her lips began to shape the name "that your sister had her struggles."

Joshua's eyes were veined red, his voice raw. "And she beat them. That time in rehab last year, that did the trick. We got her into a program that uses traditional healing. They gave her an eagle feather when she completed it. She was so proud."

Lola saw again the dark feather clutched in Judith's frozen hand, swiveling like a weathervane with each snowy gust. Her hands stilled.

Angela took the dough from her, worked it briefly, and dropped it into the hot lard.

"Have you talked to Charlie yet?" Lola asked.

"No. Tribal police is all. Why?"

"Just talk to him," Lola said. And turned away to avoid the question in Tina's wide eyes.

CHAPTER THREE

The numbers on the clock glowed one in the morning when Lola heard the front door open. A candle burned on the nightstand. Its flame crouched low before the rush of cold through the house, then leapt high as the door closed, rendering Charlie's shadow monstrous as he crept into the bedroom in stocking feet. Lola watched in the wavering light as Charlie reversed his morning routine, standing on one leg, then the other, to peel off the layers of socks, the pants and the long johns, the wool shirt and sweater.

"You're going to burn the house down someday with those damn candles of yours." His voice was fond.

"I like them." She'd never told him why. They were a reminder of her years in Kabul and its unreliable electricity, when it was deemed better to use candles for light and save the generator's precious power for the computers, the cameras, the satellite phones. She'd come to appreciate the way soft candlelight rendered spaces intimate, forced people to huddle close, threw up a barrier of darkness beyond that made the nightly pop-pop-pop of rifle fire—as likely from bandits as insurgents—seem insignificant and far away.

"Go ahead. Get it over with." Charlie didn't mind the candles so much as the way she put them out.

Lola touched her tongue to thumb and forefinger and positioned them on either side of the flame. She counted down slowly, moving her fingers closer together. "One thousand one, one thousand two, one thousand three, one thousand four—ow!" She pinched out the flame and blew on her fingers as Charlie slid into bed in his T-shirt and shorts. "Your feet are freezing."

"Says the woman who plays with fire. Why such a wimp about cold? Besides, your feet would be cold, too, if you'd been standing out in the snow for the last few hours. Move over and give me the warm spot."

Lola nestled deeper beneath the layers of star quilts hand-stitched by Charlie's grandmother. Their pointed crimson, orange and gold patterns reminded her of the candle flame she'd just extinguished. "Like hell. Make Bub move. You can have his spot."

"His spot? I was under the impression this was my bed." He yawned and put icy soles to her calves. "It feels good in here. You feel good."

Lola turned on her side and he spooned against her, pressing his chest to her back, an icy slab slowly thawing. "Tough deal about Judith," she said.

"And the truck driver."

Lola didn't much care about the man who'd died in the crash that had kept Charlie out much of the previous night. But she didn't want to seem too eager about Judith. "What about him? It sounded pretty straightforward. The truck went off the road in the storm, right?"

"Looks that way. Impossible to tell. Snow filled in his tire tracks and then the wind played hell with everything. I called in the snowplow, but there's no skid marks on the road. If it had happened on Deadman's Curve, I could understand. But he was a few miles past it, on the straightaway. And then there was his neck. It was—" Charlie's voice trailed off.

"What about his neck?" She shifted, and felt him jerk awake.

"Broken. Twisted clean around. I've seen plenty of broken necks in crashes, but never one like that. And there was a footprint."

Lola raised her voice to keep him from drifting off again. "I thought you said the wind blew snow all over everything."

"There was a lee spot, where the trailer jackknifed. One print there, clear as day."

"Let me guess. It didn't match the driver's shoes."

"Boots. Not even close."

"Maybe somebody stopped to see if he could help and left when he realized he couldn't. Who called it in?"

Charlie's words came slow and sepulchral, dragged up from whatever small part of him was still awake. "Unidentified male. Said he was too busy trying to keep his own rig on the road in all that snow to give us any more than the location. Actually, what he said was, 'all that fucking snow.'"

The house shuddered within the wind's renewed attack. Snow pinged like gravel against the windowpanes. These Montana storms were nothing like the gentle snowfalls of Lola's childhood on Maryland's Eastern Shore, with their fat flakes seesawing lazily toward the ground, settling in soft sparkling heaps, clinging to each twig and bit of brush, creating postcard prettiness in tired oystering towns too far from Washington, DC, to have been revived by tourists. In Montana, the wind slammed snow against earth frozen hard as iron and then packed it tight enough to hold cattle on a surface so glazed and brittle that when the occasional steer broke through, it emerged with legs sliced and bloodied by the sharp edges.

"I know how that guy feels. I hate the snow here," she said to Charlie, trying to keep him awake, surprised when he responded.

"What about Afghanistan? You said it was a lot like here in terms of weather. So the snow must have been the same, too."

"I was hardly ever there in the winter." The various warring factions, made pragmatic by a quarter century of war with the Russians, then one another, then the Americans, generally put away their rifles and grenades and IEDs when winter fell. Ever wary of an underemployed reporter, Lola's editors promptly sent her on the road to other war zones in a constant churn of travel that she'd complained about at the time, but now found she missed. Other than near daily trips back and forth to the reservation, she'd barely left Magpie since her arrival.

Charlie's breath puffed against her back, a prelude to the easeful snores whose rise and fall would compete with the wind's low howl. A lifetime insomniac, Lola considered the finality of Charlie's sleep a thing of wonder. She'd tried various experiments in their time together—turning on the light, the radio, even one memorable night running the vacuum cleaner across the floor—only to see Charlie pull his pillow over his head and plunge more deeply into slumber. She pressed her thumb and forefinger together, feeling the calluses of her nightly experiments with the candles. "That brand on her arm. It was creepy."

"Gang sign, I guess." The words floated on a long, slow breath.

Lola knew that gangs had launched operations on reservations around the country, having divined with criminal efficiency the opportunities existing within the vacuum created by the wrangling among law enforcement agencies. But still. "A heart? That's way too girly for any gang I know. Not the Crips or the Bloods, for sure, nor the Nortenos or Surenos, either. Not the Mongols or the Angels or the damn Pagan's." The last, a motorcycle gang, particularly irritated Lola with its grammatical flaw.

Charlie's chest quivered with a deep chuckle. Lola relaxed. He wasn't as far gone into sleep as she'd feared. "Here all this time I'd been worried that you might be a terrorist, given how much time you've spent in all those bad places," he said. "Now it looks like you might've been a gangbanger. How do you know this stuff?"

"Live where I did in Baltimore and you learned about gangs fast. Plus, I covered courts for awhile before I went overseas. I sat in on every bullshit drug trial there was. Man." Lola shook her head, remembering. "I earned that Kabul posting." Which she had, but never was able to shake the conviction that the only reason she got the job was because no man at the paper had been crazy enough to want to go to Afghanistan—or if one had, his wife's objections had trumped ambition. She pressed her fingertips against her temples, erasing the memories. She needed Charlie's attention while he was at least half-awake. "I went over to Joshua's tonight. He doesn't think his sister ran away." Lola turned onto her back and lifted herself on her elbows. Cold flowed beneath the tented quilts.

Charlie snatched at them and drew them tight. "Dammit! I was almost asleep."

Lola lifted the quilts again. "The women tonight were talking about some other girls who ran away, too."

Charlie pulled her back down beside him and wrapped the covers tight. "There was a rash of them for awhile. These things come in waves. A few years back, it was suicides. That was bad."

Lola took his hand and held it to her lips, warming it with her breath. "How do you know they ran away?"

"Because it's what kids do. And because nobody turned up dead." His words caught on a yawn. "I'm off the clock. And you're off the beat. Let it go."

Lola lay quietly, doing math as Charlie's breathing slowed again. Half a dozen girls, maybe, from a school of about six hundred kids. Half of those students, girls. Probably the girls who went missing were older, maybe juniors or seniors. By the higher grades, the classes would have been decimated by the reservation's gut-punch dropout rate. So, maybe six girls out of a hundred, max. A number to be noticed, absences keenly felt. Lola jostled Charlie. "Just because I'm asking about something doesn't mean it's for a story. Anybody would be curious. Four or five girls go missing in a year, that's scary." He lay motionless beside her. "Faker," she said. "I know you're not asleep."

He put his hands on her shoulder and turned her to face him. His hair still smelled of cold. "These were very troubled young ladies. I was aware of them before they went missing and I'm even more aware of them now. Painfully aware. But I'm not going to share the details with you. Look. We promised each other we wouldn't talk about work. That's the only way to keep either of us from getting in more trouble than we're already in. Everybody already expects this thing to blow up in our faces."

Lola knew he was right. Dating a source broke every rule in the book. Except that she hadn't been working for the Magpie paper when she'd started seeing Charlie. The job came later, and she'd almost lost it on her first day, when the editor had expressed relief that he'd finally have someone to cover the police beat, vacant since the murder of Lola's friend Mary Alice. Lola had looked at the editor's expectant face and gave two seconds thought to not telling him about her budding relationship with the sheriff. The words were out of her mouth before the thought was even completed. "I'm afraid the police beat won't work," she'd said.

The editor had cursed so vehemently that she'd been halfway out the door, lecturing herself that she'd been a fool to consider working even temporarily in a place like Magpie. Then he called her back. "You'll cover the reservation. I'll put Jan on cops. I'm going out on a limb here. You so much as look sideways at a crime story and you're gone. Got that?"

Lola got it. His caution was fair, she had to admit. But she hated the feeling of being on some sort of long-term probation, of having to tiptoe around any number of topics with Charlie. She pulled the covers all the way over her head and let them muffle her words. "If we don't talk about work, then what are we going to talk about?"

Charlie dove beneath the quilts and ran his hands, warm now, from her shoulders to her thighs. "We're not going to talk at all."

CHAPTER FOUR

A row of tricked-out double-cab duallies took up the parking spaces in front of Nell's Café. Lola parked her own pickup down the street behind some displaced ranch trucks, their original colors obliterated by layers of frozen mud. Their drivers had left the engines running, wreathing the café in blue-tinged exhaust. Winter-furred cattle dogs rose stiffly from the beds and aimed perfunctory barks her way. Joshua stood outside the café, the smoke from his cigarette adding to the general miasma. Lola yearned toward the warmth of the interior, but paused beside him. "What are you doing at work today?"

Joshua looked at the cigarette in his bare hand as though he'd never seen one before. "Funerals cost money. I just finished paying off her rehab. She swore she'd pay me back if it took the rest of her life. I never wanted money from her. I just wanted her healthy and safe. Goddammit."

"When's the funeral?"

He lifted a shoulder, let it fall. "Same as always. Four days after. That's what our ceremonies require. But we're worried about the uncles in the patch. They're trying to arrange for at least three days off. A day to get here, a day for the funeral, and a day to drive back. They might not have time for the vigil, the rosary. People are almost as upset about that as they are about my sister."

"Come inside. You'll freeze to death out here." Lola put a hand to her mouth, too late to block the words. "I'm sorry. That was awful."

He dropped the cigarette into the snow. Its tip flared, then turned black. "Everything's awful today." He followed Lola back inside.

A rotating group of locals usually presided over the café's large center table throughout most of each day, but on this morning young men in steel-toed boots crowded around it. Ranchers bundled into quilted canvas coveralls perched on the edges of their chairs at side tables, as if waiting to reclaim the natural order of things. Lola went straight to the counter, where Nell studied order slips fanned like poker hands before her. "Coffee and a cinnamon roll to go?" she asked without looking up.

"Better make it two. Jan's mad at me again."

Nell swept the slips into a stack. "A cinnamon roll should do the trick. What have you done now?"

"I haven't done anything. She gets territorial with stories."

"Hah. Reminds me of someone else I know. I can't keep up with you two. One minute you're best friends, the next you're each sneaking around, trying to get something over on the other." She punched a couple of buttons on the cash register. The café had yet to switch to a computer. "I'll ring you up before I get started on these guys. Otherwise you'll be here all day."

Lola put down a ten. "Keep the change and put it with Joshua's tips. What's with the crowd?"

Nell smoothed her pink nylon skirt over the generous hips she termed the best advertisement for the café's cooking. "Bunch of roughnecks on their way back to the patch from Idaho. I guess they usually drive straight through, but they ran into that storm and got held up overnight. Those boys got more money than God. Every last one of them ordered steak and eggs. Good thing you don't want steak. We're out." She rang up Lola's order and slipped the change into her apron pocket. "I'll see that Joshua gets this. You're not the only one today."

"All the way from Idaho?" Lola whistled. "That's a long way to go for work."

Nell slid a to-go cup across the counter. "I thought you were supposed to be some sort of trained observer. We get guys from Seattle stopping here on their way to jobs in Dakota. They say they make almost as much on the rigs as they did in those tech companies that went bust."

Lola nodded toward the bunch at the center table. To a they looked hard and capable and—given the volume and an tion of their conversation—well versed in the proper calibrat of amphetamines to mileage. "Don't tell me a single one of tho guys ever held a desk job."

"You'd win that bet," Nell acknowledged. "My guess? Ranch hands who don't care if they never buck another bale of hay in their lives."

Lola took the cup and crossed the room to the coffee urns behind the table of roughnecks. She caught a whiff of booze amid the scents of charred steak and fried potatoes and wondered if the men were sweating off the previous night's excesses, or if they'd dosed their morning coffee from the hip flasks she saw protruding from a couple of pockets. The *Daily Express* was spread out before them. One of the men flipped through it, stopping at the obituaries. Judith's photo took up two columns. Lola had to remind herself, as she always did when she saw Judith, that her model's cheekbones were the result of the near-starvation resulting from drug abuse; that such beauty came at too high a price to be admired. The men staring at her photo had no such perspective. "Damn," one said, his voice low and appreciative.

Another drew the newspaper closer. "Hey. I seen that girl before."

Lola jerked, then gasped as the hot coffee hit her hand. She redirected her cup beneath the stream and then busied herself adding the cream and sugar that she never used, as a way to linger within earshot. Joshua, mopping nearby, stroked the linoleum with infinite care. So he'd heard, too.

"You have not," another man said. "You've never been here in your life until today."

"Not here," the first one said. His tangled reddish muttonchops curled toward fleshy lips. A scratch clawed its way across his cheek. "Back in Burnt Creek. She's one of them girls from the man camp—you know, the trailer." He twisted a hand into his crotch and grunted. "Made me go back for more."

"She scratch up your back the way she done your face?" His friend was smaller, rabbity, with protruding eyes and teeth. His shoulders twitched in nervous laughter. "Either way, won't be any scratchin' to go back for now. This here's an obit. Looks like you fucked her to death, Swanny."

"You couldn't fuck that girl long enough to fuck her to death. The way she turned it on, it's a wonder that's not my obit. I damn near had to kill her myself just to get out of there alive."

Joshua's hand slammed into Lola's back, shoving her out of the way. She staggered and flung out her arms to catch her balance. Her cup flew from her hand. Coffee sprayed the wall. Joshua grabbed the rabbity guy by the scruff of his skinny neck and flung him aside. He planted his foot in Swanny's chest and sent him and his chair backward. He reached down, seized the muttonchops and hauled at Swanny's head and smashed a fist into his nose. Gouts of blood patterned Nell's linoleum. The man came up fast, and Lola saw how much bigger he was than Joshua. Rabbit Face latched onto one of Joshua's arms and someone else wrestled the other one behind his back. Joshua's head whipped back and forth from the force of the bleeding man's blows.

"Stop!" Lola yelled. She took a step forward and someone straight-armed her and she hit the floor as Swanny resumed his methodical demolition of Joshua's face. A sheet of soapy water fell over the scene. The knot of men drew apart and came up gagging. Nell stood with Joshua's mop bucket in her hand.

"Out of here. Every last one of you."

Swanny dragged a hand across his face and wiped it on his chest, leaving scarlet streaks. "This asshole jumped me. For no reason."

Lola clambered to her feet. Her hip ached where it had struck the floor. "Idiot," she hissed. "That's his sister."

The man jerked a bloody thumb toward Nell. "Her?" he said, his disbelief clear.

Lola limped to the table and put her finger on Judith's photo. "No. Her."

The men coughed and shuffled their feet and moved muttering toward the door. Lola and Joshua and Nell waited motionless until the last of the trucks had passed before the window. "Shit," Nell said. "I forgot to make them pay. All that goddamn steak, right down the drain. I don't even have any left to put on your eye. Are you okay? What about you, Lola?"

Joshua turned his head to one side and spat a tooth into the mess on the floor. "Sure. Everything's great." He spoke around a hard lump in his jaw.

Lola winced. "I'm fine."

Nell kicked the bucket away. "Go on home, Joshua. I'll pay you for the day. I'm already out so much money, what's a little more?"

The door banged behind him. Lola reached for the mop. "I'll help you clean up. I've got a little while yet before I have to be at work."

Nell disappeared into the kitchen with the bucket and came back with it refilled with water so laced with bleach that Lola's eyes watered. She dipped in the mop and squeezed it against the side of the bucket and drew it across the floor. The blood ran pink and gradually disappeared. Nell righted the chairs and swept the broken dishes into a dustpan and tossed them with a clatter into a trashcan. She picked up the newspaper and hesitated over Judith's photo.

Lola looked over her shoulder. "Do you think she really went to the patch?"

Nell wadded the paper into a ball and hurled it toward the trashcan. It bounced off the rim and lay uncrumpling on the damp floor, revealing Judith's face by degrees. "Could be. The way these things usually go, the men make their money off the rigs and the women make their money off the men. It's tough to think about Judith that way, though. She was a sweet girl who got dealt a hard hand, what with losing her parents and then her grandmother. No surprise that she started using. A lot of people do without half the reasons she had. But she worked so long to get straight. Never thought she'd end up like this."

Lola stooped and picked up the newspaper and shook it out. Judith's face was wet and blurred. Lola threw the paper away. She wished she'd gotten a chance to ask the men about Judith before Joshua had started in on them. She said as much to Nell.

"They probably wouldn't have told you anything, anyway," Nell said. "Half the guys working there are running away from something. The last thing they want is somebody nosing around about their personal lives. You could be something even worse than a reporter. A parole officer, maybe. Or somebody's ex-wife, trying to collect child support. You want to find out about the patch, you need to know somebody who works there."

"I don't know anybody like that."

"Yes, you do." Nell stood the mop in the bucket and wheeled the contraption across the floor, letting Lola work it out for herself.

"The uncles," she said to Nell's retreating back. "They'll be at the funeral. And so will I."

CHAPTER FIVE

The uncles made it back for the funeral, just, the scents of clean snow and dirty industry accompanying them as they eased into pews beside their families just before Father Szczepanski raised his arms in benediction. Somehow he'd managed to avoid being rotated to another parish, as was customary. He often speculated that was only because the church hierarchy had assumed he'd been dead for decades.

He and Alice Kicking Woman, the tribe's oldest member, were contemporaries and great friends besides. In warmer weather they sat at the picnic table outside the rectory, reminiscing about earlier times as they softened biscuits in glasses of syrupy unconsecrated communion wine. Over the decades, every last hair had fallen from the priest's head, leaving its surface as shiny and smooth as the marble baptismal font that was the pride of St. Anthony's, paid for with years of bake sales. Lola suspected that his hair hadn't actually fallen out, that instead it had somehow wormed its way under his scalp and reemerged from his brows, dense white thickets that grew so long and snarled they threatened his vision and negated the need for his impossible name. People from outside referred to him as "that priest with the—" accompanied by a vague gesture toward their foreheads; on the reservation, everyone knew him simply as Father Eyebrows.

He peered from beneath them now, pausing to allow the men to take their places. They apparently had come straight from the rigs, faces and hands bearing telltale dark smears, as though they'd halted for the quickest of truck stop washups before barreling back onto the two-lane highway paralleling the railroad tracks that carved their way across the top of Montana, just below the Canadian border. Because of the railroad, the region was called the Hi-Line, a term understood by the rest of the state to be synonymous with wind and desolation. Given time, Lola knew, the men would have gone home first and showered until the hot water ran out before donning starched snap-front shirts, knife-creased jeans, boots polished to a high gloss, and stiff-brimmed felt hats brushed free of every last speck of dust and parked with solemnity atop hair gleaming with fragrant oil.

"Let us faithfully remember our dear child," Father Eyebrows began, somehow infusing his wobbly old man's voice with extra warmth, as though to reassure the men their presence was the important thing. A sort of sigh went through the congregation, an exhalation of both grief and respite, an acknowledgment that even if they'd lost yet another of their own, the men had returned to help bear the weight. Several moved their lips along with the liturgy they'd heard too many times. Death on the reservation was, if not a friend, at least a constant companion. People drank themselves into permanent oblivion, or drove old cars with bald tires on bad roads, or signed up for the military and came back in flag-draped boxes, or were too intimidated by the brusque and overworked Indian Health Service doctors to mention that strange lump or cough until the cancer had raged throughout their bodies. Obituaries from the reservation outweighed those from the rest of the county three to one in the pages of the *Daily Express*. Charlie once told Lola that as a child he'd been to so many vigils in the high school gym that he was shocked to attend his first basketball game there. He'd had no idea of the building's real purpose. The night before Judith's church funeral, Joshua had held reluctant court in the gym as people crossed the varnished wooden floor to pay their respects before her casket, those mourners no doubt thinking of the youngsters in their own families, offering silent thanks that their children had chosen a different road, or saying prayers that they would find their way back to sobriety before sharing Judith's fate. From her pew near the rear of the church, Lola craned her neck for a better view of Joshua. He looked as though he hadn't slept, crossing himself sluggishly, intoning the responses to Father Eyebrows's prayers a beat too late. He uttered his own "amens" barely above a whisper, but they sounded throughout the church during the pauses in the interminable service, each lagging a little longer behind the prayers than the last, until Lola feared Joshua had fallen asleep from sheer exhaustion. The mass ground toward completion. "As we grieve over the loss of one so young," Father Eyebrows intoned, "we seek to understand Your purpose."

"Ha! What purpose?" The congregation stirred as Joshua pushed himself to his feet, shoved past the others in the pew and headed for the church door. Father Eyebrows rushed through the final few phrases of the service. He made as if to follow, but Charlie intercepted him, whispering something into the old priest's ear, leaning so close that he risked entanglement with those fearsome brows. Lola saw Charlie's eyes scanning the crowd over the priest's gleaming pate, tracking Joshua's beeline toward the men who'd returned from the patch. Lola moved with the rest of the mourners as though she hadn't seen Joshua backing one of the uncles into the stairwell that led to the church's postage-stamp choir loft. The stairwell housed what was, to Lola, the church's most remarkable feature, a long-neglected statue of Saint Lucy. The plaster image was a relic from the days when the church more enthusiastically celebrated the martyrdom of unfortunates like Lucy, whose eyes were said to have been gouged out before she was put to death for her refusal to marry and give up the virginity she'd dedicated to Christ. Lucy the statue cradled a saucer with a pair of blue eyes, the whites veined red, the orbs trailing scarlet stalks. Another pair, miraculously intact, gazed serenely from her face. Lola looked over her shoulder. Someone else had claimed Charlie's attention. His back was to her. She hurried toward the stairwell, stopping just outside.

Joshua had cornered Josephine deRoche's husband, Roy. "I told you, I never saw her there," Roy said. "What kind of question is that for a man to ask about his sister?"

"She wanted to pay me back for rehab." Joshua's voice was low and miserable. "Where else do people go to make money these days? And how else do women make money over there?"

"Stop that talk. First of all, if I had seen her, that'd mean I'd have been in one of those places. If they even exist. I've never heard of such. But then, I wouldn't. None of us would. We work, sleep, keep to ourselves, away from the whitemen. Safer that way. Besides, people make money in all sorts of ways over there. Motel maids, waitresses, that sort of thing."

"The guy who said he'd seen her—he wasn't talking about any motel maid."

"What difference does it make now? She's gone. We've all had our losses. At least you've got somebody to bury."

Lola wondered at the level of grief that could make one grateful for the knowledge that a loved one was actually dead. One of the missing girls, she remembered, was related to Josephine's husband. The girl had been gone for nearly a year, but pain stabbed through Roy's voice. Lola imagined that agony multiplied exponentially among all the relatives of all the missing girls. Joshua apparently had the same thought.

"I'm sorry, uncle," he said. "I forgot myself."

Lola heard the thumps and exhalations that marked men hugging. "You understand why I've got to get home to Josephine. I need to spend some time with my family before we head back to Burnt Creek."

So much for visiting the uncles, Lola thought. None would appreciate an intrusion into precious family time. She flattened herself against the church wall as Roy escaped the stairwell's confines. She stepped into the place he'd fled. "You really think your sister was in the patch? Those roughnecks could have mistaken her for someone else."

Joshua leaned against Lucy's pedestal, clutching one of her sandaled feet. Lucy watched over them with all four eyes. The wine-colored paint of her gown had faded to pink and had flaked away in places, exposing the crumbling plaster beneath. Lola wondered if someone touched up the veins in the detached eyeballs, which remained vivid.

"You heard Roy. What does it matter?"

Lola took his hand. He pulled away. "Listen to me, Joshua. It matters because she isn't the only one. You know that. Finding out what happened to her over there might help us find out about those others." What was that shopworn term? "You know, so people could have closure."

It was the wrong word. "You got closure on Mary Alice yet?"

And just like that, the words conjured Lola's friend Mary Alice, tossing her head in her throaty laugh, giving Lola good-natured shit about some story or another, a posture mimicked when Lola had found her body, neck arched, head blown back by the force of the gunshot that killed her. Lola blinked hard. Maybe Lucy's eyes hadn't been dug from her head. Maybe she'd cried them out after seeing all the loss around her. Lola picked at the scabbed plaster, widening a gouge in Lucy's foot. "No," she said. "No closure."

Indian people considered it rude to look someone in the eye, but Joshua's gaze met Lola's and held it. She looked away first. But stuck to her guns. "It matters, Joshua. Not just because of those other girls, too, but for your sister herself. Otherwise, we'll never know how she ended up dead in the snow not five miles from home."

CHAPTER SIX

Lola moved her reporter's notebook across the upper quadrant of the large Montana map that took up most of one wall in the *Daily Express* newsroom.

Jan Carpenter propped booted feet on her desk and watched from two desks away. Those desks, purchased decades earlier at a government surplus sale, were two of the four that housed the *Daily Express* news staff. Lola had to tamp down memories, whenever she walked into the building, of her old newsroom in Baltimore. Despite taking up most of a city block, it had felt cramped—at least before being decimated by layoffs and buyouts—with the feral ambitions of five hundred reporters and photographers and editors, all of whom firmly believed they belonged at the *New York Times* or the *Wall Street Journal* or the *Washington Post*. Lola had snatched the brass ring of the Kabul posting, only to have it torn away when the newspaper shuttered all the foreign bureaus, ordering her back to a job in the Baltimore suburbs.

More and more these days, she fought the uneasy suspicion that she'd been too quick to avail herself of the shelter that the *Daily Express*—and Charlie—had offered after the one-two punch of being downsized, and then discovering Mary Alice's body during a consolation visit to Magpie. When it came to Charlie, Lola considered herself a realist about the temporary nature of most relationships. And the *Express*, she reassured herself, almost certainly would turn out to be a rest stop, the place where she'd figure out what to do with the rest of her life. In the meantime, she had to contend with the unnerving presence of Jorkki Harkannen, the cadaverous Finn who'd edited the paper long enough to remember printing Jan's birth announcement. When Lola first heard his name, she'd thought of a small, incessantly yapping dog. But Jorkki spoke in monosyllables, glowering through the pale forelock that hung lank over no-color eyes and skin like bleached linen. Brian Finch sat beside him, round and pink and glistening as a canned ham, an oppressively cheerful counterpart to Jorkki's near-transparent presence. Finch worked the night shift, compiling the police blotter, along with the marriage and divorce listings, the birth announcements and obituaries, after which he put the paper to bed before vanishing into the night. Never once had Lola seen him around town—not stopping for coffee at the café, or picking up a quart of milk at the convenience store, or pumping gas into his sea-green cruise liner of a Cadillac, an eye-popping anomaly in a town of serviceable pickups and Subarus. Magpie was small enough that, even after only a few months in town, Lola knew most people by sight and generally where they lived. But Finch locked the door behind him at midnight and materialized at his desk every afternoon at two, his face already glazed with sweat as though his very exuberance were its own exertion. He took his vacation in two-day increments, one long weekend every month. Speculation about his whereabouts during those longer disappearances comprised a longstanding guessing game at the *Express*. Lola didn't mind him, much, but he drove Jan to distraction. She seethed as he chirruped in Lola's direction.

"Planning a trip?"

"What the hell are you doing, Wicks?" Jan spoke over him.

"Math," Lola said without turning. She held the notebook against the map and jotted some numbers on its cover.

"Come again?"

"If it's eight notebooks from here to the patch, how many miles is that?"

Jan's auburn hair trailed down her back in a thick braid. When something bothered her, as apparently was the case at the moment, she chewed on the end. On the rare occasions when she undid the braid, her hair cascaded around her face in chorus-girl waves that caught the light and held it. Lola thought, not for the first time, that it seemed to be her own fate to be the pretty girl's gawky friend; everything about Lola herself *too* by comparison—jaw too strong, shoulders too broad, chest too flat, butt too skinny. Mary Alice had been tiny and blond and distractingly rounded; with Jan, there was the added insult of her youth and ranch-girl fitness, the shoulders-back, light-on-her-feet stance that casually proclaimed her ability and eagerness to kick some ass.

Jan wrapped the braid around her neck and pulled tight, sliding down in her chair. "Better get ready to hire another reporter, Jorkki," she choked out. "I'm going to kill myself out of despair for the stupidity that surrounds me." One pointy-toed boot thudded onto the execrable carpet, followed by its partner as she sat up. Jan wore her cowboy boots throughout the winter, somehow retaining her slick-soled footing even on Magpie's icy streets. She hammered at her keyboard and read Lola the results. "Four hundred seventy miles, depending on where you're going once you get there. This time of year, allowing for weather, better count on ten hours minimum. Maybe more." Her eyes narrowed. "Why the interest in the patch? Isn't that a few hundred miles outside your territory? Or maybe you've decided to go to work there?" She feigned—maybe—a hopeful tone. "You could make twice as much slinging ten-dollar burgers for greenhorns and roustabouts as you could working here."

"Knock it off, Jan," Jorkki rasped. He didn't smoke, but to Lola he always sounded like he was on his tenth cigarette of the day. "The last thing you need is for Lola to leave. Your work has gotten about one hundred percent better since she got here. Besides, who'd you pal around with after work if she were gone? I figure the two of you are like checks and balances, keeping each other more or less in line."

Pleasure and indignation fought one another to a draw across Jan's features. "I thought it was your job to make me better. Not hers."

"Way I see it, you watch what she does and then you do the same thing. My job gets easier as a result. It's a win-win." He threw Jan a bone. "Pretty soon, you'll be giving Lola a run for her money."

Finch spoke up. "I'd pay to watch that."

"Shut up, Finch." Something Jan said to Finch several times a day.

Lola returned to her desk. She and Jan sat next to each other, facing Jorkki, whose sole form of exercise, as far as Lola could tell, involved bobbing from one side of his chair to the other, peering around his computer monitor to see which of them was available to do his bidding. Sometimes he turned to Tina Kicking Woman, who came by after school to help Finch with obituaries and the occasional feature story on the days when Jorkki was either feeling magnanimous or desperate. Tina made a space for herself and her secondhand laptop at the long table at the back of the room where the newspapers were stacked according to week. That gave her the advantage of turning her back on Finch, who beamed moistly whenever she made the mistake of glancing his way. She hunched over her laptop, but Lola could tell by the way her fingers stilled on the keyboard that she was eavesdropping.

"I thought I might head out to the patch for a story," Lola said.

Jorkki raised his head an inch. "Oh? Jan, I expected that autopsy story an hour ago."

Jan hit a couple of keys. "There. It's all yours. But it's just the coroner's initial report. The autopsy results will take at least a couple of weeks."

"If it was done, why didn't you send it to me?"

"Because I like watching you break into a sweat. It's good for that delicate Finnish complexion. Look at Finch. Soon you'll be just as rosy as he is." She walked to the map and put her left hand on Magpie and stretched her right as far as it would go, across the state line into North Dakota. "You're talking a hell of a mileage bill," she said to Lola. "Betcha Jorkki says no."

"Jorkki says yes," Jorkki said. "What's the story?"

Jan spoke before Lola could answer. "If it's in the patch, it's one that's already been done. Repeatedly. The fracking boom has been written to death. Besides, Lola probably doesn't even know what fracking is."

Lola hoped she sounded more authoritative than she felt. "I do, too. It's a way of going after oil."

Jan's grin anticipated victory. "And gas, too. What's it mean?"

Lola tried to joke her way out. "Damned if I know, but it sounds like a cuss word. Which seems to be how people think of it."

"Hydraulic fracturing," Jorkki informed her. "They blast liquid into deep rock to break it up and release the oil. Or, as Jan pointed out, gas. And not everybody thinks of it as a cuss word. Before the boom, that area was losing people so fast the census folks classified it as frontier again. You've got counties out there with fewer than one person per square mile. Fracking means salvation for entire towns. People are working jobs with living-wage pay and benefits for the first time in their lives."

Lola shot a triumphant grin of her own at Jan. "And that's exactly the idea of my story. Those towns aren't just in the patch. A lot of the Blackfeet people are going over there for work. I thought maybe I'd do a story"—Lola calculated—"maybe a whole series of stories, about that fact. They've got to leave their families for three-week shifts. Then, when something happens like Judith's dying, they're away when their families need them most. I'd like to see what their lives are like so far from home." She wandered to Jorkki's desk and tried to look over his shoulder at Jan's story on the screen.

Jan joined her and reached around Jorkki and hit "store." The screen went blank. "Half of Montana is driving back and forth to Dakota for work. There's nothing new about that." She sat back down at her desk.

"But it's different on the rez," Lola said, warming to her own nascent idea. "The money they're bringing home, it's changing everything there. People can finally afford to buy things, real things, like furniture and houses." She stopped, aware that she'd made a fine argument for doing a story on the reservation, but had yet to justify a trip to the patch. "But at what cost? Extended family is such a big deal. Now you've got family men living on their own in—what do they call them?—man camps."

"She's right." A soft voice came from the back of the room. It had taken months for Tina to realize that deference was something she had to shed along with her coat and schoolbooks whenever she walked into the newsroom, but she was learning.

"Did you hear that, Jorkki?" Finch asked. "Tina said she's right. And she should know."

Tina grimaced obligingly in Finch's direction. He felt around on his desk for a stray paper napkin and mopped at the freshet on his brow.

"Good lord," Jan said. "The man is going to blow an aneurysm."

"How long?" said Jorkki.

Lola wished she'd done a little more preparation. "I think people from the reservation have only started going over in a big way for about six months or so. Just about the time I got here. Long enough now so that Josephine's husband just started up a van service to run people back and forth."

"I don't give a shit about Josephine's husband."

Lola slumped, avoiding Jan's eyes.

"Scratch that. It'd make for a nice sidebar. I meant, how long will you need?"

Lola let out a long breath. "Couple, three days. Not counting the driving. Four. Five."

"Three. And the driving's on your own time. Jan's right. The mileage alone is going to wipe out petty cash."

"We've got a petty cash fund?" Jan asked.

Jorkki ignored her. "Leave Monday so you're back by Friday."

"What the hell?" Jan bounded up from her desk. "Why does she get to go? You've never sent me anywhere and I've been here three years. She's here all of what—three months? Besides, how am I going to write the whole paper by myself?"

Something shifted in Jorkki's face, not quite a smile, but a shade less dour than his usual death mask. "You never asked. We reward initiative here. Or at least we would, if anyone ever showed any. As for writing the paper, Tina's been doing just fine on feature stories. Time we threw some news her way."

Tina glowed quietly. "That's a great idea," Finch enthused. "One of your best ever."

"Shut up, Finch," Jan and Lola snapped in unison.

"Can't I at least go along and watch? I want to see how Lola here handles that bunch over on the eastern plains and beyond. They're a different breed of human. Tough. More than tough. Got to be, to live in that godforsaken place."

Jorkki spoke to Lola. "How do you feel about sleeping in your truck? Because there won't be a vacant motel room within a hundred miles of where you're going. Oh, and pack your woollies. You think it's cold here? That wind's been rolling across the Hi-Line for five hundred miles with nothing to stop it by the time it hits the patch. When you get back, this place will feel like Phoenix."

Lola doubted it. But she was too relieved to care. Even if it meant nothing more than trading one frozen wasteland for another, she was finally escaping the increasingly suffocating confines of Magpie.

CHAPTER SEVEN

"Why the sudden interest in the patch? Can't it wait until spring?" Charlie stood in the bedroom doorway as Lola added underwear and socks—and then more socks—to a duffel bag. Bub shadowed her, alternately radiating suspicion and excitement. The candle flickered beside the bed, redundant in the glare of the overhead light that Lola had switched on so that she could see as she packed.

"It's a better story in the wintertime. Shows how desperate people are for work. Jorkki said it would be even colder there than it is here. How is that possible? Do you think I should get one of those facemasks that make people look like bank robbers? Do you have one? Can I borrow this?" She reached for the coyote-fur-trimmed hat that sat on Charlie's nightstand and put it on. She unfolded the earflaps, tied them beneath her chin and stood before the mirror. The brim came down over her eyebrows. "I look like an idiot. But maybe if I wear my watch cap under it, it'll fit." She took off the hat and tossed it beside the duffel, then rooted through the contents of the single dresser drawer she'd allowed herself at Charlie's. Most of her possessions were in boxes in the barn. Lola may have acquiesced to Charlie's pleas to join him in Magpie, but she'd insisted to him and to herself, too, that their living arrangement would last only until she found her own place. But summer had turned to fall, and then winter arrived with a ferocity that made any effort beyond work and simple survival unthinkable. When Charlie suggested she delay her house hunt until spring, she'd shoved another log into the woodstove that kept the living room bearable and agreed that was a fine plan.

Now, noting the rigidity in Charlie's shoulders, the set to his jaw, she wasn't so sure.

"Jorkki liked the idea," she told him.

"Jorkki doesn't know you like I do. He's about to find out. You won't stop at anything when it comes to a story."

"That's generally considered a good thing."

Bub whined, looking from Charlie to Lola. He had belonged to Mary Alice, but had finally transferred his loyalties to Lola. Bub had one brown eye and one blue, and guilt shot through Lola when he trained the blue one on her. She dropped to her knees and stroked him. "It's okay, Bub. I won't be away for long."

"You're leaving the dog with me, too? Did you even think to ask?"

"He'll just slow me down. Besides, he's better off here than hanging around in the truck all day." Lola zipped the duffel shut and turned her attention to her book bag. Laptop. Notebooks. Pens—and, of course, pencils, along with a small sharpener, the kind she'd used in elementary school. Chargers and spare chargers. When Lola had been stationed in Kabul, she'd had to lug a camera, too, in the event she couldn't find a photographer to accompany her to an assignment. But smartphones were everywhere when she returned from her overseas posting, making her life considerably less burdensome in that regard. The *Express*, like so many papers, had long ago dispensed with photographers, relying on Jan and Lola and Tina to provide photos and videos with their own stories—although Jorkki ran Lola's cluttered, off-kilter photos only as a desperation measure. Lola went into the kitchen and retrieved Charlie's Thermos, the size of a small fire hydrant, from a cupboard. A steady supply of caffeine was the only solution, she told herself. She could sleep when she got home. She held open the cupboard doors, seeking more plunder. Charlie's kitchen was a place of mystery to her, stocked with all manner of ingredients in rows of mason jars. Flour, both white and whole wheat. Cornmeal, again white, and yellow, too. Rice, white and brown; likewise with sugar, and a veritable rainbow of beans. The problem, Lola had learned early on when she went looking for snacks, was that everything required some sort of preparation and assembly.

"It's called cooking," Charlie said when she'd remarked upon that fact. "Maybe you've heard of it." After which, dinner became his responsibility.

Lola located a jar of almonds and shook a handful into a baggie. Useless to hope that Charlie would have squirreled away a bag of chips someplace. He blocked her way back to the bedroom. "I just think it's interesting that you chose to focus on workers from the rez."

Bub wormed his way between them and leaned against Lola's legs. Lola nudged the dog away and stepped around Charlie. "I cover the reservation. So it makes perfect sense. All of those jobs have affected the rez in a big way."

Charlie's voice followed her. "I ran into Joshua. That's quite a shiner he's got. He said he punched out a guy who called his sister a whore. Guy told him she'd been working someplace. But I forget where."

Lola turned around. Charlie had a hand to his head, as though trying to remember. "Wait. It's coming to me. The patch. What a coincidence."

"Yes, it is. And that's all it is."

Lola sat on the bed and looked at the clock. It was eleven. The hours before her departure stretched dark and interminable. She never slept well the night before heading out on a story; preferred, in fact, to leave the night before and drive through until morning. But when she'd said as much to Charlie, he'd threatened to report her to a suicide hotline. "Bad enough you've got almost no experience driving in this kind of weather and now you want to try it at night? Do you want to end up like Joshua's sister? Or that poor trucker?"

Lola had to concede the point. She'd already experienced too many days in which even the short commute between the newspaper and Charlie's small ranch just outside town turned eerie and unrecognizable in wind-driven snow. "Fine. Come to bed." She switched off the overheard light, and wet her fingers and framed the candle flame between them, counting down and smiling as the fire licked at her calluses before she pinched it out.

Charlie walked to the window and scraped at the icy ferns patterning its surface. "Stars are out. If it's clear, it'll be even colder. Lola, I need you to promise you'll stick to the one story. If this thing with Joshua's sister turns into a criminal investigation, you could really screw things up by poking around the way I know you like to do. You could wreck the investigation and you could wreck things for us, too."

The investigation into Judith's death? Or was Charlie also talking about the missing girls? Lola started to ask, but thought the better of it. She slid under the covers and peeled out of her clothes and kicked them onto the floor. Of course it had crossed her mind that her trip might provide some information about Judith and the girls. Even if she couldn't do the story herself, she relished the thought of presenting her gleanings to Jan. But she'd be damned if she'd admit as much to Charlie. "Do you take me for a fool?"

Bub leapt onto the bed and burrowed beside her. Charlie's voice rang emphatic in the darkness. "Promise."

Lola crossed her fingers beneath the blankets.

"I promise."

CHAPTER EIGHT

Lola woke at midnight, at two, at three. At four, she gave up trying to sleep and lay sandwiched between Charlie and Bub, stiff with impatience. Dawn was hours away. Twilight would arrive too quickly behind it, grey at four in the afternoon, full black by five. Lola had long used her nighttime sleeplessness to good effect, making mental lists of questions she'd ask in coming interviews. But as much as she tried to focus on the men from the reservation, her mind strayed to the missing girls. In her experience, men who went walkabout tended to show up eventually, sometimes worse for the wear, but not infrequently better. It was different for women, especially young ones. Predators homed in on them like wild dogs to scraps of raw meat, sniffing out their need and vulnerability. Too many ended up like Judith. The lucky ones lived. Although, given what some of the survivors endured, Lola thought that maybe "luck" wasn't the right term.

"Did the *Express* ever write about any of those girls who disappeared?" she'd asked Jan.

"No." Jan avoided Lola's eyes. "People go missing, they turn up. We'd go crazy if we tracked every single one of those stories."

"But they never turned up."

"Right." Spoken past a larger-than-usual section of braid.

"No story even after the third or fourth girl? Or the fifth?"

"Nobody would talk."

Jan's misery was so obvious Lola almost felt sorry for her. Of course they wouldn't talk. Leaving the reservation was, for all practical purposes, a nonexistent problem. The bigger issue usually involved people coming back. No matter how generous the academic scholarship to the University of Montana—or Dartmouth, or Harvard—no matter how high a college basketball profile, no matter how sweet the offer of full partner in the big-city law firm, the pull of home too often proved more powerful. There was some shame in that, inflicted mostly by the white world, but pride, too. What family wouldn't luxuriate in drawing their own back home again? A dynamic that made a true disappearance unimaginable, and airing it in the press unthinkable.

Tina's fingers had rattled over her keyboard, loud in the silence. Lola resisted an impulse to stand and look over Tina's shoulder, to confirm her suspicion that nothing but rows of x's marched across the screen as Tina tried to mask the fact that she was once again eavesdropping. "Roy deRoche seems to think those girls are dead," Lola said.

Tina dropped all pretense of work and spun around in her chair. "Or not. You yourselves said how hard it is to disappear a body. Let alone several bodies. You told me. All of you. So they could still be alive." Her soft voice shook with the boldness of the accusation.

When Tina first started working at the *Express*, so nervous she fairly trembled as she walked through the door each day, Lola and Jorkki—and even Jan despite her relatively short tenure in the newspaper business—had treated her to a friendly hazing, regaling her with gruesome stories from their years in the business, in which abortive attempts to hide bodies figured prominently. Mary Alice's murder the previous summer had been the only one in the county in forty years, but Montana's other fifty-five counties provided plenty of fodder. Even if *Express* reporters hadn't actually covered those killings, they pored over the details in preparation for the day someone in Magpie went homicidal—and creative.

"No matter how well people plan a murder, they always seem to forget the fact that there'll be a body to deal with afterward. Forget wood chippers. Bone fragments and DNA from here to Sunday," Jorkki advised.

"Same for garbage trucks," said Jan. "They can smash the junk from your kitchen trashcan, but a dead person just ends up in big chunks."

Lola's own contributions harkened to Baltimore, or as she had described it to Tina, "the town where nobody ever reported a bad smell."

"People were forever shoving bodies into closets or under the bed or some such, and just leaving them there. Somebody would finally find them and all the neighbors would say, 'We thought a mouse had died in the walls.'"

Nothing, of course, could fully prepare Tina for the day when she'd cover one of those stories on her own. But she'd learn to turn it into a tale later, to rely on the fiction that a good barroom recounting could stave off the shock and horror of those initial facts.

Now Lola shifted uneasily beside Charlie, wondering if Tina had thought of the missing girls—she'd grown up with them, after all—and despite her defiance on their behalf, wondered if her friends had ended up as nothing more than fragments in a DNA lab somewhere. Lola rued her own part in planting such images in Tina's head. She checked the bedside clock again. No matter how she timed it, she'd drive a significant part of the way to the oil patch in the dark. Better to make that part early, given that the truck traffic would only worsen the closer she got to the patch. She moved her leg experimentally and Bub jumped to his feet, instantly alert. Charlie stirred and flung an arm around her. There'd be no sneaking out of bed without waking him. She pictured his arm across her small, pale breasts. When she'd first met him, she'd thought him tanned by the sun that shone as fiercely in the summer as the winds blew in the winter. His last name came by way of earlier generations of French fur trappers who married Indian women, but his mother was Blackfeet, mostly, the algorithms of blood quantum qualifying him for tribal enrollment. For his children to meet the quantum, though, he'd be best off marrying within the tribe. Which Jan had pointed out to Lola.

"Bad enough you slept with a source," she'd said, speaking over Lola's protestation that she hadn't even been working for the *Express* when she'd started seeing Charlie. "But no white woman has a future with that guy. You're just asking to get hurt."

"Jesus, Jan. Nobody's getting hurt, and for sure nobody's having kids. It's just a good time."

Jan spoke with the authority of someone raised in a small town where secrets were nonexistent. "I know a whole lot of babies who started out as a good time. I hope you two are taking precautions."

Lola's face had grown warm, as much from pride as embarrassment. She'd held several friends' hands through any number of pregnancy scares, had driven more than one to a clinic, trying to ignore their obvious resentment at her own clockwork biology that was, apparently, foolproof. Now, she checked a mental calendar, sighed, then nudged Charlie. He woke instantly, as fully alert upon waking as he was oblivious while asleep. Alert, and ready, too. "Condom," she whispered, as he pulled her to him. The clock said five. Lola wound her arms around him, almost as grateful for the distraction of lovemaking as she was for the fact that she'd be on the road minutes after they'd finished.

THE THERMOS rolled from atop the pile of gear in Lola's arms and clanged against the frozen ground. Lola retrieved it and shook it, relieved not to hear the rattle of a shattered liner.

"Lucky." The whisper floated toward her through the darkness.

Lola spun around, almost dropping the Thermos again. "Joshua! What are you doing here?"

Joshua stepped from the truck's shadow. "Waiting for you. About an hour now. Mind if I have some of that coffee? I'm near froze."

Lola handed him the Thermos. He unscrewed the top and poured. The coffee gurgled and steamed. "God, that's good. I didn't think you'd ever come out."

A whicker sounded from the direction of the barn. A spotted horse, curious about the hushed commotion, ambled through the open door and stretched his neck over the fence, seeking the packets of sugar Lola usually filched from the café for him. Lola waved him away. "Go back inside, Spot." The Appaloosa, like Bub, had been Mary Alice's. Lola had given him to Charlie after Mary Alice's death, then had ended up with him, anyway. She'd come to learn that his curiosity was insatiable. She glanced toward the house, where Charlie was cleaning up after the breakfast he'd insisted upon making. The last thing she needed was for Spot to neigh and draw Charlie to a window, where he could see her talking with Joshua.

"How'd you get here? I didn't hear anything," she said to Joshua.

"OIT."

"What?"

"Old Indian Trick. We're always creeping up on you white people in our moccasins."

"Hah." Indian people were unrelenting jokesters, but Lola never knew when it was appropriate for a white person to laugh. She usually settled for the same forced smile she now turned upon Joshua, hoping he hadn't noticed that she'd actually glanced toward his feet to ensure he was wearing boots. "Seriously, how? And why?"

"Heard you were leaving this morning for Dakota."

Of course he had. Lola had mixed feelings about the gossip in Magpie, which was nearly as accurate as it was widespread. As a reporter, it was a great help. But she didn't like being the subject.

"When did Dakota lose the North?"

Joshua ignored the question. "I parked down around the bend and walked up here. I wanted to talk to you before you headed out." In the harsh black and white of moonlight, his injuries looked even worse, the swollen jaw leaping to prominence, the space gaping darkly where his tooth had been, eyes cavernous and haunted.

"About your sister," Lola said, "Charlie already told me not to go asking about her. Or those other girls, either."

Joshua's mouth stretched into a grotesque semblance of a smile. "But you will, anyway."

"Maybe."

He reached for the Thermos, took another swig. "Look. I thought about what you said. About the other girls. I don't care if it ends up in a story or not. I just want to know what happened to my sister. And if knowing what happened to her helps find out about them, too, maybe that's a good thing, closure or no closure."

Lola thought of the man in the café, his ugly words about Judith. It was entirely possible, she thought, that Judith had endured worse abuse than the simple beating the man had delivered to Joshua, something so cruel as to make fleeing into a blizzard in street clothes seem the only way out. There were the track marks, the brand. The autopsy report still hadn't been released. She confessed her reluctant second thoughts to Joshua. "Are you sure you want to know the details?"

The front door opened. Lola turned to see Charlie silhouetted in the doorway. A whisper barely reached her ears.

"Disappearing now. Another OIT. And, yes. I'm sure."

"COULDN'T WAIT to hit the coffee?" Charlie shook the half-empty Thermos. "I can't believe I'm letting you take it. I've had that Thermos since I was a boy." He handed Lola her duffel bag. She tossed it into the space behind the pickup's seats. The moon was still high, its silver light so bright that Charlie hadn't bothered to turn on the outside light. He looked toward the horse. "Nice of Spot to see you off."

"He's just waiting for a treat. I forgot to bring him one."

"Tank full?"

"I stopped at Howard's last night."

He moved to the front of the truck and unplugged the long cord that kept the battery from freezing during the night. The cord's twin ran to his cruiser. He wrapped the cord in figure eights from his elbow to wrist and tied it off and sat it atop the duffel. "Try to find a place with plug-ins at night. I don't care if you have to pay somebody. Speaking of which—got enough cash?"

"You sound like my mother." Lola stood on one foot, then the other. First Joshua and now this. She'd been ready to leave twenty minutes earlier. "I'm fine." When she'd first met Charlie, she'd thought him homely, with his deep-set eyes, blade of a nose, and wide full mouth warring for dominance between a broad brow and uncompromising chin. In repose, he could look almost angry, something he knew and used to good effect when questioning suspects. Now those same features twisted in concern. Lola was relieved that his eyes were in shadow.

"You'd better take this," he said.

She almost dropped it when she realized what it was. "The last thing I need is a gun."

"I'm not saying you have to use it. It was my mom's. It's just a little thing. It probably wouldn't even kill anybody unless you got right in his face, but it would stop him. It's already loaded. You'll feel better, knowing you've got it."

"You mean you will." She'd hoped for a laugh. None came. "You're as bad as Bub, the way you make me feel guilty."

"Speaking of which." He handed her another bag. Was there no end to the delays he'd manufacture?

"Now what?"

"Bub's food and his bowls." He took a couple of steps back and opened the front door. Bub streaked past him and into the truck, turning three times before settling himself into the passenger seat, panting in delight.

"What the—?"

Charlie boosted her into the truck. He reached in and turned the key. The engine caught on the first try. Lola had a good idea, looking at his expression, how criminals felt when they realized the sheriff had gotten the better of them. "Best to share your space with another beating heart," he said. He closed the door behind her and raised his fingers to his lips and put them to the glass.

She thought of his own heart, beating alone in the cold house. What about you? she wanted to say. She touched her fingers briefly to the window, pressing hard against his on the other side, and put her foot to the accelerator.

CHAPTER NINE

Magpie lay at the intersection of mountain and plains, spaces abruptly changing from vertical to horizontal. Lola loved the juxtaposition, the headlong sweep of prairie to the east, the way it made her feel at once small and soaring, while behind her rose the bracing immensity of the Rocky Mountain Front, the sheer limestone reefs seemingly so close that she could put a hand to them to steady herself. Until Lola drove east out of Magpie, she hadn't realized how much she'd come to take that defining backdrop for granted.

Sixty miles out, her sky-gouging landmark disappeared from the rear-view mirror and the world became entirely too vast. The sky slowly lightened into roughly the same clotted-milk shade as the snow, making it impossible to tell where land left off and clouds began. "Do you think if I stood on my head it would look much different?" she asked Bub. She was already grateful for the company. Not, she thought, that she'd ever give Charlie the satisfaction of knowing that. She dug a hand into Bub's fur, and felt for the stump of his missing leg. It ended in a hard knot of scar tissue that Bub gnawed when he was bored. She reminded herself that the dog had almost died because of her, flinging himself at the man who had killed Mary Alice and then had tried to kill Lola, too. So what if Bub's presence meant a few extra stops so that he could do his business? She scratched at his ears. He thumped his tail against the seat. The pickup's interior was toasty, and she'd long ago shed her parka and hat and mittens and glove liners. Still, the dog—the warm, living mass of him—provided a different kind of comfort, warding off the psychic chill imposed by her frozen surroundings. She kept one hand on Bub's ribcage, with its reassuring rise and fall, and scanned the landscape, picking out features—a dense shelterbelt heralding a faraway ranch, the inevitable grain elevators marking a town—as a way of breaking it into manageable proportions.

Handfuls of houses, the remnants of railroad towns, sprang from the prairie at regular intervals and receded behind her before she could take comfort in the knowledge that other human beings shared the boundless space around her. Angus cattle stood motionless in fields of wind-whipped snow, like black barges in icy bays. At least, she thought, the road itself was largely clear of snow, scrubbed as it was by the merciless wind. Fellow travelers were such a rarity that she took to counting passing vehicles as a way to combat boredom. When that proved insufficiently distracting, she ignored Bub's reproachful stare and warbled off-key tunes, starting with radio sing-alongs and then, when the dial went to static, a cappella versions of every song she could remember, including patriotic anthems and Christmas carols. She'd have recited poems, but all she could remember were dirty limericks and "Under the spreading chestnut tree," its line about the smith's large and sinewy hands leading her back to the limericks. By the time she reached the North Dakota border, she'd refilled the Thermos twice and stopped four times at gas stations whose bathrooms made her long for a fine healthy tree, if only such a thing had existed on the bald land and the mercury hadn't stopped its daytime ascent at zero. She wondered what Judith had thought on her own long journey east, the mountains and trees vanishing behind her, exchanging the sometimes-stifling warmth and caring of her own people for the disinterest of strangers. Even if Judith had gone willingly, it must have been daunting.

Everything changed at the North Dakota line, starting with the road. The pickup had jounced over tarred seams that stitched the pavement together for more than four hundred miles when the ride smoothed, the tires rolling over new macadam, the unbroken coal-black surface startling against the snow. The road widened to four lanes. The distractions she'd so wished for hours earlier made a belated appearance. She'd passed the occasional oil rig in Montana, but here they grew in profusion, stabbing at the sky, a veritable forest cloaked year-round in green—not the verdure of leaves, but the rustling come-hither of ready cash. First came the ubiquitous pump jacks common even around Magpie, grasshopper heads ducking rhythmically as metronomes toward the earth as their mechanisms turned slow-motion revolutions. Closer to the patch, flames heralded Lola's approach, waving like flags atop flare stacks beside rigs, burning off the natural gas that was a byproduct of oil drilling. Traffic picked up. Lola goosed the truck up an incline and steered it into a turnout. A supersize truck hauling a proportionate flatbed was parked there. Lola looked up and up. The equipment it carried—something round and metallic; part of a tank, maybe, or a pipe seemingly large enough to funnel the ocean—towered three stories above. She pulled her gaze back to the road with its surge of tankers and pickups and big rigs like the one parked behind her. There were panel trucks and fifteen-passenger vans, standard tractor trailers dwarfed by the double- and even triple-trailer varieties, too, along with the rare lone sedan moving low and squashable behind its high-riding cousins. That, she thought, was her horizon—not the indefinable line between snow and sky, but the river of trucks converging from all directions, ferrying oil and all of the things that went with it, the pipes and the gear and above all the manpower, across the rolling sea of prairie.

Night fell fast and hard. Floodlights appeared beside the road, glaring above a series of roadside campgrounds with travel trailers and RVs and pickup campers sardined into spaces meant for a third their number. The man who'd spoken so crudely of Judith in the café had called her "one of the girls from the trailer." Lola had thought she might end up knocking at the doors of a trailer park in Burnt Creek. Most towns had one. It hadn't occurred to her there'd be too many to count. A painted plywood sign heralded the town itself. "Burnt Creek. Population 700. Home of the Dinosaurs. 1972 Class-C basketball champs." Somebody had crossed out Dinosaurs and written in Drillers, sketching a hard hat with an oil company logo atop the cartoon T-Rex that balanced a basketball at the end of one of its tiny, useless arms. Lola thought it impossible that a town of seven hundred people would bring the profusion of neon that lit up the road into Burnt Creek like a Las Vegas boulevard. Lola crawled along with the traffic that backed up three blocks beyond what appeared to be the town's only stoplight. Lola shielded her eyes against the oncoming headlights. Most of the neon signs turned out to be for motels and, just as Jorkki had warned her, every last one said, "No Vacancy." There was a camper shell on the back of her pickup. Her tattered old sleeping bag that she'd used far too often in her travels around Afghanistan was back there, along with the newly purchased luxuries of a foam pad and a pillow and down comforter, as well as a plastic tub packed with a lantern and some canned goods—also, the can opener she'd belatedly added after a teasing reminder from Charlie—and a camp stove and toilet paper, standard equipment between September and May for every vehicle in Montana. She didn't want to have to use any of those things, least of all the toilet paper. She imagined herself crouched by the side of the truck, buffeted by wind and snow, and decided that if nothing else, she'd park next to a twenty-four-hour fast-food place with bathrooms she could bogart. Even though, in her experience, towns of seven hundred people didn't have twenty-four-hour anything. "But there's more than seven hundred people here now," she said to Bub. "A lot more."

She was already taking mental notes, years of habit kicking in, the frisson of a new place and a new story chasing the fatigue from her bones. People spilled from the door of a bar that looked a lot like a railroad car. Lola squinted. It *was* a railroad car. She belatedly took note of the name. "The Train," it said. And, in smaller letters, "Pull One." She worked it out in her mind and flinched. Pull a train. "Otherwise known as gang rape," she told Bub. He whined at her tone. The Train had to be a strip bar. She wondered if Judith had ended up in a place like that. Tried to imagine the clientele. She reached below the seat, where she'd stashed the little revolver. "You'll feel better having it," Charlie had said. Suddenly she did.

The lights grew brighter still, the street more crowded. She and Bub were in Burnt Creek proper now. Bars, bars and more bars. Lola had yet to see a church. There had to be one, if not several. The longer she lived in Montana, the more she marveled at the way even the most far-flung hamlets harbored a variety of congregations, sometimes all in a row, the Seventh-Day Adventists next to the Presbyterians next to the inevitable Catholic church that had begun as a mission guaranteed to try the faith of even the most sacrifice-addicted cleric. It was almost as if some long-ago law had mandated bars and churches in equal numbers, providing the balance of a Sunday morning recovery from Saturday night's revelries. Maybe North Dakota was different, she thought.

An American flag, standing stiff in the wind above a frame building, caught her attention, along with the most welcoming sight of the very long day. Homestead County, a sign said. And, below it, a smaller sign: "Sheriff's Department." Lola flicked the turn signal and pulled into a parking lot and found her notebook and Judith's photo from the newspaper. She flipped through the notebook until she came to the notes she'd made about Burnt Creek. The sheriff's name was Thor Brevik. She'd met just enough sheriffs in her brief time in Montana to know that Charlie's youth made him a rarity. Brevik was almost certainly one of those leathery-skinned specimens whose tarnished belt buckle from his rodeo days would likely outdo his badge when it came to grabbing attention. She imagined him tall, the beginnings of a stoop, another pale Scandinavian like Jorkki, the hair already so light as to render the transition from blond to white unremarkable. She looked at her watch. It was just before five. No matter what Thor Brevik looked like, if his workload were anything like Charlie's, he'd be at his desk another hour yet.

CHAPTER TEN

The man in the sheriff's office wasn't particularly old. And it was impossible to tell if he was leathery, despite the discomfiting amount of flesh on display. Tattoos from wrist to shoulder wrapped bare arms that bulged like boulders from a denim shirt with the sleeves ripped out and buttons long gone. The visible strip of chest and stomach appeared to be similarly adorned, albeit covered with such an impressive mat of hair—she'd been right about the blond, at least—that it was nearly impossible to make out the designs that twisted like so many snakes through the shrubbery. An inked strand of barbed wire provided the only demarcation between neck and jaw. In some trepidation, Lola shifted her gaze upward. Thor Brevik's blond curls framed a cherubic face that in no way went with the body below it. His pretty pursed lips parted in a smile of surpassing sweetness. A gold tooth shone. Lola blinked.

"Aren't you cold?" she blurted, looking at the exposed arms and flesh.

"Wouldn't be if you'd shut the door behind you." Something soft and Southern in his voice, a little syrup to flow pleasingly over all those crags.

Lola slammed the door shut. "Sorry. I don't know what's wrong with me."

He waved her apology away with a hand weighted with silver rings that reached to the knuckle of every finger, including his thumb. Lola saw a skull, a cobra, a Stars and Bars, and one featuring two carved silver women, hands grabbing one another's ankles, mouths bent to . . . she looked away. Each of the rings stuck up at least half an inch, rendering Brevik's fist a fearsome weapon.

The tooth flashed again. "Help you?" *He'p.*

Lola slid her hand into her pocket, ran her finger along the ragged edges of the clipping with Judith's picture. It seemed obscene to show the photo to this hulking aficionado of girl-on-girl action. If the people of Homestead County had elected this man as their sheriff, the county was rougher than she'd thought, reluctantly conceding to herself that Jan may have had a point.

"Y'all probably want the sheriff, right?"

"You mean—" Lola's sentences kept stopping before she was finished with them. The final cup of coffee, just before she drove into Burnt Creek, probably hadn't helped.

The man's laugh exploded in the small room, ricocheting off the walls, blasting Lola back against the door. She felt for the knob. "You thought I"—*Ah*—"was the sheriff? That's a good one. I'm Dawg. This here"—the rings beat a drum solo on an inner door—"would be Thor."

THOR BREVIK, like Charlie, was still at his desk. All resemblance ended there. Charlie's style with anyone, whether criminal suspect, stranger in town, or lifelong acquaintance, was to let the other person start the conversation, and also do most of the heavy lifting once it was under way. But Thor came out from behind his desk in a half-crouch, hand extended, talking, talking. "You must be Lola. Thought you'd never get here. Of course, it's a rotten drive. But we were starting to worry anyway." He urged her into a chair. Lola twisted. Dawg loomed behind her.

"Told you she'd get here fine. Y'all get acquainted now."

Thor flapped a hand as the door to the outer office was closing behind Dawg. "Don't forget, we roll at seven tomorrow, Dawg." He turned back to Lola. "I've been listening to the weather station all day, figuring you might run into snow. A front's supposed to blow through any time now. But it sounded like clear sailing all the way for you. How about some coffee? You're not one of those people who can't drink it after noon, are you? I can't imagine you are, not in your line of work. You reporters are the only people I know who drink as much coffee as cops. Take our local gal, Susie Bartles. I swear she goes through a gallon a day. Says she drinks a cup at bedtime to help her sleep. Sugar? Cream? Powdered is all I've got."

"Black is fine." When he brought the coffee to her, his back remained bent as though in a bow. But whatever was wrong with his back, the rest of Thor Brevik was just fine. More than fine. Lola thought of old movie posters, the square-jawed guy in the white hat, one arm curled around the waist of a little lady who stared adoringly into his handsome face. Lola yanked her own stare away, fearful that some adoration of her own might have crept into it. "How'd you know who I am?"

"Why, your sheriff, of course."

Lola choked on a mouthful of java so strong it put her own muscular brew to shame. "Charlie?"

Thor swung his arms behind him and hoisted himself up onto his desk. He wore the belt buckle she'd expected, showing a bull flinging its hind feet high in the air, a cowboy balanced improbably on its back. "He called to let me know you were coming. Told me to keep an eye on you. Burnt Creek can be hard on new folks."

She could have sworn he winked. She raised the mug to her lips. With anyone else, the long sip would have been a delaying tactic, a way to keep the person talking. But Thor Brevik didn't need tactics to keep talking. "It didn't used to be this way. Time was when we were mostly just a bunch of dirt farmers barely hanging on. Now you've got folks who've been here their whole lives taking vacations in places like Paris. Coming back all prissy and perfumed. And the likes of the people showing up looking for work—well, they're from whatever the opposite of Paris is, I suppose. Your Sheriff Laurendeau is right to worry."

My sheriff? Lola stopped herself from saying it aloud. What in the world had Charlie said? She took another sip and looked at the clock. A half hour had flown by. She wondered how long it would take her to find a place to settle for the night.

He rubbed his hands together. "Is it cold in here? I swear as soon as it gets dark, the temperature drops ten degrees inside for every twenty outside." He hopped down from the desk and fiddled with a thermostat. Heat curled around Lola's ankles. She leaned toward it. Thor Brevik snapped the cover back over the thermostat. "How can we help you while you're here?"

Judith's photo, deep within a hip pocket, burned against her thigh. Lola hesitated. He'd already had one conversation with Charlie. What if he had another? "I'm assuming I won't be able to get a room tonight, or any night while I'm here," she stalled. "Is it okay if I park my truck in your lot for the night?"

Thor flung his arms wide. "Be my guest." A phone buzzed on his desk. He leaned back and hit a blinking button. Dawg's voice came tinny through the speaker. "I'm calling it a night, sheriff."

Lola had thought him already gone. She wondered if he'd lingered at the door, listening. She was glad she hadn't asked the sheriff about Judith yet.

"I'm right behind you." Thor hit the button and the phone went dark.

Lola gestured toward the phone. "That guy. Dawg. He's—"

"He's what?" Thor parried. The corners of his eyes crinkled, as though the two of them were about to share a delicious joke.

Lola thought any number of words could apply to Dawg, none complimentary. She went with tact. "He's *unlikely*. What does he do here?"

Thor chuckled. "Little of this, little of that. He's sort of a deputy. That's where he gets his nickname. You know—Deputy Dawg."

Lola thought the nickname an insult to the portly cartoon character. "What do you mean, sort of a deputy?"

Thor leaned toward her and stage-whispered, bringing her into a cozy conspiracy. "I call him a reserve deputy. He can't be a real deputy, of course. He didn't pass the background check. But he's a tremendous help." He patted his belt buckle. "Back in the day, a bull stomped right on my backbone. The older I get, the harder it is to deal with. But Dawg deals just fine. And then there's the way he looks. What with the element we've got coming into town, it actually works to my advantage to have him along on some of the calls we get. Otherwise it's just me. Towns like Williston in the next county up from here, they've gotten big enough to justify extra law enforcement. But Homestead County's still too small, at least when it comes to permanent residents. The old-timers here might not like the looks of Dawg, but until they approve the money to let me hire a real deputy, this is what they're stuck with."

Lola thought that if she lived in Burnt Creek, she'd be banging on her county commissioner's front door, demanding he raise taxes or do whatever it took to get Dawg out of the sheriff's office and a real deputy in. Then she thought of the bar she'd seen on the way into town. The Train. She imagined the sort of clientele it attracted. Maybe Dawg had his uses after all.

Thor watched her, expectation in his eyes. "Anything else I can help you with?"

She pulled the clipping from her pocket and smoothed its creases on the surface of Thor's desk. "You can help me by telling me anything you know about this girl."

CHAPTER ELEVEN

Lola had trimmed the clipping free of copy, so that only Judith's photo remained, with no way to tell that it belonged with an obituary. Judith usually pulled her hair away from her face with a thin headband and further tamed it into a ponytail, the way she wore it for basketball games, but in this photo her hair swung free, flowing over her shoulders. Even in the slightly off-register black-and-white newspaper photo, it shone, vying for brightness with the smile so wide it farther lifted the corners of her uptilted eyes. It was the same photo that had accompanied the announcement that in her senior year, Judith had yet again made the National Honor Society.

That was the thing about Judith. Somehow, even through the worst of her drugging, she'd managed to keep up with her studies. It wasn't unusual for Joshua to bond his sister out of juvie on a weekend, and then show up at the café the following week brandishing another one of Judith's tests with an A+ scrawled across the top. "Why can't she ace the rest of her life the way she does school?" he'd ask, glaring at the test paper as though it somehow refused to give him the answer.

The furnace knocked a few times and fell silent. The heat went away. Thor held the clipping like a piece of evidence, pinching its far corners between his fingertips. He stared at the photo for a long time. Lawmen, thought Lola. They were all alike. Give them something perfectly obvious and they focused on it as though it held the key to a serial murder case. Lola had seen Charlie turn the same look on a menu, presumably scanning it for the thing that didn't fit. "The cheeseburger did it," she said once. He hadn't laughed.

"Indian girl?" Thor said finally.

"Blackfeet."

"Beautiful."

"Yes."

Warm air whooshed again from the heating vents with an asthmatic gasp. Lola gave the furnace another year, tops, before the county got stuck with a big replacement bill. The county courthouses Lola had seen so far in Montana, even in Magpie, were imposing affairs, built of blocky stone with soaring clock towers, meant to impress a harsh land with the fact that civilization had arrived. Civilization apparently ran out of steam in North Dakota. The courthouse containing the sheriff's office was a low frame building shaped like a squared-off C, town offices on one side, county on the other, paint peeling on both. Thor's window faced the city offices. That side of the building was black. Lola thought it likely that at this hour, she and Thor were the only two people in the whole place.

"We don't get a whole lot of Indians over this way."

Lola shifted in her seat. "Actually, you do. Or, at least you're getting more. That's why I'm here. To write about all the people from the Blackfeet reservation who are coming over here for work."

"Ah. That explains it."

"Explains what?"

"What you're doing here. Your sheriff didn't say."

Lola wished he'd quit calling Charlie *her* sheriff. How was Thor Brevik supposed to take her seriously if he saw her first and foremost as the sheriff's girlfriend? "I'm a reporter. That's what brings me here." She heard the edge in her voice and tried to soften it. "I was hoping you could help me. Are there places in town where Indians hang out? Where they maybe feel more comfortable than others?" It had taken Lola about five minutes in Montana to figure out that attitudes about Indian people were sometimes delivered word-for-word in the same disparaging phrases that white people directed against blacks in Baltimore. She didn't expect much difference in North Dakota, but worried nonetheless that her question might offend Thor. Instead, he laughed. "We got the woo-woo Indians—so you tell me—we got India-Indians, we got colored, we got Mexican, we got Chinese and Japanese and every other kind of 'ese' you can think of coming here for work. People would go crazy if they try to keep to themselves."

Lola told herself that Thor was a product of his environment, his characterizations of other people due to the fact that, until the oil boom, every single person around him most likely had been white. She'd met people in Montana who'd gotten all the way to high school without having seen a black person. "Men, mostly. Right?"

"That is a fact. Fifty-to-one men-to-women, I'd say. Maybe a hundred-to-one. The other day I told the Chamber of Commerce they ought to start marketing Burnt Creek as the marriage capital of the world. If a girl can't find herself a man here, she might as well hang it up and join a convent."

Lola tiptoed toward her next question. "That must pose some law enforcement problems."

Thor was ahead of her. "You want to know if there's whorin'."

Lola checked a wince. "It seems logical."

The furnace clanked with the finality of a jail door slamming shut. The chill moved in fast, brushing Lola's fingertips, the end of her nose. Thor rubbed his hands together. "You want me to kick up the heat another notch? Or are we about done here?"

"We're about done. But—prostitution," Lola reminded him. The word sounded prim. She thought of the roughnecks who'd wreaked such havoc at Nell's. Given the clientele, whoring seemed the more appropriate team.

"It stands to reason we've got it. I've kept an eye on the titty bars, but they seem clean enough. Wouldn't surprise me if some of the dancers set up dates on their own, though."

"What about"—what was the phrase the man at the café had used?—"the man camp?"

"Which one?"

"Which one what?"

"Camp. We got a new man camp just on the edge of town and then all the damn campgrounds—excuse my language—that might as well be man camps now, too."

Lola slumped in her chair. "The new one. I guess."

Thor's denial was swift and decisive. "Not a chance. They got security guards, everything. That place is tighter than a tick."

Lola decided it was too soon to ask him about the trailer that the man in Nell's had mentioned. If he didn't know about it, the question would only embarrass him. And if he did know, his denial of problems in the man camp meant she'd need a lot more information before she hit him with a question. Thor, however, had one for her.

"Was this girl a hooker?"

"Maybe. It's not important." Stupid, she thought, as soon as she said it. If it hadn't been important, she wouldn't have brought it up. And, by the way Thor's face went all bland and accommodating, she knew he realized that, too. No use even mentioning the other girls at this point. She'd already tipped her hand too soon. Lola reached for her coat. She retrieved the clipping from Thor's desk and shoved it into her pocket. It seemed rude to talk about Judith in such terms with her smiling up at them.

"If she was a hooker," said Thor, "she never got caught. I've never seen that girl in my life." His gaze slid sideways when he said it.

Some liars, Charlie had told Lola, look you straight in the eye when they spin their tales. That's how you know. Other ones, they glance away at the last minute. How do you tell, Lola asked him once, which is which? "Instinct," Charlie told her. "You've got to trust your gut."

Lola did a gut check. It told her nothing at all.

CHAPTER TWELVE

By the time Lola left Thor's office, the storm he'd mentioned had started. She let Bub out of the truck for a minute, then ran the engine awhile to warm the cab before shaking some kibble into his bowl and going in search of her own dinner. She ducked her head against the stinging flakes and dodged semis as she crossed the street to a bar called The Mint. As far as Lola could tell, every single postage-stamp town across northern Montana into North Dakota had a Mint Bar, along with a Stockman's.

"The Mint harkens back to the railroad days," Thor had told her when she'd asked for a recommendation. "In the old days, you'd never have sent somebody to a railroad bar, especially not a lady. But some of the characters we see these days make those old brakemen and gandy dancers look like Sunday school girls. Lucky for all of us that they don't favor The Mint."

The Mint was all warmth and light and shouted conversations. Every table was taken. Lola elbowed her way to the last counter stool, brushing past a hesitant man of about fifty whose coveralls still bore the store shelf's creases. His work boots looked stiff and blister-making; his haircut careful, his belly soft. She wondered what sort of work he'd done before taking a run at the patch. Cubicle rat, probably. At the counter, she pushed away the proffered menu and ordered a steak and a beer. Then she thought of the long night facing her in the back of the truck, the roll of toilet paper stashed there, the need to limit her liquid intake. "Better make that wine," she said. That, at least, would give her a fighting chance of making it until morning with her dignity intact.

The waitress held a jelly glass beneath a box for a long time. She slid it cautiously across the counter toward Lola, who bent her mouth to it for the first sip. "That's what I call a pour," she told the waitress. The girl, who didn't look more than fifteen, blushed beneath a plastering of makeup that failed in its attempt to mask the acne that ridged her cheekbones and clustered in a volcanic mass on her chin.

"Did I do something wrong?" She sounded as though she was used to being told yes.

"No." Lola took another sip, lowering the level just enough to allow her to actually lift the glass without spilling. "You did just right."

"That one's on me."

Lola turned to look at the man on her right who had spoken up. He sat with elbows planted firmly on either side of a plate mounded high with starchy things, knife in one hand, fork in the other. A drop of gravy hung from the end of his walrus mustache. Beneath it, his lips moved. Lola thought maybe he was smiling.

"No, thank you."

The man turned his attention back to his meal, scraping a dollop of mashed potatoes onto the fork with his knife and shoveling it under the mustache.

"Well, then, it must be on me."

Lola swung to her left. The man there was younger, clean-shaven, a toothpick at a jaunty angle in the corner of his mouth. The overhead lights glinted off his Oakleys. Hopped up on something, Lola thought, not wanting anybody to see those telltale pinpoint pupils.

"More your style than Grandpa over there, right? Go ahead. Have another glass. Whatever you feel like drinking, I'm buying." The toothpick swiveled to the other side of his mouth.

"No." Lola put some spin on it. "Thank you."

He winked and pointed his finger at her. Made a *tch* sound against his teeth. "Can't blame a fella for trying."

Can't blame a woman for trying to eat a meal in peace, she thought. But she kept it to herself. No use prolonging the encounter. A heavy hand fell on her shoulder. She turned and saw the man who'd been waiting for a seat when she came in. She looked down at the hand. It was soft and pink, the nails trimmed and clean. She wondered if he'd gotten them manicured in his former life. She'd heard that, while she'd been in Afghanistan, men back home had taken to doing such things.

"Sorry those men are bothering you," he said. "I just got a table. Perhaps you'd like to join me there. You might enjoy the company more than—" He glanced from one side of Lola to the other.

"No." Her patience fled. "Go away." The hand slid from her shoulder. He trudged back to his table accompanied by guffaws from the counter crew.

"Is it always like this?" Lola asked the girl behind the counter. "Because when I checked the mirror this morning, I looked the same as I always did. It's not like I turned gorgeous sometime in the middle of the day."

"You here alone?"

"Clearly."

The girl leaned across the counter and whispered. "You packing?"

Lola thought of the toylike revolver beneath the seat in the truck. "Sort of."

The girl slid her gaze to the men on either side of Lola and kept her voice low. "Good. You want to keep that thing on you day and night. We only live two blocks from here, but my dad doesn't even let me walk to work alone. He drops me off and picks me up. And when my mom wants to go up to the big stores in Williston, he sticks to her like glue. Women have gotten felt up in the aisles, raped in the parking lot. I don't know a single woman who doesn't carry pepper spray, but most of us go for something stronger."

Lola thought that sounded farfetched and said as much.

"All I know," the girl said, "is I don't go anywhere alone anymore. And if you're smart, you won't either."

"Hey, Ellen." The shout came from the other end of the counter. A knot of men, balancing their plates in their hands, called again to the waitress. "When are we going to see you down at The Train? Nice, healthy girl like you, you'd make three times in a night there as you do in a week at this dump. Over there, nobody'd care about your face. Hey. C'mere." One of the men waved her toward him. Ellen plodded the length of the counter. The man reached across it and slid a bill beneath her apron strings. The girl jerked away. Their laughter drowned her gasp. "There's more where that came from, girl."

Ellen disappeared into the kitchen and came back with Lola's steak. Patches beneath her eyes shone clean and damp, entirely free of the makeup that would have disguised the redness of recent tears. "You know," Lola whispered, "you don't need to hide under all that gunk. And you don't need to listen to those jerks."

Ellen slammed down the plate. "Go to hell. You don't know what you're talking about."

Lola sawed at the steak, her jaw already aching in expectation of the prolonged chewing that awaited. Her months in Montana had accustomed her to the fact that no matter how she ordered it, her steak would arrive well done. "Yes, I do." She worked a bite of steak from one side of her mouth to the other, and spoke around it. "You find out, eventually, that looks are the last thing that matter. Maybe not the last thing. But not always the first either."

"You want to know what matters?" Ellen reached into the rear pocket of her jeans. The motion threw her shoulders back. Even beneath the disguising apron, Lola could see a lush figure. She hadn't noticed, but the men at the end of the bar had, and from a distance, too.

Ellen withdrew her hand from her pocket. She thrust it beneath Lola's nose. Let her fingers unfold. The bill that one of the men had tucked beneath the apron lay there, creased lengthwise. "Go ahead," Ellen urged. "Look at it."

Lola expected to see a phone number on it, maybe some crude message. She shook it open. "Holy shit."

"Yeah," said Ellen.

Lola had thought they'd given her a five or even a twenty, but she held a hundred-dollar bill in her hand.

Ellen snatched it back. "You were right. My looks don't matter at all. And they were right, too. I could make way more there than I can here. And I turn eighteen this summer." She turned her back on Lola and headed back down to the other end of the counter, hips swaying, chest outthrust.

If a girl could score a Benjamin with her clothes on, Lola thought, how much would a dancer who took them off make? And what about someone who not only took off her clothes but lay down with a man? That whiskery, redheaded guy back at Nell's had as much as said Judith was a whore. The lure of easy money had led stronger people than a drug-addled teenager down the wrong path—especially when that teenager felt painfully indebted to her brother. The wine went sour in Lola's mouth. She pushed the glass away and slid the remains of her steak into a baggie that she kept on hand for scraps for Bub. The girl came back.

"More?"

"I think I've had about all I can handle for one night," she said, happy to let Ellen think she was only talking about the wine.

CHAPTER THIRTEEN

At three in the morning, Lola kicked off the quilt she'd draped atop her sleeping bag. The thermometer on the bank clock across the street had read fifteen below when she'd crawled into the back of the truck with Bub. It had to be colder now, but to Lola's grateful surprise their combined body warmth had heated the truck to something nearing comfort. Headlights swept across the window with rhythmic regularity; workers heading out on the day shift. People in The Mint the previous night had told her that some of the roughnecks drove as far as fifty miles to their rigs. The lucky ones from the man camp rode old school buses that had been painted white and pressed into service as shuttles. Bub whined. Lola struggled out of the sleeping bag and into her parka. She thrust her feet into boots and opened the back of the truck and slid out. Bub shot to a corner of the municipal building. Lola followed him and kicked fresh snow over the yellow circle he created. A pickup on steroids pulled off the main street and stopped beside her. The window lowered.

"You working?"

The man who spoke had a square pleasant face. He may have been headed for a twelve-hour shift in the weather, but he'd shaved and combed his hair. Another unemployed insurance agent, Lola thought, come to the patch to support a family back in a sprawling suburban house with an underwater mortgage. "Excuse me?"

"I wondered if you were working. I got an early start this morning, so I've got a little extra time. My truck's already warmed up. I could pull over right there, out of the light. I'm pulling a double shift today. Be good to start it with a smile."

Lola wanted to crawl back into the truck and fall into sleep again before the wind woke her all the way up. Maybe he didn't mean what she thought he did. He dispelled that notion fast.

"You know." He poked a forefinger into his fist, the crude gesture at odds with his outward decency. "You work for yourself? Or are you one of those girls from the camp? Heard somebody new was coming in. You take care of me now, you can keep all the money for yourself. I know the place takes its cut." He checked his phone. "I'm still okay on time. I'm not looking for anything fancy."

He could have been discussing getting a cup of coffee. Which Lola wished, very badly, that she had. She needed her brain to kick into gear. What had the redheaded guy said back at Nell's? "She's one of them in the man camp. You know the ones I mean. From the trailer."

"The camp," she said. "I'm looking for somebody there. I didn't want to try to find it in the dark." She unzipped her parka, hoping the cold would shock her synapses into firing. "Maybe you can tell me how to get there."

"Who would that be?"

He looked like a family man. Lola thought of Joshua and played the sibling card. "My sister. She fell in with a bad crew. I'm trying to get her to come back home." She scuffed her feet in the snow.

He looked at his phone again. "That's about as bad as a crew gets. You don't want to deal with them. I'd go to the police if I were you. About time somebody did."

Lola tamped down a flare of interest, hoping it hadn't shown on her face. "Then you know what I'm dealing with. I can't concentrate on anything else right now. Although I appreciate the offer. I really do."

He rolled his eyes. "Right. But maybe I'll see you around again. Name's Dave. You ever feel like making a little extra on the side, I take my dinners at the Grub Steak. You can find me there after ten."

"That's late."

"So's my shift."

Lola raised a hand. She'd left her gloves in the truck, and she cut the wave short, curling her fingers against the cold. "I'll be sure and keep an eye out for you, Dave." By the time she and Bub had settled themselves back in the truck, all the heat fled the camper. She held the dog tight, shivering within the layers of sleeping bag and quilt, until the late-breaking dawn.

THE CELLPHONE ding-donged in her ear, seemingly minutes after she'd finally fallen back asleep. Lola held the phone close to her face in the grey light. It was eight-thirty. The phone sounded again, annoyingly cheerful. She reminded herself to find a new ringtone. She cleared her throat. "This is Lola."

"Lola, what in hell do you think you're doing?"

"Charlie?"

"You know damn well who this is. What are you up to over there?"

Bub inched his way from his spot across her feet until he lay upon her chest. Lola forced her words past the fifty-pound weight compressing her lungs. "What are you talking about? You know I'm working on a story. A series."

"But what story? Thor Brevik said you started right off asking about Judith."

Lola made a mental note to kill Thor Brevik. Or, at least not say more than "Hello," "Goodbye," "Please" and "Thank you very much for ratting me out."

"For God's sake, Charlie. It's a logical question. If I get any information, I'll pass it along to Jan. How are you today, anyway? What's it like to have spent the night in a nice, warm bed? And what's the deal with Brevik? He's got this freak working for him.

Do you know anything about that?" Trying to change the subject, and maybe get some sympathy, too. Neither worked.

"Let's just say it's a relief not to have spent the night with someone I apparently can't trust at all. When you get back, you might want to think about getting your own place. It's not like it'll take you any time at all to pack. You never really moved into mine. I should have known."

"Charlie—" The phone was dead at her ear. Lola kicked open the back of the truck and let Bub do his business by himself. "Damn." She lay back in the twisted sleeping bag and tried to remember the last time she'd had anything resembling a relationship, let alone what seemed to be a relatively healthy one. She'd spent years in Afghanistan limiting herself to practical, prescriptive sex, preferably with colleagues getting ready to rotate to another assignment or aid workers winding up their tours of duty. Which, she'd told herself when things started with Charlie, was how things were likely to go with him, too. But she'd been secretly pleased as the weeks accumulated with neither insecurities nor drama, and passion limited to bed, which was where it belonged. She'd thought they were comfortable together. Apparently, she'd been wrong. Bub touched an icy nose to her neck just as the phone rang again.

"Jesus!" she shouted. Then, "Charlie, I'm sorry. That wasn't meant for you."

"This isn't Charlie. But you owe that man an apology. And me, too."

"Jan." Lola held the phone away and glared at it, then put it back to her ear. "What do you want?"

"What do you think I want? I want you to stay the hell away from my story. Charlie just called me and said you were all over it. Jorkki is going to fire your ass."

The dog was back on Lola's chest. Which, she thought was a good thing. The effort required to speak made her words seem slow, measured. "Jan. I'm going to tell you the same thing I told Charlie. And if Jorkki tries to fire me, I'm going to tell him, too.

It's crazy for me to be over here and not ask about Judith. Besides, I think this is about more than Judith."

Lola could practically feel Jan's struggle to control her curiosity.

"How's that?" Jan spoke past a yawn whose fakery came through loud and clear.

"I think it's about all those girls. Too many of them, you know? All from the same place. All in trouble with the law. Now one of them's dead. You know what we say—"

"There's no such thing as coincidence," Jan broke in with the oft-repeated lesson.

"Exactly," Lola said. "So why don't you do some poking around back there, and I'll do some here. Get their photos. Check the school library. The yearbooks should have them." Lola knew that the minute Jan put faces to the names, found out the barest facts about the girls, they'd be real to her and she'd be hooked. "I'll feed you whatever I find out here. Think what it would mean to people for you to get to the bottom of whatever happened to those girls." She gave Jan a moment to salivate over the irresistible possibilities that lay on the silver platter she'd just extended. "Now, if you don't mind, I've got a story—my own story—to work on." This time, she made sure that she was the one who hung up first.

She spit on her hands and ran her fingers through her hair. It was growing out in ways that reminded her why she'd cropped it so short for so many years. Now she had a good three inches of unruly curls, one more layer of insulation between her and the cold. Silly to even worry about her hair, really, given that it would spend most of the day hidden in a hat. Which she located and pulled onto her head with a jerk, making sure it covered her ears. Weeks earlier, she'd returned from a careless outing with one lobe white and frozen. The thawing-out process was something she never wanted to repeat.

"Come on, Bub. Looks like we'd better go track down Judith's uncles." Could she help it if any of them might have run into Judith in Burnt Creek, or at least heard through the Indian Country grapevine about what Judith was up to in the patch? More to the point, the places she needed to go to ask about Judith—the strip bars like The Train and its ilk—probably wouldn't be open until later in the day.

Bub shoved his face against hers, something he did whenever she became agitated. She ruffled his fur. "Everything's going to work out just fine." But just to be sure, she held her finger over the phone's on/off button until its screen went black.

CHAPTER FOURTEEN

Roy deRoche and assorted relatives and friends—Lola had long ago given up trying to track relationships—had somehow managed to snag one of Burnt Creek's rare apartments, where the sixteen men split the twenty-five-hundred-dollar-a-month rent on two shoebox bedrooms, a closet of a bathroom, and a microwave and minifridge. They lined up four cots in each of the bedrooms and duct-taped blankets over the windows so that the eight men coming off the night shift could tumble onto still-warm, just-abandoned cots and sleep through the day's weak light. The blankets served as extra insulation against the icy winds that sliced through the gaps between window frame and walls, but also served to hold in the mingled odors of sweat and farts and feet that had spent twelve hours and more in heavy work boots.

The smell greeted Lola as the door swung inward. She clutched an armful of plastic containers closer to her chest. She'd stopped by Josephine's house the day before she'd left for Burnt Creek, collecting frozen offerings of stew and casseroles so that the men would have a taste of home, a gesture calculated to win the good will of both the women and their men—altruism that she hoped would make them more likely to talk with her, and with Jan, too, about matters normally too sensitive to discuss with outsiders. "I sent Roy off with plenty of food," Josephine had assured Lola, as though she might assume otherwise. "But those guys work so long and so hard, they've probably inhaled every last bit of it by now."

Lola had hurried to be at the apartment early, thinking to catch the night shift crew before they hit the sack, but instead the apartment was impossibly crowded. Some men sat two to a cot, testing the limits of the threadbare canvas. Others rooted around beneath the cots, stuffing belongings into duffel bags. Lola squinted into the dimness, searching for Roy. He emerged from the second bedroom, carrying a bundle of what appeared to be clothing wrapped in a sheet.

"Lola," he said. "I forgot you were coming."

A couple of the men looked her way, but most of the others continued what they were doing, even if that involved nothing more than staring into space. Roy reached for one of the blankets over the windows and ripped it away. The light did the room and its occupants no favors.

"Damn, Roy," one man said. "Why you got to do that?"

"You can sleep in the van," Roy said to him. "Come on. We've got to clear out. They've got some renters coming in tomorrow."

"What's going on?" said Lola.

"What's it look like?" Roy shrugged into an oil-stained Carhartt coat and slung the bundle over his shoulder. "We're out."

"Out?" Lola could think of only one meaning—but one so unimaginable that she asked anyway, hoping for a different answer.

"Fired," Roy said.

"Shitcanned," another man chimed in.

"Don't let the door hit you in the ass on your way out."

"There's sixteen more where you came from, and another hunnerd sixteen waiting to take their places."

Lola flung up her hands to stop the barrage of euphemisms. The plastic containers tumbled like frozen bricks onto a vacant cot. "But why?"

One of the men laughed, a short barking noise. "The patch is like the army. If they'd wanted someone in your family to go and die, they'd have killed her themselves."

The men were on their feet now, looking toward the door.

"Wait. Please. You got fired because you took time off for Judith's funeral?"

"That's about the size of it," Roy said. "Guess the van's gonna get repo'ed. Doesn't matter, really. No use for it now, anyway."

A burly man ran his right hand over his face. It was missing two fingers, the scar still red and raw, coarse black stitches poking up from the skin. "Easy for you to say. I took out a loan on an addition to the house so my daughter and her husband and our grandbaby could come home and live with us instead of being jammed into that apartment and working shit jobs down in Great Falls. There goes my credit. Think they'll repo the sheetrock?"

Grim, knowing smiles passed around the room. Lola thought of the new trucks, the cow-calf pairs meant to fatten on summer grazing, the seed money for a spouse's coffee cart—the reservation's first. The new clothes for kids instead of hand-me-downs, the spill of presents beneath Christmas trees, the occasional dinner out at the local café, ice cream for the whole family. The debts paid off, the savings accounts started. The clutch at the bottom rung of the ladder, the daring gaze upward. She sat down on one of the cots with a thump and pulled out her notebook.

"Whose decision was this? What did they tell you? And when?"

Roy motioned for her to stand. "That cot's coming with us," he said. "No time to talk now. Call us when you get back to Magpie. Maybe people will feel like talking. Maybe not."

The men filed past her, stooping to retrieve the containers of food, and stashed the casseroles and the cots and their duffels and small sad bundles into the van and climbed in after them. Roy started the engine and lifted a hand to Lola as she stood on the sagging steps and watched the story that had brought her to Burnt Creek vanish in a swirl of exhaust and snow.

Lola lingered in the yard, uttering every curse word she could think of. She started with the good, solid Anglo-Saxon ones, all sex and excrement, then moved on to profanity, a vocabulary that had increased considerably during her time in Afghanistan, where all manner of deities were cursed, a rising flow of invective halted only by the slam of a door on the other side of the house and the appearance of a red-faced bowling ball of a woman waving a broom at Lola as if to sweep her off the very face of the planet.

"Shame! Shame! Decent people live here. Begone!"

"Begone?" Lola said. "Begone? Who talks like that?" She headed for the truck, where Bub's nose had smeared the passenger-side window nearly opaque, calling back to the woman. "Forsooth. As it happens, I was just taking my leave." But she spun on her heel at the woman's next words.

"I finally get rid of those filthy Indians and now this." The woman stomped back toward her side of the house, rolling sailor-like as she walked, the broom trailing behind her in the snow.

"What did you say?" Lola ran to confront her, blocking her way. "What about the Indians?"

The woman dropped the broom and folded her arms across her chest. She'd left the house without a coat and her face purpled dangerously, whether from the cold or indignation Lola couldn't tell. "Crammed into that place on top of each other. Living like animals. If they hadn't gotten themselves fired, I'd have had to evict them."

"No, you wouldn't have." Lola's voice rose. "You'd have kept right on taking their rent money every month, overcharging them for living in that hole just like you're going to do the next people. Shame? The shame's on you." She heard herself shouting, her face inches from the woman's, blasting all the morning's frustration at an ignorant woman who probably for the first time in her life was on firm financial footing and whose only experience of Indians was likely the seemingly rough men who outnumbered her sixteen-to-one on the other side of her home's too-thin walls. Lola headed for the truck. "Sorry," she muttered. Which, she thought to herself, was more than the woman deserved. Bub whomped against her as she got into the truck, keening as he sensed her agitation. Lola stroked him until he quieted and her own breathing settled. The woman was back inside. Lola saw the curtains stir on her side of the house. She started the truck and drove away, turning down one street and then another. She wondered how long it would take Jorkki to find out that the reason for her trip to Burnt Creek had vanished. Someone on the van had no doubt already texted a relative with the news, which meant it was all over the reservation. Tina would know, but might not volunteer the information at the office. Lola knew she could go home and write a story about the men's firing, about the effect on the reservation's economy. But her trip to Burnt Creek would supply nothing more than a few paragraphs of description of their brief time in the patch. She thought of Joshua, materializing beside her the morning she left, begging for news about his dead sister. About one of the uncles, wishing for a body for a proper burial. She didn't have anything for them, either.

"A thousand-mile round-trip deserves more than a few paragraphs," she assured Bub, whose worried look had disappeared, replaced by his typically agreeable manner, now that her voice was back to normal. "Jorkki probably won't hear anything at least until tomorrow. We're already here. Might as well ask around about Judith and those girls."

CHAPTER FIFTEEN

Even though Thor had said he thought some of the strip-club dancers might be turning tricks on the side, Lola couldn't face The Train. She opted instead for a place called the Sweet Crude, driving three times around the block before she worked up the nerve to walk inside. The Sweet Crude was in one of the prefab buildings that seemed to comprise half of Burnt Creek proper and all of its outskirts, set so low to the ground that a dancer who forgot herself and flung up an enthusiastic arm risked bruising it against the ceiling. Music pounded Lola's eardrums. It wasn't yet noon, but every barstool was taken by men who didn't even look away to place their drink orders, so focused were they on the young woman whose very presence seemed a contradiction of physics, given that she remained upright when the size and weight of her breasts should have toppled her forward. Men crowded behind the stools, jostling for a better view, both of the dancer and of the levels in the drinks at the bar, hoping a near-empty glass signaled a soon-to-be-vacant seat. Bowls of peanuts sat beside the drinks, and the men dug into them with hard scarred hands and cracked the shells between their teeth. They spat them out without aiming, justifying the presence of a bikinied waitress whose sole job appeared to be to sashay behind the barstools with a whisk broom and dustpan, bending and presenting her impertinent bottom at regular intervals, sweeping diligently until someone tucked a bill or two beneath her thong, at which point she moved on to the next pile of peanut shells. Lola recognized one of the men at the bar as Dawg, the sheriff's deputy, who turned on the dancer the same moist devoted gaze he'd bestowed upon the sheriff. Lola, trying to skirt the walls of the room, was glad he was so preoccupied. Yet despite the gravity-defying assets of Miss Double Derricks, the morning's advertised entertainment, Lola still managed to attract attention. She willed an approaching man to walk past, but he blocked her way. His lips moved. "What?" Lola mouthed. Maybe she actually said it. She couldn't hear a damn thing over Salt-N-Pepa's shoopin'. The man took her arm and steered her toward the door.

"Sorry," the man said when they stood in the cold. A couple of roughnecks shoved past, openly assessing Lola before going inside. "I know it's cold, but I can't hear over the music. Here's the deal. Sixty a night. That's what you owe me for stage time. Plus a cut of tips. And don't think you can squirrel them away somewhere. That's what Summer thought and that's why she's gone and we've got ourselves a job opening."

The tip of Lola's nose was going numb. "Sixty seems high," she ventured.

"Miss, we're talking a thousand or more a night in tips. We're the closest thing in Burnt Creek to a class act. You don't like this deal, get yourself on down to The Train. You can keep your tips and pray to God they'll cover the hospital bill you'll end up with when that place is done with you." He imparted the information with all the matter-of-factness of a conversation about the weather. Lola felt a chill that went beyond the thermometer reading.

"I'm not here for a job. Look, is there someplace inside where we can talk—and hear ourselves think, too?"

"Damn." He turned and spat into the snow. "Miss Double-D isn't going to like it when she hears she's got to be Miss Double Shift today. You sure you aren't looking for work? Haven't you ever danced even a little? Maybe at your high school prom?"

"Yes, I'm sure, and I didn't go to my prom." She led the way back into the bar, until he finally maneuvered himself around her and steered a course through the whiskey-soaked crowd into an office whose walls didn't exactly muffle the din, but at least kept it manageable.

DENNY BLAIR very nearly guided Lola right back outside again when she confessed to being a reporter. Only when she assured him, and then reassured him, that her story had nothing to do with his bar did he settle into a wooden swivel chair that would have looked at home behind a schoolroom desk. And in fact, Denny told Lola, he'd been a high school social studies teacher before the boom. "I got more sociology in fifteen minutes here than I did in twenty years of teaching," he told her. "Back then, you wouldn't have caught me dead in a place like this, even before I was married. Now look at me. I paid off my house in my first year at the Sweet Crude. When the owner took me in as a partner, I got a big enough bump so my wife could retire. You put your scruples aside real fast when it comes to things like that."

Lola could see him back in the classroom, a pilled cardigan hanging off his scarecrow frame, the chalk dust settling in his wispy hair. If Burnt Creek was anything like Magpie, it had never made the jump from blackboards to dry-erase panels.

"It really doesn't bother you?"

"Only when my old students come in. Funny thing is, it doesn't seem to bother them a bit. I guess we're all making so much money now the old rules don't apply." He fiddled with a loose thread on his sweater.

"Speaking of rules—what about the dancers? Is dancing their only . . . duty?"

Denny Blair threw back his head and laughed. His sagging neck briefly tightened. Lola calculated that he was about the age her father would be if he had lived. She tried to imagine that gentle man, who treated cancer as though it were an annoying relative to be tolerated with an excess of civility, running a titty bar. She shook her head. Try as she might, the image wouldn't come.

"Do you mean are they hooking? Damned if I know. I'm sure some of them freelance. As far as I know, there's only one place in town that does it in any kind of organized fashion and believe me, you don't want to get crosswise with them."

"You mean the trailer," Lola said.

Denny's eyebrows shot up. "For somebody who appears to have just walked into town, you sure figured things out fast."

"Not fast enough," Lola said. The heat in the office made her drowsy. "Where would I find the trailer?"

Denny was on his feet, holding the door open. The music rushed in. Sleepiness fled. "You wouldn't," he said. "Not if you know what's good for you."

Onstage, Double Derricks swung sideways from a pole and twined her legs around a man's neck, her crotch a mere inch from his face. The man's hand moved automatically from his pocket to her G-string, slipping one bill after another beneath it. Denny made a little noise of satisfaction.

"Wait," said Lola. She pulled the clipping from her pocket.

He studied the photo. "Don't know her. Wish I did."

"Yes. She is—was—lovely."

"That, too. But that's not the best part."

In a place like this, Lola wondered, what else is there? Judith hadn't been particularly well endowed. But before she could frame the question, Denny pointed. Double Derricks retrieved a satin bag at the rear of the stage and transferred money from her G-string into it. Another woman pranced into the room and wiped down the pole with a hand towel. A long soft feather fluttered from a nipple ring; an abbreviated breechcloth flapped from her G-string. Her tan was spray-on orange; her black braids pulled away from a part whose roots appeared to be quickly reverting to their original blond. She shimmied toward Dawg and wound her fingers in his curls, pulling his boyish face close to her breasts, pushing it away just before contact. "Our very own Poke-a-hotness," Denny said with a bit of a flourish.

Lola wondered if she'd heard him right. Denny had the grace to apologize.

"You wouldn't look at me like that if you saw her tips. A real Indian girl could make more still. And if we could find a black girl, a Queen of Sheba—no, let's call her Nefertitty—what can I say? I know it's not politically correct, but these men are a long way from home. Everything else is different, so why not a little dark meat, too? But this girl"—he handed the clipping back to Lola—"she looks young. Too young."

Judith did, wide-eyed and smooth-skinned despite what already had been years of drug abuse. Lola had seen her share of addicts, and always marveled at the way it hit them all at once, especially the women, still some mother's baby-faced girl one day and then haggard and haunted beyond their years the next. Judith had died before that happened. Denny was right. Judith could have passed for a high school freshman. They were at the door. Lola braced herself for the cold.

"Double D's on break. Maybe you want to talk to her, too. She might know that girl."

CHAPTER SIXTEEN

Lola stepped back from the door before the words were out of his mouth. "Yes. Yes, I do. Where?"

Denny didn't even bother to shout over the music, just pointed to one side of the bar. A mountain of muscle sat on a stool beside a door, arms crossed over his chest, eyes nearly closed. "It's okay," Denny mouthed in his direction. The man twitched away from the door. Lola edged past, glancing over her shoulder for Dawg. His back was turned and he appeared to be shouting into a cellphone. She hurried through the dressing room door before he could turn and see her. She found herself in a long narrow space that was all mirrors and heaps of clothing, glittery G-strings mixed with mittens and heavy sweaters. Miss Double Derricks sat in a chair before the mirrors, leaning forward to rest her breasts on the counter.

"Hand me that bucket, would you?" A child's plastic sand bucket sat in a corner of the room. Lola retrieved it. The bucket was full of snow, barely melted. Miss Double Derricks scooped out a handful and rubbed it atop her breasts. "Ahhhh. That's good. Mind putting some on my shoulders? My back's killing me. If I'd have known how much it'd hurt to hold these puppies up, I'd have gone for C-cups."

Lola held the bucket over the girl's freckle-splotched shoulders and shook out some snow. "For God's sake," said Double D. "Rub it in." Lola patted at the snow. Double D twisted to look at her and Lola saw more freckles on her tilted nose and across her cheeks. Along with her wide blue eyes, they gave her the look of a curious child—at least from the neck up.

"Those are huge," Lola said, finally looking directly at Double D's breasts.

"Uh-huh." Double D sat up and threw her shoulders back, bringing her breasts to attention. Lola thought of all the comparisons to cantaloupes and beach balls and, of all the improbable objects, jugs, and decided none did justice to the creamy globes rising from Double D's seemingly inadequate torso.

"Go ahead," Double D said. "Touch them."

Lola shook her head. "No way." But Double D already had caught Lola's hands, bringing them to her breasts. "Squeeze."

Lola squoze. She'd expected a rocklike quality, much as if she'd grabbed the bicep of the bouncer by the dressing room door, but the flesh gave easily beneath her fingertips. "They feel real!"

"Yep." Double D nodded and her breasts rose and fell gently beneath Lola's hands with the motion. "I paid extra for the high-quality job. Worth every penny, don't you think? And just look here." Double D traced the pink outline of her nipples, showing a threadlike white line halfway around each. "You can barely see where he made the incision. I had to go to Denver to get this kind of work. I wasn't going to trust any old Dakota surgeon who grew up looking at cow titties. Took me a year to save up for them and they paid for themselves within my first few weeks back at work. Mr. Blair told me they'd be a smart investment and he was right."

"Mr. Blair?"

"Denny."

Lola fished for tact. "It just seems odd that you're so formal with someone who—"

"With someone who sees me nearly nekkid every day? I know. But he was my teacher in high school and I can't get over the habit of calling him Mr. Blair."

"Your teacher?" Lola tried to imagine prancing in a G-string in front of one of her own high school teachers. "Now that's odd." She joined Double D's laughter. Double D had an appealing forthright manner, nothing like the weary cynicism Lola would have expected from someone in her line of work.

"How long have you been doing this? My name's Lola, by the way."

Double D leaned forward and rested her breasts on the counter again and smoothed more snow onto them. "What's your real name? You here for the job? God knows, we could use an extra body or five." She sat up and slid a hand under each breast and jiggled them, a regular cataclysm, then patted them dry with a towel.

"That is my real name."

"And DeeDee's mine!" she said, genuine delight in her voice. "That's part of the reason I went for Double-Ds. It seemed like a natural. You know, most girls here use a different name for work." She fished through a pile of brightly colored scraps of cloth and selected a bikini top whose abbreviated cups were shaped like yellow hard hats. "Tie this for me, will you? Not too tight—I've got to lose it halfway through the dance."

Lola knotted the strings loosely at DeeDee's nape and in the middle of her back. "I'm not here for a job," she said. "I'm a reporter." And there it was, the look she'd expected all along, the wariness and suspicion and all the other emotions that added up to rejection.

"Reporters," DeeDee said. "We get nearly as many reporters in here as we do horny guys, and there's hardly any difference. You all want something from us. Only difference is, the guys offer to pay. The reporters come from all over the country—even from foreign countries sometimes—to do stories on the patch. How it's caused the breakdown of society out here. The dancers are Exhibit A. Me, I think they just want to see a little free snatch. That how it is for you? You like girls? Because we can just cut to the chase and you won't have to waste your time asking me your bullshit questions." DeeDee stood up, dusted gold glitter onto her eyelids and breasts, peeled off her G-string and selected a new one, bright yellow to match the hard hats. She threaded it between buttocks as high and firm and perfect as her breasts—without, as far as Lola could tell, the benefit of silicone—and adjusted it over her absolutely hairless crotch. Lola, who remained defiantly unwaxed, crossed her legs.

"That's all you get," DeeDee said. "That do it for you?" She headed for the door, giving her ass a final defiant swing as she strode away from Lola.

Who was so flustered she forgot to ask about Judith.

It probably didn't matter, she told herself when she was back in the truck, waiting in the warmth while Bub took a break to romp outside. Denny had recoiled from the reality of Judith's youth. He might have made the considerable adjustments necessary to accommodate Burnt Creek's new standards of morality, but the man had limits. Which, Lola thought, might not have been good news for Judith or any other young girl seeking her fortune, willingly or otherwise, in the patch. Lola sensed that beneath his tolerance of offensive names like Poke-a-hotness and Nefertitty, Denny still possessed an innate decency, one that would make work at the Sweet Crude bearable, if only just.

Which left The Train.

CHAPTER SEVENTEEN

The music in The Train was louder, the crowd bigger, and the room darker than the Sweet Crude. Lola patted a hip pocket. The revolver nestled like a talisman within. The bar and stage stretched the length of the old boxcar. On one side, the room opened into a flimsy addition, nothing more than a large space where men milled like cattle when the hay wagon comes around. Some lined up outside a curtained area. Lap dances, Lola surmised. There were no bowls of peanuts, no actual drink glasses. Cups at The Train were plastic, a fact Lola appreciated when one flew past her head and bounced off the chest of a man behind her. The cup was followed by its owner, fists windmilling toward his target. The bouncer chasing him down looked capable of murder. Lola peeled her feet free of the sticky floor and dodged, bumping into a man who raised his arms. To steady her, she thought, until his hands landed on her breasts.

"Knock it off!" Lola shoved him away. He grinned. Lola checked an impulse to reach for the gun. She looked around for the bouncer. But he was preoccupied with separating the cup flinger and the fling-ee. "I don't care what she told you," said the bouncer. A black beard bypassed his chin entirely and sprouted directly from his neck, reaching to the middle of a chest whose breadth was outdone only by his stomach. Lola thought of the starch-heavy meals she'd seen at The Mint, and figured the bouncer for one of their best consumers. His bulk was an immovable object between the men. "You got to wait your turn. Unless," he said to the man who'd thrown the cup, "you want me to pull a girl off the pole." His beard lofted into the air as he spoke, then lay back against his chest. "Maybe that one. What's she calling herself these days?—Cherry. Yeah, that's a good one. Anyhow, it'll cost you fifty bucks more."

"Thirty," the man said. "Cherry, my ass."

"Thirty," the bouncer agreed. He beckoned a woman flailing around a pole like a trout on the end of a fly. She dropped to the stage, breasts flopping as she landed. Lola suddenly appreciated the structural benefits of silicone. Her hair was either soaked with sweat, or badly in need of washing. It hung in strings around her shoulders as she sidled through the crowd, letting hands land where they may, whether accompanied by dollars or not. The woman who replaced her hopped onto the pole without wiping it down, as the dancers in the Sweet Crude had done. Cherry stopped before the bouncer, wobbling a bit, seeking her balance. Her eyes wandered before finally focusing on the man in the bouncer's grip. "Aw," she said, "not him again. He's a cheap bastard."

The man wrenched free of the bouncer's grasp. "And you do one sorry excuse for a lap dance. More like a lap nap. Let's see if you've gotten any better." Cherry stumbled behind him toward the row of curtained compartments. A hand landed on Lola's ass. She twisted away. "Make them stop," she said to the bouncer. "I need to talk to the manager. Where can I find him?"

"You're in the wrong place if you don't like guys playing grab-ass. And we're not hiring," he said. "At least not today. Come back tomorrow. The way the turnover is here, there's always a chance."

Hot breath gusted into Lola's ear. An unshaven cheek scraped her neck. "Less youn I get outta here," a voice mumbled. She brought her foot down on his. Her soft snowpacs had exactly zero effect on the man's work boots.

"Keep these assholes away from me," she said to the bouncer. "I only need one more minute here." The newspaper clipping had acquired creases that sectioned Judith's face. She held it up so the bouncer could see. Other men crowded in. The appreciative noises they made sent her closer to the bouncer. "Do you know her?"

"Didn't fuck her, if that's what you mean. Against the rules."

The answer acted like caffeine on Lola's frazzled nerves, concentrating her focus. Distractions receded. She jerked away from yet another intrusive hand and grabbed the bouncer's forearm to keep him from leaving. "But you know her. Did she work here?"

The beard flapped. "Yeah."

"Dancing?"

"Yeah. We done here? Because I got to get back to it. Look a there." Three men ducked into a curtained booth, separate from the larger lap dance area. "That's trouble." He turned his back on her and bulled toward the booth, elbows up, plowing through the crowd. Lola fit herself into the space behind him.

"How long did she work here?" she shouted. "Can I talk to somebody who knew her? Maybe one of the dancers?"

"Sheeeit," he threw back over his shoulder. "They're too drunk or high to make any sense, and anyhow, weren't none of them here when she was. That girl's been gone for months." He dove through the curtains. Men came flying out, as though propelled by a boot to butts. Lola heard a slap from within. "Goddammit, Destinee. No whorin' on premises."

Lola parted the curtains an inch. "But she was in Burnt Creek just recently."

A woman stumbled out past Lola, adjusting her G-string. Her lip was swollen. Fingerprint bruises polka-dotted her breasts. She smeared her hand across a slick spot on her thigh and wiped it on a man's sleeve as she headed back toward the stage.

The bouncer stood before Lola. "You see what it's like? Imagine this place at midnight, two in the morning. If things start getting out of hand now, it'll be hopeless then."

"Wait. Do you know where she went?"

He flung meaty arms wide. "Could be anyplace. Lotta towns in the patch, lotta dancers. I tell you one thing, though."

"What's that?" Lola held her breath in prayer for a single snippet of useful information. Just one, she begged whatever discredited saint had been assigned to look out for reporters.

"A girl hits The Train, she's at the end of the line, at least in this part of the world. Doubt you'll find her in any of the clubs.

Now I got to get back to work. And you got to go back to wherever you came from. Which is what your friend did, if she was smart."

"She *was* smart," Lola said to his broad, departing back. "She just didn't get back there soon enough."

CHAPTER EIGHTEEN

"I'm batting a thousand here," Lola told Bub as she fumbled with the key, trying to open the door with mittened hands. He bounced back and forth between the driver's and passenger's seats, impatient for release. A man stumbled out of The Train and past Lola, almost knocking her off her feet in his rush to the middle of the street. He put a hand against her truck and bent over and threw up into the snow. Bub hurled himself against the window in a frenzy of barking, teeth clicking against the glass. The man straightened and wiped his mouth. "Shut the fuck up, dog."

"That's my dog. And that's my truck. So maybe you're the one who needs to shut the fuck up." Lola liked situations where she could use her height to advantage and this was one of them. She drew herself up and put her hands on her hips and raised her voice over Bub's din. "Move along."

The man turned and regarded her out of reddened, bulging eyes. He opened his mouth as if to say something, but took in the fact that Lola stood a good head taller. He closed his mouth. His front teeth protruded, tugging at his bottom lip. "I was just leaving." He attempted a smile as he backed away.

Lola looked at the splatter in the snow. It appeared to have missed her truck. "Lucky," she said. The man hunched back toward the bar. Bub calmed as soon as she put her hand on the door. The street was lined with trucks, but the sidewalks were nearly deserted. Night shift workers, Lola thought, already in the bars, drinking the day away, thawing from the inside out. The man who'd upchucked by her truck stood a moment outside The Train, taking deep breaths, face in profile, chin an afterthought.

Something plucked at her memory. "Wait," she said to herself, then called out, "Wait!"

She ran down the street after him, trying to avoid patches of ice. Burnt Creek's sidewalks weren't so much cleared as flattened, snow stomped into grimy submission by hundreds of pairs of boots. A man emerged from the alley next to the bar and walked toward her, looking, she imagined, much as she looked herself—shoulders rounded forward, head down, hands jammed deep into pockets, wreathed in clouds of his own condensed breath. As he neared, she saw with envy that he wore a ski mask. Her own cheeks were already tingling, the tip of her nose a stinging rebuke. They passed one another wordlessly, and Lola would insist later that she had no warning at all—no telltale grunt, no swish of air—of the blow that landed on the back of her skull, sending her face-down into the filthy snow, where she lay helpless as his steel-toed boots slammed over and over into her ribs.

"Lady. Lady. Hey, lady." The face swam out of focus above her own, so close she could smell the reek of vomit on his breath. She turned away. "Hold on just a minute here while I call 9-1-1. They'll take care of you."

Lola snatched at his wrist, proving at least that she was capable of movement. Very painful movement. But she had to keep him with her until they could talk. She groaned. "I'm fine."

The man sat back on his heels and Lola drew a deep and grateful breath—only to regret it when her ribs screamed even louder than the protest her arm had just registered.

"You are not fine. That guy whaled on you six ways to Sunday. I almost missed it. Two seconds later and I'd have been back in the bar. I heard something and turned around and hollered. Didn't even know he was beating on a woman till I got to you. That's just wrong. You got to let me at least call a doctor. Police would be better."

"No doctor. No police." They'd never get a chance to talk if he called in the cavalry. Lola rolled onto her side and pushed herself up into a sitting position and waited until her head spun more slowly. "Help me up." She had never realized so many separate motions were involved in getting to one's feet, each and every one of them involving a new variation on pain.

"You got to let me help you somehow. The way he went after you, there's no way you're not hurt bad. He knew what he was doing."

Lola let go of his arm, swayed, and latched on again. "What do you mean?"

"Just look at you. Well, you can't. But he didn't touch your face. Guy's a pro."

Lola didn't want to think about how he might know such a thing. "You want to help me? Buy me a drink." Even through the pain pulsing behind her eyeballs, Lola could see the flash of interest in his eyes as the unexpected opportunity presented itself. She wondered how badly she'd have had to be hurt to have extinguished that. Blood? A broken bone or two?

"You see," she said to forestall whatever it was he might have been about to say, "I think you and I have met before."

THEY SAT at the far end of the bar in The Train, distant enough from the ceiling-mounted speakers that they could talk at something just below a shout. The dancers took one look and saw a man and woman together and avoided their end of the stage in favor of more lucrative territory. Lola's request for Jameson's had been met with a blank stare. She settled for her companion's request of well tequila, outrageously overpriced and vile enough to remind her why she hated even the good stuff. "No salt? No lime?" she said to the woman who slammed down the plastic cups with a shot's worth—maybe—sloshing around in the bottom.

"You wanna do that college shit, find a bar over in Grand Forks."

"We don't need none of that. Just keep those shots coming," the man said. Lola forced down three before her companion—his name, he told her, was Ralph—deigned to remember the breakfast at Nell's. "That place." He hooked his front teeth over the edge of the plastic cup and gulped another shot. He rubbed the back of his hand across his mouth. "Some crazy guy jumped Swanny."

Lola maneuvered her swollen fingers—her attacker must have stomped on her hand—to unfold the newspaper clipping. "He was looking at her."

Ralph's bleary eyes brightened. He smacked his lips. "I remember. You stay out here any amount of time, you're just glad for a warm body. Looks, too—now that's a bonus."

Lola braced herself and knocked another shot, but it failed to erase an image of Judith beneath a squirming Ralph, his face against her shoulder, those teeth digging into her too-prominent collarbone. Please God, she thought, let him have been as quick as his rabbitty looks indicated.

"So you knew her." She congratulated herself on her noncommittal tone, and a moment later fought hard to conceal the relief that washed through her at his reply.

"Not me." Lola's gratitude vanished with his next words. "Swanny claimed that one. And if you know anything about Swanny, you don't want to be between him and something he's got his eye on."

"Someone." Lola couldn't help herself.

"Come again?"

"She was a person. Not a thing." Oh, Judith. She spoke quickly to cover up her lapse. "If I wanted to talk to Swanny about her, where would I find him?"

"You wouldn't, not today. He's working an extended shift out on the rig. He won't be back until tomorrow afternoon." He waved to one of the dancers. "Some beer here." The woman who brought it leaned across the bar. Her breasts dangled almost to its surface. Crow's feet fanned out from the corners of her eyes. Her roots were long past the touch-up stage.

“Party room?” the woman asked, the words automatic. “We do lap dances for ladies, too. Equal opportunity, you might say.” She stuck a cigarette-yellowed finger into her mouth, drew it out slowly, and ran it across Lola’s lips.

Lola laid down a ten for Ralph’s beer and a five for a tip. “No, thanks.”

Even as Lola pressed her lips together to rid herself of the nicotine taste, Ralph’s hand crept along her thigh. Lola slapped her own hand over it. Was there no end of insults she could endure in a single afternoon?

“I was thinking maybe you and me could get dinner tonight,” he said.

Lola wondered what his idea of dinner was. A fast-food burger in the backseat of his truck? She directed a tight smile at him, still holding his hand in a death grip. “Swanny,” she reminded him. “I need to talk to him about Judith. She had a name, you know. Or maybe you don’t.”

His look was both rueful and sly. “All the women want to get with Swanny. Even though he’s a prick. I’m the nice guy. But ain’t nobody asking about me.”

There was a commotion by the booths. The bouncer blew past. A dancer at the other end of the room noticed his distraction, and crouched quickly on the bar in front of a group of men. She said something to them. One lay a bill on the bar. The woman pulled her G-string aside. The man leaned forward and licked. The rest whooped.

Lola turned away. “What makes Swanny a bastard? And who’s the one getting free drinks off a woman right now?”

He raised his cup in acknowledgment, but reminded her, “Looks like drinks is all I’m getting.”

Damn straight, Lola thought. She wanted nothing more than to swallow about a bottle’s worth of ibuprofen and sink into a hot bath, although at this point, even her sleeping bag in the back of the truck looked good. Still, she needed to get to Swanny. “Seems like I owe both you and Swanny for that breakfast mess back in Magpie. How about if I buy the two of you dinner at The Mint? Maybe tomorrow night? That'll give you time to check with Swanny"—she forced a wink, handed him a business card—"and see if he minds coming along on our little date."

CHAPTER NINETEEN

Lola almost wished she'd asked Ralph to stick around and help her climb into the truck. She'd never realized how far off the ground the driver's seat was. Once there, the simple act of raising her arms to the wheel caused a rush of agony. Bub, who'd jumped out for a quick break, returned with senses on full anxious alert, whining and tentatively swiping her face with his tongue.

"That guy got me worse than I thought," she told him. "Prob'ly a good idea to go to an emergency room." Or, more likely given the size of Burnt Creek, a clinic. But she didn't know where one was. She fumbled with her phone, thinking to look up the address. Its screen swam before her eyes. The tequila, she thought. "I'm in no shape to drive," she said. The long muscles in her back howled when she bent over the steering wheel. "But I just can't sit here until I freeze." She started the truck. Bub leapt to his usual post, front feet on the dash, back leg braced, alert to whatever came next. The sheriff's office was two blocks away. The pickup weaved toward it on streets that were, for one brief blessed moment, largely free of traffic but for an elderly man in a sedan who braked and leaned on his horn until Lola wrestled the truck out of his lane. Lola swung wide into the sheriff's office parking lot. The truck stopped at an angle. She turned off the engine. Opened the door. Eased one leg out, clung to the wheel, worked the other leg over toward the opening. Lost her grip. Fell into the snow. Made an abortive attempt to push herself up, then lay back and waited for the warmth that survival manuals had assured her came to freezing victims, wondering if that warmth had come to Judith at the end.

SHE CAME to in Thor's arms, his face close to hers, green eyes fixed on her own grey ones, mouth nearly close enough to kiss. She closed her eyes again, and a second later, was glad she had, thus avoiding the inevitable look of disgust on his face.

"Miss Wicks! You're drunk! You reek of liquor."

"Tequila," she mumbled. "Awful stuff. Hate it."

"Apparently not. Let's get you on your feet."

"No!" But she was too late. He hauled her upward. The moan that escaped her turned into a full-fledged scream.

Thor paused, his face considerably out of kissing range. Lola dangled above the ground. "Miss Wicks?"

"Clinic. Please." Each word took a great effort. She forced more. "I. Got beaten. Up."

He lifted her again, more gently this time, to her feet. "Lean on me. Can you walk? Who did this to you? When did it happen? Here. Hold onto me. Like this." He wrapped her arms around his waist and took a step. Lola dragged her feet through the snow. They worked, a welcome surprise. Thor took another step. When they got to the building's front steps, he simply lifted her. Lola and Thor groaned in unison. She had forgotten about his back. "I'm sorry," she gasped.

"We're a pair, aren't we?" he said through whitened lips. "Me all stove up, you beat up. Not much farther now. You owe your dog a treat. He stood out there and barked and barked. Otherwise, there's a good chance nobody would've found you until quitting time."

Dawg was in his usual spot in the front office and stayed put when Thor and Lola staggered in, Bub at their heels. Dawg's nostrils flared. "She's drunk. And what's that dog doing in here?"

"That may be." Thor's breath came ragged from exertion. "But she's hurt, too. And the dog seems to go wherever she goes. Help me out here."

"No. I can manage." The last thing Lola wanted was Dawg manhandling her aching body. She put a hand to the wall and followed it to the open door of Thor's office and eased none too gracefully into a chair.

"Don't go anywhere," Thor said to Dawg. "I'm going to need you to help me find whoever did this to Miss Wicks." He closed the door and turned to Lola. "Do you think you can answer a few questions before I get you some help? Because the quicker I jump on this, the quicker I can get this guy." He handed her a cup of coffee, and poured a second one. "Drink this. And when you're done, drink that one, too. We need to get you sober."

LOLA TOLD him the same thing three times in a row. *Cops*, she thought on Round Three. Always trying to trip you up. "No. I didn't know him. Or if I did, I couldn't tell. He came out of the alley. Started"—how had Rabbit Face put it?—"whaling on me. He didn't say a word. And I never saw his face. He wore a mask. He was big. And he hit me really hard. That's about it." She was just about to relax, thinking he was done, when Thor got around to the topic she'd hoped to avoid.

"What were you doing over there?"

"Interviewing someone." Which was true, she thought.

"On the street? In your truck? Where?"

Lola ran one hand over the other, her fingers thick, the skin tight and shiny over burst blood vessels. "In a bar."

Thor waited.

She lifted a hand before her face. Her thumbnail was black. She was probably going to lose it, she thought. "The Train."

Thor's expression changed not at all. It occurred to Lola that there was probably an entire session in the police academy on poker faces. "Indian guy?" Thor asked. "Because that's what your story is about, right?"

Lola poked at the thumbnail. It wiggled. The man's pale skin had showed through the eyeholes in the neoprene balaclava. "White guy."

"Do you always drink heavily during your interviews?"

Bub curled a lip and rumbled. Lola wondered how long it would take Thor to call Charlie and impart the news that his girlfriend had gotten drunk at lunchtime with some stranger in a titty bar. Charlie would probably ask the same questions Thor just had, and would know that her interview at The Train had nothing to do with a story about Indian workers in the patch. Thor voiced that same conclusion now.

"You were talking to him about that girl. What'd you find out?"

Lola thought of the bouncer, how he'd at least confirmed that Judith had been in Burnt Creek, dancing. She saw no reason at all why that information might help Thor catch whoever had lit into her.

"Nothing," she said. "I didn't find out one goddamned thing."

CHAPTER TWENTY

"Oh, my dear. Oh, my word. I'm so sorry, Miss Wicks. This is going to hurt."

"Call me Lola. Please. You and Thor both." Lola sank deep into a flowered sofa in Thor Brevik's living room, succumbing without protest to the ministrations of his wife. Charlotte Brevik was a nurse, Thor had told Lola, and would give her far better care than anything she'd find at the clinic. Lola had expected a rodeo queen with a sticky sprayed cotton-candy poof of hair, jeans Saran-wrapped around a hard little butt. But where Thor was spare, a twist of barbed wire, Charlotte was like a stack of plump pillows challenging the double-stitched seams of her nurse's scrubs. For a woman so ample and soft, her touch was firm as she probed the lump on the back of Lola's head. "May I?" she asked before easing up the layers of Lola's shirts. "You turn around," she commanded her husband. Her tone was playful, but a flush crept up her neck, patching her delicate skin like a rash. Thor hovered in the doorway of a living room crowded with occasional tables and display shelves, all forested with porcelain figurines. Lola wondered how Thor and Charlotte—especially Charlotte, with her excessive dimensions—negotiated it daily without sending things crashing down. Charlotte pushed her fingers against Lola's breastbone. "Does that hurt?"

"Hell, yes, it hurts." Lola slapped Charlotte's hand away. "Stop that. Where's my dog?"

"He's in the mudroom. It hurts because there's a bruise. A lot of bruises, bad ones. But beyond that—below it, internally—do you feel any sharp pains?" Lola shook her head.

Charlotte pressed the small of Lola's back, her abdomen. "There?"

Lola's stomach twisted. Her head spun. She spoke through clenched teeth. "Same. Hurts, but not the way you said. I feel more nauseated than anything."

"That's the stress. And it's good. It means we don't have to worry about internal injuries. You can thank that big coat of yours. If this were summertime, we'd be looking at broken ribs at the very least. That knock on your head, though. That's worrisome." She produced a tiny flashlight and shined it into Lola's eyes. "Don't blink." Her face was inches from Lola's, eyes so brown they appeared black, cheeks pink with a dusting of blush, lips tinted with gloss, just enough makeup to disguise the faint lines that too soon would become the claw marks of time. She smelled of lotion and face powder, undercut with something tangy and familiar that Lola couldn't quite place. She put Charlotte at about forty, only a few years older than she was. Lola touched a hand to her own face and wondered when she would have to start taking makeup seriously.

Charlotte caught the gesture. "Does your face hurt? Did he hit you there?"

"Told you she was good," Thor called to Lola from across the room.

Charlotte simpered. "That's how we met. I took care of Thor when he was in the hospital after the bull got him. He called me the prettiest little thing he'd ever seen."

"That bull knocked me in the head," Thor said.

Charlotte pressed her lips together and turned away. "Sometimes it takes the bruises awhile to come up. You've got some dandy ones on your back. Take a look." She rose heavily from the sofa, and returned with a hand mirror and raised Lola's shirts again. "Thor! Honestly. Go into the kitchen and make coffee. And make sure the dog has some food and water. Get him an old blanket to lie on while you're at it." She waited until he was gone and whispered to Lola.

"Honey, I can tell you've been drinking. It's awfully early in the day. Do you need help with that? There's a good AA group in town. I've sent plenty of people there. I'm sure you've got one back where you're from."

Lola fished for an explanation that would make sense to someone like Charlotte. Doing tequila shots during an interview in a topless bar probably wasn't going to cut it. "Someone spilled it on me," she said. Charlotte's pitying expression told her the lie hadn't worked.

"Look." Charlotte held the mirror inches from Lola's back. Bruises bloomed like peonies. "You think they're bad now, give them a couple of days. They'll turn colors you never knew existed. You'll want to take ibuprofen, four tablets every eight hours, for the next few days. And if you have the least bit of dizziness, you get yourself to a doctor right away. And if you change your mind about that meeting—"

She stopped as Thor emerged from the kitchen with three mugs of coffee on a tray, along with a cream pitcher, a sugar bowl, and little spoons. The cellphone clipped to his belt rang. He put down the tray and detached the phone. "Dawg," he announced. He turned his back and spoke briefly. "She's fine. Or she will be. I'll be back in a few and we can head out. We don't have much to go on." He rang off. "He wanted to know how you're doing."

"That Dawg," said Charlotte. "Bet your first look at him was a jolt."

Lola minimally lifted a shoulder. She was learning to conserve movement.

"Speaking of looks," said Charlotte, "did you get a good one at the guy who did this?"

Lola took a coffee mug, hoping that neither Thor nor Charlotte saw her fingers quivering. "No. As I told Thor, he was all bundled up. He even had on one of those ski masks."

"That describes about half the men—and a good number of the women—in Burnt Creek this time of year."

Lola heard again the harsh breaths, the grunting exhalations in rhythm with the kicks. "I'm pretty sure it was a man. He was so big." She nestled into the deep cushions, and sipped at her coffee with her eyes closed, waiting for the shaking to stop. It didn't take long. The Breviks kept their home a good ten degrees, maybe more, warmer than Charlie's. It had been weeks since she'd been so comfortable. Something drifted around her shoulders. Lola opened her eyes to see Charlotte Brevik arranging a crocheted afghan over her.

"You drink your coffee and then you take a little rest. It's the best thing for you. Thor's going to go back to work and try to figure out who did this, and when he comes home, we're going to have a nice dinner to help you get your strength back. Oh, and take this." She dropped a round white pill into Lola's palm.

"What is it?"

"Something for the pain. It'll help you sleep. I'll give you another one to take before you go to bed tonight. Tomorrow, you'll need to start working through the stiffness, but this will give you a bit of break before then. You'll hurt for a couple of days, but you'll be surprised how fast you heal."

Lola gulped it down and handed over her empty mug. She stretched out on the sofa, the bruises screaming at the movement, but stopping as soon as she'd settled. She'd barely murmured her thanks before she fell asleep.

CHAPTER TWENTY-ONE

Lola lifted another forkful of chicken and dumplings to her mouth and closed her eyes as she savored the lightness of the dumplings, the peppery gravy that coated them. "I can't thank you enough."

Charlotte patted Lola's arm with a soft hand graced with unexpectedly long, slender fingers, their nails filed to perfect ovals and painted the same shade of peach as her lip gloss. "Oh, my dear. When I found out that Thor had sent you to The Mint—we like to go there, of course, but it's no place for a single lady, not these days. Thor, you should be ashamed."

Thor grimaced obligingly on cue across a round table groaning beneath the platter of chicken, a loaf of homemade bread, a bowl of iceberg lettuce enhanced with cherry tomatoes and bacon bits, and a casserole of creamed butterbeans that Charlotte assured Lola she'd grown in the backyard garden and canned. "Seems like nobody wants to can anymore. But I think there's nothing better in the middle of a Dakota winter than a little reminder of summer's goodness. Don't you agree?"

Lola wondered if she could agree without admitting she'd never so much as successfully nurtured a houseplant in her life, let alone planted a garden and preserved its bounty. She solved the issue by taking another mouthful. Focusing on the food had the added benefit of keeping her from staring at the Jack Sprat disparity of Thor and Charlotte. Despite her good intentions, a question escaped.

"Do you eat like this every night?" She bit her lip, too late. Tried again. Made things worse. "Everything is so delicious. I'd be big as a house if—" She stopped. There was no recovering from that one.

"Oh, yes. Charlotte's a wonderful cook." Thor's voice was flat. Lola couldn't tell if Thor was coming to her rescue, or his wife's. Layers stacked his own plate. He appeared to have one of those constitutions that withstood calories and cholesterol and sheer volume. Lola wondered what Charlotte had looked like when they married; if she'd cooked to keep up with her husband's galloping metabolism, sacrificing herself on the altar of being a good wife, the bright sparkling girl she'd been slowly dimming beneath pads of fat. Lola speared a butterbean and ordered herself not to think about the mechanics of their sex life.

The red patches reemerged on Charlotte's face, creeping up her throat, finding purchase in her cheeks. She reached for the butter dish. One, two, three pats were deposited atop a dumpling. Charlotte poked at them with her fork, speeding their transition into a golden pool. She lifted the gravy boat and swamped the little butter pond with a tidal wave. Back to the fork, a sodden mouthful scooped up and deposited. Eyes closed in defiant bliss. The flush subsided. A row of Hummels watched from a sideboard, their wide innocent eyes a rebuke to Lola's uncharitable thoughts. A seated porcelain boy took shelter under an umbrella nearly as big as he was; another boy also held an umbrella, this one furled and resting on his shoulder. He toted a portmanteau in his other hand and strolled along whistling. With their round eyes and rounder cheeks and winsome blond locks, the Hummels looked like miniature versions of Charlotte. Or, Lola thought with a start, like Dawg. Pre-ink and steroids, of course. She cleared her throat. She needed to say something to cover her gaffe, but had no idea what. She'd forgotten how Thor tended to fill in any silence, no matter how brief, with bursts of verbiage.

"Charlotte makes sure to keep my strength up. Which is a good thing because the things that are happening in Burnt Creek these days have me running day and night."

Lola broke in before he could build up verbal steam. "What sorts of things?"

He ladled a helping of butterbeans onto his plate. Lola thought it one of the paler meals she'd ever consumed, the yellow beans swimming in their cream, the bread and dumplings whiter still, the lettuce almost startling with its hint of green, the tiny red tomatoes downright shocking. A chandelier tinkled overhead in the steady hot breath from the furnace, its crystals refracting shards of light across the dishes.

"You, for starters. Some animal attacking a woman right on the street, in broad daylight. Nothing like that ever happened here before. That's not Burnt Creek, that's big city stuff. If that's the kind of life we wanted, we'd move to Denver or Chicago or someplace, and Charlotte could take herself shopping in fancy department stores every day."

"How are you feeling, dear?" Charlotte dished more chicken onto Lola's plate. "Let's get some more protein into you."

Lola was pretty sure all the protein had been cooked out of the chicken, but she dutifully took another mouthful. "Sore. A little headachy, but no dizziness, none at all," she added quickly as Charlotte's features creased in concern.

Charlotte sat back. "Good. Then you should be able to drive home tomorrow."

Lola slid a dumpling through some gravy. She wanted nothing more than to leave this frozen, confounding place. But returning to Magpie wasn't much of an improvement. She'd have to explain to Jorkki that she'd wasted time on a story that had vanished. Charlie would no doubt assume that her injuries had been caused by Lola doing something she shouldn't have. And she'd have to tell Joshua she hadn't found out a damn thing about Judith, and admit to Jan that she hadn't even asked about the other girls.

A thought pushed through the haze of carbohydrate overload. "I can't leave tomorrow. I set up a meeting with a couple of people. I'm trying to find out what happened to a friend. I'm afraid she ended up in one of the bars out here."

CHAPTER TWENTY-TWO

The Breviks exchanged looks. Charlotte pressed a hand to her chest. She had the sort of generous bosom that Lola associated with dental technicians and elementary school teachers, a comforting place to press one's head, a refuge.

"I feel bad for any girl who ends up in one of those places. You could just cry," Charlotte said. "I go to the high school every year, talk to the girls—nowadays, the boys, too—about nursing. It's a good job, pays well, and you can take it anywhere in the country. The world even. But when I tell them the pay, they just laugh at me. The same way they laugh at me when I try to tell them the downside of working in the patch. The girls, you see how they end up. And the boys, sure they make great money. But it's dirty, dangerous work. You can end up hurt bad, dead even."

Thor ladled more dumplings onto Lola's plate before she could object. The tightness in her stomach was beginning to rival the bruises on her back in terms of discomfort. "Now, Mother," he said. "Think of all the ways you can get hurt ranching. Just look at me. I've been all busted up since I was in my teens. And it's not like I made any real money for my pains."

The response had a well-rehearsed air. "For reasons that escape me, he felt obligated to ride those bulls when he was young," Charlotte told Lola. "As far as I'm concerned, he brought his injuries upon himself. Good thing he married a nurse." Thor, unsmiling, raised his glass to his wife. The light caught the golden cider within. Lola craved a wine, or even a beer, but as far as she could tell, the Breviks were teetotalers.

"We interrupted you," Charlotte reminded her. "You were talking about your friend. If you're trying to find her, it shouldn't take too long. Burnt Creek's grown, but not so much that it should take you more than a day or two to track somebody down here. Besides, maybe if you're lucky, you'll find her working in one of the fast-food places or cleaning the motels. There's lots of ways to make money here, good money, and still keep your dignity."

Thor shook his head before Lola could reply. "Lola already knows where her friend is. I expect she's just trying to find out how she got there. Am I right?"

Charlotte clapped a hand over her little mouth as Lola explained the circumstances of Judith's death. "I think she got into some kind of trouble out here. I'm supposed to have dinner tomorrow night with a couple of guys she met here. One of them seems pretty rough. Don't worry," she said in response to Charlotte's look of alarm. "I'm meeting them at The Mint. I know you don't like it, but it still seems safer than any other place in town."

"Do you know their names?" Thor asked. "Maybe I've run across them. If that's the case, there might be some information in the files you could use. It's all public record. But you being a reporter, you already know that."

Lola could have kicked herself. What the sheriff said made eminent good sense. "All I've got is Swanny. Big red-haired guy from Idaho. Elvis sideburns. His friend is Ralph. I don't know either of their last names. Ralph looks like this." She sucked her lower lip beneath her teeth. "Hangs out at the Sweet Crude. And The Train, too. At least, that's where he was today."

Charlotte's eyes grew avid. Lola thought that you could take a church organist, a Sunday school teacher, a maiden aunt, people as far removed from the world's hard realities as possible, people who insisted they avoided newspapers and television because the news was simply too upsetting, and yet every last one of them reliably lit up at a hint of scandal.

"The Train! That awful place. Do you think they killed her?" A shred of lettuce, drenched in ranch dressing, fluttered from her fork onto the tablecloth unnoticed.

Thor answered. "The sheriff back there thinks it's natural causes. I can tell you for a fact he doesn't appreciate Lola poking around. He called me again today, wanted to know what she'd been up to. Luckily, it was before Lola ran into trouble."

Lola coughed, dislodging a butterbean in the back of her mouth. She spit it into her napkin. "He called again?"

"Even all the way out here, your Sheriff Charlie Laurendeau has a reputation for being thorough."

"Charlie Laurendeau." Charlotte rose to clear the table. She paused with the platter of chicken denting her side, the dish of butterbeans in her other hand. "Isn't he the one—there was something with a woman. A child, too, if I remember correctly."

Lola stared at her lap. As far as she knew—which, she realized now, wasn't very far at all—Charlie had never been married. Which of course didn't mean he hadn't had serious relationships before, let alone a child. But he might have told her. And even if he hadn't, she was surprised that neither Jan nor anyone else in Magpie had informed her about it the very second her involvement with Charlie became public knowledge. Which appeared to have happened about five minutes after the first time she slept with him. She made a mental note to herself to go online and check birth announcements from the reservation as soon as she got a free minute.

"Lola and the sheriff," Thor began.

"No," Lola said, even as Charlotte smothered her in an apologetic hug, "it's really not like that." Not anymore it wasn't, she thought grimly. Not until the two of them had a very long talk, both about Charlie's background and also as to why he insisted upon checking up on her work in Burnt Creek.

CHARLOTTE'S APOLOGIES only became more fulsome when she found out her husband had let Lola spend the previous night in her truck. Within moments, Lola found herself in a cozy attic room, a stack of sheets and towels in her arms, and the insistence that the room was hers for the next two nights, or however long she stayed in Burnt Creek. Bub wasn't welcome inside the house—Lola had noted the gleaming, dust-free surfaces and presumed as much—but Charlotte assured her he'd be fine in the mudroom, even after Lola warned her of the havoc a frustrated border collie was capable of wreaking upon an entire house, let alone a single small room. "I'll check on him before I go to bed," Charlotte told Lola. "Maybe give him a treat to settle him down. And Thor's up at an ungodly hour in the morning. I'll make sure he feeds him and lets him out first thing. The best thing for you right now is a solid night's rest. You don't need the dog bothering you."

"He's not a bother," Lola said, but Charlotte went right on as though Lola hadn't spoken.

"I hope it's not too quiet up here for you. We added some extra insulation and put in those triple-glazed skylights, too. See where the old leaky window was?" A tall oblong in the wall beside the twin bed had been turned into a recessed bookshelf that held a collection of Raggedy Ann dolls. "Here." She gave Lola another pill. "You'll sleep like a baby."

Lola thought of her restless night in the truck, the whine of passing tires on pavement, the metronome sweep of headlights across the windows. The two skylights, small and square, served as the attic's only windows. Lola, who could stand upright only in the middle of the room, pressed her hand to one. Her outstretched fingers barely fit within it. The idea of a good quiet night's sleep appealed. She swallowed the pill dry and bent over the bed to put the sheets on, pain flaring anew as she stretched to reach the corners. Charlotte backed out of a narrow closet with a quilt draped over her arm. "You should be warm enough, but just in case. The bathroom's across the hall. Lola—" She hesitated in the doorway. Light from the hallway haloed her head. "Do you have to go meet those men tomorrow?"

Lola had asked herself the same question, considering the worst-case scenario that the meeting was likely to yield nothing more than a few additional salacious details about Judith, nothing she'd ever pass along to Joshua. The extra day would only make

Jorkki madder. And it would delay whatever reckoning she faced with Charlie. Still. Ralph and Swanny were her only connection to Judith, and maybe to the other girls, too. The latter was the most fragile of possibilities, but Lola long ago had learned the hard way never to pass such opportunities by. "I set it up. It would be rude for me not to show. Besides, I've got no way of contacting them to cancel."

"I see." Charlotte's tone said she didn't see at all. "At least let me know exactly where you're going and when, and how long you expect to be. If you're not back by then, I'll send Thor in. Or better yet, that Dawg. He'd put the fear of the Lord in anyone."

Lola laughed with her. Even Swanny might quail at the sight of Dawg, she thought. Charlotte turned out the hallway light. "Good night."

Lola sat a moment in the narrow bed. She'd gotten used to sleeping with Charlie. Even on nights when a call kept him away from home, there was always Bub. She thought about him alone in the mudroom, no doubt reducing a row of boots to scraps of well-chewed leather. And she thought about the child Charlotte had mentioned. Check on Bub, she told herself. Then fire up the laptop and review those birth records. But even as she swung her legs over the side of the bed, the pill Charlotte had given her began its fast work. "In the morning," she promised herself as she fell back. She scanned the row of grinning Raggedy Anns and chose one that looked old and well loved. She turned off the light and fell asleep with the doll clutched to her chest.

CHAPTER TWENTY-THREE

About the only sound Lola hated more in the morning than the alarm was that of her cellphone.

Yet there it was, shrilling in her ear, a good fifteen minutes before the alarm was supposed to go off. "What do you want to bet Jan's got a wild hair again?" she said, talking to Bub out of habit before realizing he wasn't there. And indeed, Jan didn't even bother to say hello. "Jorkki wants to know how your story's coming. The one on the folks from the rez working in the patch. Isn't that what you're working on?" Which meant, Lola assumed, that Jan knew good and well the men from the reservation had lost their jobs.

Until Judith's death, Lola and Jan had approached friendship. No real confidences, and certainly no talk of shared vulnerabilities as women and journalists, but the occasional beer after work, hikes or horseback rides when Charlie was out of town for training. Jan made a few abortive attempts to teach Lola to fly-fish. Lola liked it well enough, the dreamlike combination of still, pellucid air warming her face and shoulders as the cool water coiled around her thighs. Swallows skated off the limestone cliffs that leapt from the far side of the creek. At the cliffs' rocky base lay deep pools with the dimpled surfaces that spelled trout. Or so Jan said. Even when Lola, lashing the air with her line, managed to place a whimsically named fly in the general direction of where she'd aimed it, the fish disdained her offerings. "They jump right out of the water at yours," Lola pouted as Jan, with a mere flick of her wrist, put down her fly wherever she pleased and pulled in fish after fish. Lola admired their startling colors, the bands of emerald and ruby, the way they hung suspended in the water for a moment when Jan released them before flicking their tails and disappearing.

When the weather turned, Jan had tried to talk Lola into some snowshoeing or cross-country skiing. "Maybe next winter," Lola had protested, thinking privately, if there *is* a next winter. "So does that mean ice-fishing is out?" Jan pressed. Even Jorkki had hacked up a laugh at Lola's expression.

But apparently, even in Magpie, ambition trumped friendship, Lola thought now. "If Jorkki wants to know what I'm working on, why doesn't he call me himself?"

Jan's reply was fat with satisfaction. "He will. I get the feeling there's a number of things he wants to talk to you about." If they were guys, Lola thought, and actually facing each other instead of talking on the phone, they'd be circling, fists raised. Sometimes she envied men, the simplicity of a punch over endless slashing words.

"I need to know when you'll be back," Jan said. She waited a beat, then drove in the knife. "So I can head out there." Twisted it. "To write about Judith. And Maylinn and Carole and Nancy and Annie, too."

Lola suppressed a smile out of habit, then remembered that Jan couldn't see her. She grinned back at the Raggedy Anns. Her advice to Jan had worked. Once Jan had determined the girls' names, she was off and running. Lola was willing to bet she'd talked to their families, too. Maybe the *Express* had waited too long to do the story. But sometimes the wait turned into an advantage. By this time, pure raw fear over the girls' fate would have trumped shame over their disappearance. And publicity—at least this was what Lola always told families in such circumstances—could always help. She tried to sound dismissive when she replied. Jan always worked better when she felt competitive. "Why does Judith suddenly rate a story? Did the autopsy show something?"

"She froze to death, just like Charlie thought." Lola imagined Jan twirling the end of her braid around a forefinger, the way she did when she was particularly pleased with herself. Lola thought about hanging up.

"Then why a story?"

"I had a long talk with Joshua the other day. You know, he and Judith and I practically grew up together. They went to the reservation school and I went to the white school, and I was a few years ahead of them besides, but I was the leader for the 4-H group they were in. I taught Judith how to rope calves. She and I are still the only two girls to compete in calf roping. Before that, they stuck girls with goat tying. All I'm saying is it helps to have a history here."

Lola had never considered the possibility that growing up in a place like Magpie might provide any sort of advantage at all. "What did Joshua say? Maybe it's something I can start checking. Seeing as I'm here already."

"Nice try. Read my story when it comes out. Which is never going to happen if you don't get your ass back here. Which will be when, exactly?"

"Nice try yourself. I know a bluff when I see one. You don't have a story at all, do you?" She started to say something else, then realized she was talking into a dead phone. The Raggedy Anns goggled at her with black button eyes. She sighed, then took a deep breath and sniffed. She took another breath. Yes, she definitely smelled coffee. She eased from the bed, and grabbed at the door. It swung open to reveal Charlotte, swathed in yards of fluffy pink, holding a steaming mug. Until that moment, Lola hadn't realized that people actually wore bunny slippers.

"Black, right? Breakfast is ready whenever you are." Charlotte floated away, a cloud of pink.

Lola eased into jeans and a couple of sweaters. The bruises shrieked. As Charlotte had promised, they'd turned green and yellow and a shade of purple that was nearly black. One just above her knee, below the extra padding of her coat, featured a row of clearly outlined triangles. She inched down the stairs. Thor sat at the kitchen table, his head in his hands, a plate of eggs and sausage untouched in front of him. Charlotte busied herself at the stove. "Lola, how do you take your eggs? Thor, you've got to eat."

"Over easy," Lola said. "Is the dog all right?" She headed for the mudroom without waiting for an answer. Bub greeted her with an enthusiasm that threatened new injuries, but to Lola's relief, the mudroom appeared to have survived intact.

"He's already been outside," Charlotte called.

Lola ruffled Bub's fur a final time, and returned to the kitchen, ignoring the scratching at the closed door behind her. Thor raised his head. The skin beneath his eyes bagged loose. Grey bristles poked from his chin. He picked up his fork and stabbed at an egg until the yolk ran. He watched the orange tendrils as they crept across the plate. Charlotte reached over his shoulder and ran a piece of toast through the yolk and handed it to him. "Eat. Now."

He bit and chewed, the movements automatic. His gaze found focus, registering the food in front of him, sweeping the kitchen, finally alighting upon Lola. "Bad night?" she asked.

He swallowed. "The worst."

Charlotte put a plate in front of Lola, whose idea of breakfast was a bowl of cornflakes consumed while standing at the kitchen counter. On special occasions, she added a banana and sat at the table. Now she confronted three—three!—eggs, a half-dozen small sausage links and a stack of toast saturated with butter. Lola was pretty sure Charlotte wouldn't be caught dead using margarine. "I almost forgot." Charlotte set a jar of strawberry jam next to Lola's plate. "It's homemade."

"Of course it is." Lola wondered how she'd be able to move after finishing. Maybe she'd be able to squirrel away a sausage or two for Bub. She heard him pacing in the mudroom. She braced herself, then went for one of the eggs. At least they'd slide down easy. "What happened?" she asked Thor.

"Dead girl."

The egg did not in fact slide down. It lodged somewhere in the back of her throat. Lola gulped at her coffee. "Excuse me?"

"Not all nice and frozen like that girl you asked me about. No, the element we've got in Burnt Creek these days had to get creative. Terrible thing to see. Especially at two in the morning, which is when the call came in."

Lola gnawed at some toast. "I didn't hear a thing."

"I told you that room was quiet," Charlotte said. "Besides, over the years, he's learned to creep out of bed like a thief. So as not to disturb me." She joined them at the table and took one of Thor's hands between her own. He snatched it away.

Lola ate a sausage in three bites. "What happened?"

"Somebody apparently took a dislike to one of our dancers. I say 'our' in this case because she was a local girl. It's hard when someone you know gets treated like that. Anyone, actually. But worse when you remember her twirling her little baton in the Fourth of July parade."

Lola paused with a piece of toast halfway to her mouth.

"Somebody—maybe more than one somebody—beat her to a pulp and threw her into the middle of the street. Stark naked. Blood everywhere. And her neck. Broke so bad it was twisted almost backward on her body. It's like they wanted her to be found, leaving her in front of the Sweet Crude like that."

CHAPTER TWENTY-FOUR

The eggs and sausage and toast declared war upon one another in Lola's stomach. "Where was she?" Even though she'd heard perfectly well the first time.

She knew, of course. Even before Thor told her, she could see DeeDee as a freckled ten-year-old, high-stepping in white go-go boots, grinning skyward as her baton floated back down toward her sure grasp, her innate showmanship even as a child making her such a success at her later unfortunate choice of career. "I met her," she said. Something she'd said entirely too often. She'd known foreign correspondents who were killed in Afghanistan, too. But only in an across-the-room, jostling-for-position-in-the-same-media-scrum way. Not someone she knew by the color of her eyes, or—she shuddered—the feel of her fake breasts.

Color flowed back into Thor's face. "You did? How is that possible?"

"I thought that my friend might have been a dancer here. So I stopped by the Sweet Crude. I talked to DeeDee there. Then I left and some jerk attacked me."

"May I?" Thor helped himself to one of Lola's remaining sausages.

Charlotte stood. "How about I put on some pancakes?" Thor took no notice of his wife's question and spoke to Lola. "You got attacked. And then, just a few hours later, this girl gets attacked. And killed."

"It's different. I got punched in broad daylight, and then he left me alone. But—that business about her neck," Lola said to Thor.

"What about it?"

"A trucker got killed back in Magpie right before I came out here. His truck went off the road in the snow. His neck was broken, too."

Thor shrugged. "I don't see what a motor vehicle accident five hundred miles away has to do with a cold-blooded murder here. Necks get broken in car accidents all the time."

"But Charlie said he'd never seen one like this." Lola wished, too late, she hadn't referred to Charlie so familiarly.

Thor twinkled at her, letting her know he'd noticed. "That's because your Sheriff Laurendeau has only been at it a little while. Give him my years and he'll see more varieties of broken necks than he knows what to do with."

Charlotte hovered, skillet in hand. "Really," said Lola. "I'm full." A couple of pancakes landed on her plate, anyway. Lola reckoned she'd gotten off easy. Thor merited the Empire State Building of pancake stacks. He upended the syrup pitcher over it. Charlotte stood at the counter, eating directly from the griddle. She'd poured some syrup into a small bowl, swirling each forkful of pancakes through it. In between bites, she poured more batter in perfect circles onto the griddle.

"Maybe you were just the warm-up," Thor said to Lola. A thought she'd pushed away just moments earlier. "Which makes anything you can remember even more urgent. It's not unheard of, people getting killed here. Bar fights, jealous husbands, that sort of thing. But this business of somebody killing a girl and throwing her away like trash—I don't care if she is a stripper. It's going to upset people who already think the town is going to hell. When do you meet up with those people you're talking to?"

"Tonight at six. At The Mint. I already told Charlotte." Lola smiled at her erstwhile protector.

"I want you to think about what I said. Any new details come to mind, I need to know. Your truck's still back at the office, right?"

"Yes. And Bub's food is in it."

"Don't worry about him." Charlotte stood by the sink, filling it with scalding water. "I gave him a couple of sausages." Lola thought that Charlotte's version of "a couple" meant that Bub had probably gotten the equivalent of half a pig for breakfast, beyond whatever bedtime treats Charlotte had given him. No wonder he'd left the mudroom unscathed.

"Even so, you need your truck. You might as well gas it up today so you can be ready to leave first thing tomorrow. You can ride over to the office with me. Besides, I'd like you to look at some mug shots." Thor stood. His plate, improbably, shone clean. "Just give me a couple of minutes to wash up."

Thor's mention of Charlie had reminded Lola of how badly she wanted to get on her computer and see if she could find any references to a child. "I have some work to do," she began.

Help came from an unexpected quarter. "I can take her later," Charlotte said, her voice a plea.

"That would be stupid. I'm going now."

Lola flinched at the rebuke. Behind Thor's back, she offered Charlotte an eye roll at the reliable intransigence of men. But Charlotte fixed her gaze on a blank space on the kitchen wall, likewise ignoring Lola's mouthed, "Sorry."

"Do you need help with the dishes?" Lola tried. Their leavings—the sticky plates, the juice glasses frilled with pulp, the platters for sausages, pancakes, toast, the pitcher with its real cream filming over—made for a daunting display. When Charlotte said nothing, Lola gave up and followed Thor out the door, Bub pacing beside them, his uncharacteristic dignity enforced by a stomach still distended from his breakfast feast.

Lola hoped Dawg wouldn't be in the office. She saw him again on his barstool at the Sweet Crude, head thrust over the bar, trying to nuzzle Poke-a-hotness's tangerine breasts as she kept a professional but still profitable millimeter beyond reach. Lola wondered if she should tell Thor about seeing Dawg there. And she wondered how he'd react if she did.

"I JUST don't see how this is going to do any good." Lola ran her thumb across the top of the photos filling the shoebox on Dawg's desk. Even Charlie, a one-man sheriff's office, had put all of the department's mug shots online. But Homestead County apparently had yet to enter the digital age. "I mean, he wore one of those cold-weather masks."

"Look anyway," Thor said. "Maybe something will trigger a memory. The kind of coat, the detail on a collar, something like that."

Lola looked, spreading a handful of photos out before her. Hard-eyed men glared back. White men, black men, Asians, Hispanics, Indians, the most extensive array of color she'd seen since arriving in the West. She said as much to Thor.

"The patch brings them in from all over the country. We've even got foreigners, people from countries I've never heard of. All of those Stans. Before this fracking business started, it took years to fill up a shoebox of mugs. Now, seems like we start a new one every few months. Only person who likes it is Charlotte. 'Buy another pair of shoes,' I tell her. 'We're running out of space.'"

Lola stacked the first batch of photos and turned them facedown and selected more. Oil and grime darkened some faces. Others sported black eyes, split lips, open cuts along their cheekbones. "What'd they do?"

"Those you've got there? Assault, mostly. A few rapists, maybe a negligent homicide or two. We don't much get child molesters. Used to be kids could ride their bikes all over town without worrying about anything, but parents are pretty protective these days. Not much opportunity for perverts—at least, the ones of that variety—here. I didn't give you the drunks. You'd be here forever. You keep looking at that bunch. I'm going to go in my office, make some phone calls about that girl, shake the bushes a little, see if anything falls out." He closed the door behind him.

Lola flipped through more photos. Bub, who once again had accompanied her into the sheriff's office, lay down across her feet. Thor's voice came muffled from the other side of the door. She leaned toward it, straining to hear. Cold air slapped her face.

"Y'all good and comfortable at my desk?"

Dawg loomed over her. Bub jumped up. Lola forced herself not to slide back in the chair. "The sheriff wanted me to look at some mug shots. This seemed like the best place."

"Heard you got yourself beat up." The tooth glinted amid his smile.

"I didn't *get* myself beat up. Somebody made a choice to attack me." Lola pulled her attention away from his tattoos, assessing his general build, studying—as Thor had suggested with the mug shots—the detail of his collar. All she remembered about the man who'd hurt her was that he was big. Dawg was pretty big. So were a lot of men. Still. She smoothed Bub's hackles, trying to settle herself as well as the dog.

"I saw you at the Sweet Crude," she said.

"Saw you, too. Odd place for a woman. Not so much for me. So maybe I'm the one ought to be asking you the questions." A flash of intelligence beneath the corn pone. Lola had taken for granted Dawg might be dangerous. Smart, too—that was something she hadn't considered.

"I didn't ask you any questions," she parried.

"But you got 'em. That's a fact. So fire away." The door opened behind Lola. She wasn't sure whether to be grateful or sorry for the interruption.

"Dawg. You're here. Good. I need to take some air, wake myself up after that night I had. Lola, why don't you come with me?"

CHAPTER TWENTY-FIVE

Lola feared that Thor's reference to taking some air meant going for a walk. Even back in Magpie, she'd felt like she'd had enough cold to last a lifetime. Burnt Creek had, just as Jorkki had promised, made her look fondly upon Magpie's ten-below, no-wind days. Sure enough, as she and Thor left the shelter of the office, a gust whipped around the corner of the building and grabbed at her, nearly pulling her off balance. By the time she'd regained her footing, Thor was holding open the door to his cruiser. "Thank God," she said as she clambered in. "Where are we going?"

"I take a little drive around town every day, just to make sure everything's in order. Well, at least as much as anything is in order around here these days. Seems like every day or so there's something new. I feel a powerful need to keep tabs on all of it. Someday, we're going to level out, and wherever we are then, that's going to be normal. I want to get an inkling of what that'll feel like."

The cruiser crept along the main drag as he spoke, enveloped in clouds of exhaust from tanker trucks, trucks hauling flatbeds, dump trucks, and trucks whose purpose Lola couldn't begin to fathom. Bub sat in the cruiser's backseat, quivering nose glued to a window rolled down a quarter inch. The smell of diesel permeated the car. "It stinks," said Lola.

"It's like this at all hours. Come down here at four in the morning and it'll look—and smell—the same."

Lola remembered the night she'd spent in the truck just two nights before, the unbroken rumble of traffic, and believed him. But her mind was still back in his office. "I know you told me why Dawg works for you," she said. "But I don't think you told me how you found him. Did you go looking for somebody who'd scare half the people in town to death?"

Thor threw back his head and laughed. "You know, I've spent so much time around him I've almost forgotten the effect he has on people. He found me, more like. I was trying to bust up a fight one night at The Train. Whole bunch of guys, greenhorns versus roughnecks, all beating and banging on each other. I'd bust up two of 'em and three more would jump in. And it's not like I can just call for backup. The closest is the next county over. Anyhow, I was about to call it quits, just get myself out of the door in one piece and hope the lot of 'em didn't kill one other when Dawg wades in from someplace in the back of the room, throwing one guy after another out of the way, hollering to everybody to settle down and mind the sheriff. Miracle of miracles, they did. I hired him on the spot. Long as nobody ever asks for the background check, we're fine."

"What's in the background check?"

"Little of this, little of that. He's been a busy boy. Nothing too recent, though, and nothing that gave me pause. In fact, in a way it comes in handy. Let's just say he has some specialized knowledge." He changed the subject. "I want you to pay close attention these next few blocks."

"To what?"

"You'll see."

Lola hoped she would. People liked to say things like that to reporters, set little traps for them, show them they weren't as smart as they thought they were. Lola usually lost those games. She braced herself to lose again. The stream of trucks, the cruiser bobbing in its midst like a black-and-white cork, picked up some speed. They began to pass houses, large frame ones with deep eaves and generous porches. The trees in the yards, bare now, were substantial, and Lola thought that in the summertime when they leafed out and flowers grew in what were surely beds beneath the snowdrifts, this part of Burnt Creek must be welcoming, gracious. Except maybe for the trucks. "Is that it?" she asked Thor.

"All the traffic noise and stink ruins it for the people who live here?"

He made a dry noise in the back of his throat. "Close. We keep our windows closed here, even in the summer, because of it."

Lola felt inordinately pleased. She hadn't flunked the test, even if she'd only gotten a B.

"In a way, the noise and traffic—or at least, what comes with it—is what ruined it for the people who used to live along here," he said.

"Who lives here now?"

Thor didn't answer, letting her figure it out for herself. She stared at the houses. Some had gone shabby, paint faded, the walks caked with packed-down snow or shiny with ice. She'd lived in northern climes just long enough to know that only the worst of neighbors left a walk unshoveled and slick, ready to send the unwary sprawling with a sprained ankle or worse. She opened her mouth to say as much, then looked again. "I see it!" She pointed to the multiple mailboxes beside each door. Even from the street, she could see the layers of stickers on each, indicating a regular turnover of renters. "Where'd the owners go?"

Thor's smile was no more pleasant than his chuckle. "Wherever their money took them. Imagine how many people you can pack into houses this size, how much you can charge in rent. Folks who lived here figured out quick how to cut a fat hog. They sold for five times what they paid, or rented out at New York prices. Some of them went across the state to Fargo, others all the way to Minneapolis. The women especially couldn't wait to get out. These are nice houses, sure, but we're a long way from anywhere here. It's hard on people, especially women. Of course, it's a lot harder now. Look what happened to you."

"And DeeDee."

"And DeeDee. Of course, she put herself in harm's way. Doesn't excuse it," he said, as though sensing Lola's ready objection.

"Charlotte seems happy here." Lola told herself maybe she'd imagined the chill between the two. Thor dispelled that notion.

"Charlotte's happy anyplace she can get a meal."

Lola hadn't been sure what to make of Thor Brevik. Now she knew. "That's cruel."

"It's fact. You of all people should respect that. Besides, it's a fact I've learned to live with."

No, you haven't, Lola accused silently. If you had, you wouldn't be so hurtful. But then she thought of the way Charlotte fussed over her husband, despite his public put-downs. Lola wondered if that's why Charlotte surrounded herself with the knickknacks and dolls, cheerful silent figures who beamed nothing but approval as she bustled about the house, taking care of a man who seemed to have stopped caring for her long ago. Lola thought that, in Charlotte's place, she might have bounced a Hummel off Thor's head when he made one of his cracks. For sure, she mused, she herself didn't understand marriage. Yet another reason to keep things with Charlie at arm's length.

The turn signal clicked, interrupting her thoughts. Thor swung the car left. The houses grew smaller, bungalows in treeless yards. A mobile home park, three or four cars pulled up in front of each trailer. One of those campgrounds, campers packed in bumper to hitch. "No vacancy." Then, without warning, prairie. The road began to climb, working its way up a bluff.

"Where are we going now?"

"To the old buffalo jump."

"What's that?"

"Indians used to spook whole herds of buffalo, stampede them over the bluff. They could live for weeks off the ones they killed, staying put until they'd smoked all the meat, cured the hides. Hardly left anything. Then we came along and it's almost like the Indians were never here. I wonder how these oil companies are going to treat us when the boom's over. If they'll put things back the way they were or just move on and leave all their junk behind. If their stuff will cover ours so completely that nobody will ever realize we were here. It'll be like things went straight from the Indians to oil and skipped us over entirely. Makes a man doubt his own existence." He pulled the car into a parking area at the edge of the bluff and set the parking brake.

"Why, Thor." Just when she'd slotted him neatly into the Neanderthal category. "You're a philosopher."

He turned to her with a grin whose warmth stirred an embarrassing heat within her. Not for the first time, Lola cursed a mischievous libido entirely too often enthralled by the least appropriate of men. She forced herself to focus on the town below. Beyond it, rigs stretched to the horizon. Another town—or at least, something like one—lay between the rigs and Burnt Creek proper. It looked like a giant self-storage business, row upon row of prefab units gleaming even whiter than the tired midwinter snow. "What's that?"

"Man camp."

Lola started to count the rows, but gave up after she got to fifty. "How many people live there?"

"Hundreds for sure. Could top a thousand. Maybe even more people than in all of Burnt Creek. They've got mess halls, gyms, everything in there. Even a fast-food place. No alcohol allowed, so they come into town for that. It's close enough that even in this weather, those guys can walk to the bars in about ten minutes. Think about it. That many men, packed together. Working like dogs day and night, drinking even harder on their time off. No women to civilize 'em. No wonder they get rammy, beat up people, worse. Makes you wonder if maybe they didn't have the right idea in those old mining camps with their red-light districts. That probably helped keep a lid on things."

"And now you're philosophizing again," Lola teased, then changed the subject before he could flash another one of those grins at her. The last thing she needed was that sort of distraction. "Do you think the man who jumped me is down there?"

The question chased any remnants of a smile from Thor's face. "Could be. Probably. And the one who beat that girl to a pulp in the snow, he's probably there, too. Tell you what."

"What?"

"Pretty much any trouble we've got in Burnt Creek, I'll guarantee you that man camp is its source."

There it was, she thought. Her opening to ask about the trailer. But true to form, Thor was still talking.

"Now, Miss Lola." A smile to let her know the formality was affectionate. "From talking to your Sheriff Laurendeau, and from watching you work—The Train! Good heavens above—I know that you like to look around in unsavory places. So if you've got a notion to go wandering into that man camp, I'd strongly advise against it. Or at least, not without me right there with you."

First he'd told her the man camp was too well guarded for prostitution. Now he'd warned her against going into it. Lola held up her bruised hand, reminding him of the injuries she'd so recently suffered. "The last thing I want," she said, "is any more trouble."

She was the kind of liar who looked a person straight in the eye, unblinking. She just hoped Thor was as bad a judge of prevarication as she was.

CHAPTER TWENTY-SIX

Thor threw the car in reverse, the view of the subject at hand vanishing as quickly as it had arisen. Lola cast a final, dismissive glance at the monochrome vista. "What a wasteland."

Thor hit the brakes. "Wasteland? Take another look."

Lola looked. Town, rigs, prairie. White snow, grey sky. Wasteland, she thought, but decided against saying it aloud again. "It's very . . . flat."

"Not really." Thor's hand undulated across the windshield, tracing faraway bluffs and cutbanks, the washes and coulees. "We don't make it easy for people here. Don't slap them across the face with landscape the way those mountains do over in your part of the world. If you live here, you've got to develop a taste for subtlety."

Implying, Lola thought, that she didn't have it. She took a reluctant second look. "Maybe summertime improves things."

That gaze again, burning through her. Lola fiddled with the heater knob, turning it down.

"Summertime! It's fine, but you need to be here in spring. This place goes green as Ireland."

Lola had been to Ireland. She'd also spent the previous summer in Montana, which she couldn't imagine was much different than North Dakota, and had learned that the word *green* held considerably less intensity there than Ireland, more olive than emerald. She made a noise of vague assent, hoping to get them moving. But Thor was on a roll.

"And then the lupine comes. We go from Ireland to, oh, I don't know. Whatever's blue. The sea, maybe. Nothing but waves of blue flowers, as far as you can see. I grew up here, spent my whole life here, and still I never get used to it."

"A philosopher and a poet," Lola said, despite herself.

It was as though she'd granted some sort of permission. Thor leaned in and brushed her cheek with his lips. Not the safe part of her cheek, either, back toward the ear, but close in, the corner of his mouth catching the corner of hers, not a real kiss but near enough. "Everything you've been through the last couple of days, you deserve a little poetry," he said. He put the car in gear and pointed it back down the bluff, talking of matters so inconsequential as to nearly convince Lola that a kiss from a man whose wife had been nothing but kind to her was equally insignificant.

But. Lola wondered how she'd feel if Charlie took a crime victim for a ride in his car for a little tour of the town that ended in a kiss. If maybe that's how he'd met the woman who apparently had borne his child. Lupine, my ass, she thought. When Thor had first mentioned it, she hadn't thought of the flower at all, but of the word's alternate meaning. Wolflike.

"Then the lupine comes," he'd said, and for just a moment, she'd pictured a wolf, eyes fixed upon her and mouth open, the gleaming teeth, the lolling tongue, loping toward her across the prairie.

Lola scrambled out of the cruiser before Thor could bestow another not-quite-kiss. "I've got to go the library for some research before my meeting tonight," she said, refusing his offer for a ride back to the house. It would be less embarrassing, she'd reasoned to herself during the ride back to the sheriff's office, to look up Charlie on one of the library's computers than it would to use her laptop at the house, where Charlotte, ever attentive, hovered. Besides, Dawg's remarks that morning had piqued her curiosity. As a county employee, his hiring would be a matter of public record. She could get his full name, Google the "little of this, little of that" that the sheriff had hinted a basic background check would reveal. She waited until the door to the sheriff's office had closed behind him, and went to the main county office, where she waited for a clerk to tear her eyes away from her computer.

"Do you know where I could look at the county budget?"

The clerk's eyes strayed back toward a boxy monitor that looked a good decade old. Lola saw photos of beaches and palm trees and a come-on for cheap airfares. The clerk clicked on one. An array of umbrella drinks leapt to prominence.

"I'd like one of those, too," Lola said, pointing to the drinks. "More than one, actually. The budget?"

"I can print you a copy. Ten cents a page." Another click. A man and a woman reclined poolside in lounge chairs, their bodies bronzed, their bathing suits brief. The clerk's face was pale and lumpy as unevenly risen bread dough. Her sweatshirt bulged in the wrong places.

"It's not going to be like that," Lola said of the image on the screen. "How many pages in the budget?"

"How do you know? You ever been to Hawaii?" She made it two syllables. Huh-why. "That budget. It's a big, fat thing. I don't know how many pages, but a lot."

"I've never been to Hawaii," Lola admitted. She generally didn't take vacations, her trip to Montana the previous summer to visit Mary Alice a rare exception. And look how that had turned out. "How long would it take for you to make me a copy?"

"More time than I've got. I'm busy. You see these?" She patted a stack of manila envelopes that rose high above her inbox. "Building permit applications. Every one I review, three more come in. My eyes are about to fall right out of my head."

So you're resting them by looking at vacation ads, Lola wanted to say. She bit her tongue, reminding herself that she badly wanted to see the budget. She told the woman as much.

"Then whyn't you go to the library? It's right across the hall. They've got it on file. You can look there for free. 'Less you want a copy of your own. Then I'll have to do it." Her lower lip pooched out, letting Lola know exactly how she felt about that.

"The library will be fine." Lola fled.

She stopped just inside the library door. There must have been books somewhere inside the library—actually, there were, in long shelves against the far wall—but most of the floor space was taken up by rows of computers, men parked in front of them, thousand-yard stares retrained upon screens far closer at hand. Lola saw pages of e-mail, housing ads, even some porn. The place was every bit as crowded as The Mint or, for that matter, the Sweet Crude. Except that instead of the clink of beer bottles and driving hip-hop, the hum of electronics and clicking of keys provided the soundtrack. She wasn't going to get to look up Charlie's child until she got back to the house after all. There were no vacant terminals; in fact, across the room by the bookshelves, a line of men waited for their own turn at a connection with home, a crack at a better job, a chance to look at naked women without having to pay for watery cocktails. Not one, Lola noticed, pulled a book from the shelves to while away the time while he waited.

She located the information desk and asked about the budget and within short order found herself with a weighty paper copy. She leaned against a bare spot of wall, and leafed through the pages. She halted when she came to the county-run health clinic, with its lines for a physician's assistant and two nurses. Lola blinked at the salaries, thinking maybe a comma had been misplaced, a zero lost. She skipped ahead to the sheriff's department. There wasn't much to see. Some money for expenses, for maintenance. A request for a new cruiser, denied. Ditto the request for a deputy. Thor's salary was barely forty thousand dollars. Lola wondered what it was like for him to arrest men paid three times that. To watch them bond out of jail with greasy wads of cash, only to show up again the next week. It had to get under his skin. Not just his, but Charlotte's, too, as she gave them antibiotics and sent them back out the clinic door. And it had to bother the county clerk and her dreams of Hawaii as she shuffled through land deals worth more than she'd make in her lifetime, and the librarian even now rapping on her table and warning a roomful of unhappy men that their fifteen minutes of free computer time was up and would they please make room for the people waiting?

Given what the oilfield jobs paid, Lola thought it entirely possible that the entire contingent of civil servants in Burnt Creek turned over every few months. Except for Thor. For some reason, he hung on. She closed the budget book and started back to the librarian's desk and gave her a dime in exchange for a copy of a single page of the budget, the one detailing allocations to the sheriff's office. Nowhere on that page, or in any other likely spot in the unwieldy document, was any record of Dawg's presence.

CHAPTER TWENTY-SEVEN

Lola picked up her phone, put it down, picked it up again and watched until its clock advanced another minute. She'd passed an hour at The Mint waiting for Swanny and Ralph, but they had yet to show. Even given that she'd arrived fifteen minutes early, it was time to worry.

She sipped at the remainder of her second glass of wine and wondered if she should make the rounds of the bars. Ralph told her that Swanny had worked an extended shift out on the rig, spending days catching a few hours' sleep in the on-site trailer instead of returning each night to the man camp. Maybe after a stint like that, Swanny wanted quicker oblivion than a few beers over a meal would provide. Or maybe he wanted more. Lola wondered what it cost to stay with a woman an entire night. According to Ralph, Swanny had "claimed" Judith. That must have entailed more than the standard transaction. Although, Lola realized, she had absolutely no idea what the standard transaction was. The longer she spent in Burnt Creek, the more she realized how unprepared the years overseas had left her for the realities of her own country. She could identify ordnance from jagged scraps of metal, tell factions by the wrap of turban and length of beard, sneak a roadside pee and refasten her pants before her male traveling companions even realized she'd stopped. Aside from persistent wistfulness about plumbing, her years in Afghanistan had turned her recollections of home scornful.

She thought of how she and her friends used to complain about crime in Baltimore. Purse snatchings, smash-and-grabs from parked cars. Never once had any of them worried about being blown to bits as she walked from the front door to the curb to collect the morning newspaper. As for the endless discussions among women about the fecklessness of men, Lola had often passed bitterly pleasurable moments in imagined conversations comparing a broken promise to call in the morning to the reality an Afghani woman faced if she so much as looked at, let alone spoke with, a man who was not her husband or a relative. Lola had written so many stories about forced marriage and bride burnings and stonings as to earn a curt e-mail from an editor one day: "Try writing about the other 50 percent of the population once in awhile."

It seemed that an entire group of women in her own country faced equally serious repercussions for the wrong sorts of encounters with men. She thought of Judith's stiffening body, the nightgown fluttering bright beneath her sweatshirt, of the girls who'd disappeared as completely as burned brides in Afghanistan. She'd spent the afternoon before her meeting with Swanny and Ralph perched on the narrow bed in Thor and Charlotte's house, tapping restlessly at her laptop, coming up dry in her attempts to find any reference to Charlie's child, then surfing statistics as a way to fill the time. She flipped through her notebook, reviewing the data she'd jotted down. On some reservations, Indian women were more likely to die at a man's hand than afforded the dignity of breast cancer or heart disease or easeful old age. Across Indian Country, one in three was raped, but prosecution of their attackers was so rare as to be laughable and, if the men weren't Indian—as most of them weren't—legally impossible anyway. The women who survived lived in isolated areas together with the men who got away with hurting them. Lola scowled at the inexcusable numbers. The story they told, she thought, should have merited front-page news around the country. "Nobody cares about this?" she said aloud.

"How's that?" Ellen stopped in front of her and banged down a basket of rolls. Lola wondered if the girl had changed her mind about working in one of the bars. More likely, she was just waiting to turn eighteen. "You want to go ahead and order food?" Ellen asked Lola. "Looks like your friends aren't coming." Two empty place settings flanked Lola. She'd felt lucky to snag a table when she'd gotten to The Mint, but credited it with her early arrival. An hour later, though, only half the tables were full and the room was uncharacteristically quiet. Big men who'd ordered the Roughneck's Special—a chicken-fried steak with half a fried chicken and french fries on the side—pushed crispy bits of food around their plates like finicky children.

"Where is everyone?" Lola asked. "Did they all go home for their break at the same time?"

"Where've you been?" Ellen's tone was newly assertive. She'd caked on the foundation as usual, but had added cat's-eye swipes of inky eyeliner and green glitter on her lids, and switched her old pinafore apron for a waist model, showing off a clingy sweater whose neckline dipped so low Lola could see the bow on her bra. Lola fingered her own turtleneck and thought of how the cold would rush right into Ellen's shirt. On the other hand, she imagined that Ellen had doubled her tips.

"I've been working. Did I miss something?"

Ellen lowered her voice. "It's always like this when somebody dies. Creeps them all out."

Given the time the men seemed to spend in strip bars, Lola thought maybe that was understandable. Most of them probably knew DeeDee, whose face was prominently featured in that day's edition of the newspaper. Lola pulled a roll apart and rubbed a pat of butter against one of the pieces with her knife. The butter was cold, and crumbled back onto the plate. "Poor DeeDee," she said.

"Who?"

"The girl who was killed."

Ellen gave a little wave. She sniffed. "Oh. Her." Lola wondered if Ellen would feel the same way after she'd been dancing a few months. Ellen scooped up the other two place settings. "You know what they say. Lie down with dogs, get up with fleas. But I guess she won't be getting up anymore."

Lola balanced the bits of butter atop the roll and took a bite. The roll was stale. "I've got to ask. If that's how you feel, why are you considering dancing?" Knowing the answer even as she asked. Ellen thought she'd be different. Every girl probably did, at least when she started. "And how come they're all so upset?" Lola jerked her head toward the men in the room. Any direction would have worked. As usual, she and Ellen were the only women there.

"Because of the accident."

Lola abandoned the roll. "It wasn't an accident. Someone killed her."

"Not her. Those other guys."

Lola put her knife down very slowly. "What other guys?"

The ability to show off some exclusive knowledge seemed to restore Ellen's good humor. "A wire line got away from a couple of guys out on a rig today. Killed them both. You want some more wine?"

Lola's breath came fast. "What guys? What rig?" Knowing even as she spoke that it was useless. She didn't really know either of their names, and she certainly didn't know which rig they worked on.

Ellen lifted a shoulder that emerged pretty and bare from the thin stuff of her top. "Does it matter? Roughnecks come, roughnecks go. The only ones who stay are the ones who die here. Like those two." She laughed at her own joke, then tried to cover the laugh with a cough as heads lifted around the room. She drifted away.

Lola called her back. "Check." Her mouth was dry. She drank the remainder of her wine in a single swallow. She reminded herself that hundreds of roughnecks crowded Burnt Creek's man camps and sardine-tin apartments. It seemed impossible that the two men who were her sole links to Judith could have vanished so decisively. "They're in a bar," she told herself, taking reassurance from the thought that had so angered her moments earlier. She laid some cash for the wine atop the check. She'd been glad of the appointment that kept her away from the sheriff's house that evening. Now, despite her misgivings about Thor, she fumbled with her parka's zippers and toggle fastenings and hurried from The Mint, hoping to catch the Breviks before they finished their own meal. If anyone could tell her who'd been killed, it would be the sheriff.

CHAPTER TWENTY-EIGHT

The Brevik home was dark and still when she arrived. Lola tried the door and laughed. Despite the couple's bemoaning of the influx of bad characters into Burnt Creek, their door was unlocked—as, Lola suspected, were all the neighbors' doors.

She made a quick check to be sure Thor and Charlotte really were gone, then let Bub follow her into the kitchen. Her missed dinner at The Mint had left her ravenous. She stood with Bub before the open refrigerator and selected pieces of cold chicken from a platter trussed up in layers of shrink wrap. She pulled bits of meat from the bone and fed them alternately to herself and Bub until each had eaten far more than necessary. She stooped and let him lick her greasy fingers, then rinsed her hands in the sink. A grinning pig of a cookie jar beckoned. Lola lifted the lid and jumped at the loud mechanical "oink." She selected two oatmeal cookies from the neat stack and fed one to Bub and ate the other herself, breaking off a piece for Bub. "You're lucky these aren't chocolate chip," she said. "Dogs can't have chocolate." He wagged his tail.

Lola wished he'd barked. The silence in the house was oppressive, nothing to distract her from her thoughts, which returned relentlessly to the sheriff. The discovery that Dawg was working off the books. The failure of the two men to show for dinner—and the fact that Thor and Charlotte were the only people who knew she'd planned to meet them. Unless the men had talked. "It's entirely possible," she told Bub, "there's someone out there we haven't even considered." Bub ignored her and trained his eyes on the cookie jar, signaling as clearly as he was capable that another cookie was his highest priority. "Forget it," she told him. She couldn't do a damn thing about the chance that Ralph and Swanny might have been in touch with someone else who might have more information about Judith or the girls. But she could investigate Thor more thoroughly. She went into the living room and shoved heavy draperies aside. The sheriff's house sat at the far end of a street that ended in prairie, the backyard an unbroken sweep of snow past the town's boundaries. The street itself was empty, vehicles tucked into the relative warmth of garages. She knew their batteries would be plugged in for good measure. The house was too well insulated for Lola to hear an approaching vehicle, but with the drapes open, she'd see headlights well before anyone arrived. Thus reassured, Lola began a methodical search, Bub so close at her heels that she shooed him back a step or two. The sheriff and his wife slept on the main floor, in a cherrywood four-poster bed that sagged on one side. The dresser top was bare save for a set of perfume bottles on Charlotte's side, and a small wooden box on her husband's. Lola held the bottles to her nose and sniffed, transported in an instant from a bungalow on a frozen North Dakota prairie to childhood trips with her mother to the department store cathedrals of Baltimore, their glass-counter altars set as though for communion with mirrored golden trays of crystal vessels. She'd have known the scent without reading the label: Shalimar, the one her mother used for special occasions. The bottle was nearly full. She wondered when Charlotte had last lifted it to the nape of her neck, tilted her head this way and that, shivered in delight as the mist settled onto her skin. Had Thor given it to her as an obligatory Christmas or birthday or even—although Lola doubted this—an anniversary gift? Or, sadder but infinitely more possible, had Charlotte ordered it for herself, perhaps in a sporadic attempt to seduce Thor back into romance? Lola replaced the perfume bottle and lifted the lid of the wooden box, only to find pennies. She slid open drawers and saw clothing neatly sorted and folded, nothing like her own jumble. She fell to her knees and lifted the bed skirt. Nothing, not even dust bunnies. In the closet, Thor's uniforms, starched and knife-creased, hung beside Charlotte's pastel scrubs. Lola hadn't noticed a dry cleaner in Burnt Creek's small business district. She imagined Charlotte standing over an ironing board, steam rising, and dampening her face as she sprayed and pressed and otherwise took infinite care of the clothing worn by a man who seemed to have so little regard for her feelings. The fabric made disapproving shushing noises as Lola pushed the clothing aside to see if it concealed anything. It didn't. The bathroom was more rewarding, if not in a particularly meaningful way. Disposable syringes filled a shelf in the medicine cabinet. Lola guessed that Charlotte had diabetes. Not surprising, she thought, given the woman's weight and artery-clogging meals. She shook a bottle of blood-pressure medication—a few pills remained; it was time to renew—and paid closer attention to a prescription sleep aid. Charlotte's name was on that one, too, but Lola thought of Thor's frenetic talking and wondered if he had trouble winding down at night. Something flickered at the corner of her vision. Headlights.

She closed the medicine cabinet and ran to the living room and tugged the drapes shut, then hustled Bub into the mudroom, and sprinted up the stairs. She sat on the bed, then lay back and scuffled at the covers. She waited until she heard the front door open, then stood and moved slowly back downstairs, trying to make as much noise as possible on the carpeted steps. She turned the corner into the living room. Two haggard faces turned her way. "Sorry," she said. "I finished up earlier than expected. I came home and took a nap."

Charlotte pulled a chair away from the kitchen table and fell into it and let her head drop into her hands. Lola wasn't sure if the groan came from Charlotte or the chair. "It's been a hard day," Charlotte said. "For me, for once. Thor's not the only one who's overworked."

A small thrill shot through Lola at the barb. She'd thought of Charlotte as one of those beaten-down wives, too readily accepting of her husband's criticism. Lola was glad to hear she could dish out some criticism of her own. She wanted, badly, to ask about the accident on the rig, but felt as though she were intruding on a private moment. Thor took a teapot from the stove and filled it with water. He twisted a knob on the stove and the scent of gas cut the air before the flame caught. "Anyone want tea? After the day we've all had, it might be better for us than coffee."

Lola noted with increasing satisfaction that it was the first time she'd seen Thor lift a finger in the kitchen. Maybe Charlotte needed to have more bad days. Thor fussed with teabags while he spoke. "Lola, before I forget, I got a call from some girl at your newspaper."

Some girl. Lola thought how Jan would bristle at the characterization. "What did she want?"

"She asked me some questions about that same girl you've been talking about. And some other girls, too."

Dammit, Lola thought. Until now, Thor hadn't known the scope of the story. She'd hoped to find more about the other girls before she took her questions to Thor. "We like to be thorough. What did she want to know? You know—so we're not double-teaming each other."

The sheriff dragged a hand across his eyes. "I can't remember now. It was before the day went all to hell."

"Let me help," said Lola. She went through the cupboards and located the mugs and set three on the table. "I heard there was an accident," she ventured.

"Bad," Thor said. "Thought I'd seen everything 'til I saw this. Guys die in all sorts of inventive ways out on those rigs. Trucks run over them. Something sparks and there's a fireball. I had to go out and pronounce the obvious."

"Thor's the coroner, too," Charlotte said.

Her husband poured tea into her mug, Charlotte added sugar, then more, and stirred and stirred.

"I heard about it down at The Mint," Lola said. She tried to recall the unfamiliar word. "Something about a wire. Were they electrocuted?"

Thor joined them at the table. "A wire line. It's about as thick around as your thigh. Well, probably not yours. Maybe Charlotte's." Thor's payback for Charlotte's brief flash of defiance had begun, Lola assumed. She hoped Charlotte wouldn't back down. Start with small things, she silently urged her. Maybe a scorch mark on one of those uniforms. But Charlotte, snapping her teabag in and out of the water, seemed oblivious to Lola's attempts at telepathic sisterhood.

"The line goes down into the well," Thor said. "There's a safety mechanism to keep it there. But somehow this one got loose, whipped around. You can't imagine the force of those things. The head punched right through one man's chest and when his friend grabbed him, it went into the friend's gut. Killed the first guy outright, but the second one, he died hard. He was still alive when I got there, but only for a few minutes. I had to walk around afterward, bagging little pieces of skin and guts." He'd been staring into his tea while he talked but now he looked up. "Sorry."

Lola battled twin surges of nausea and impatience. She didn't know how to broach the subject of the victims' identities. "How do you tell somebody's family about something like that?"

Thor blew on his tea and took a swallow. A brown crust rimmed his fingernails. Lola's stomach engaged in more antics. "First you got to find their families," he said. "A lot of these boys don't have much in the way of roots. Their crew boss is trying to scare up next-of-kin information for me. When he does, I'll make those calls. I'll spare them the details. Oh, I almost forgot." Thor patted his pockets, starting with his pants and working his way up to his shirt, settling on the left chest. He unbuttoned the flap and withdrew a folded piece of paper. He smoothed the creases. It looked as though he'd Xeroxed two driver's licenses. Lola took the paper from him and held it beneath the tinkling chandelier.

Thor had enlarged the images, badly blurring them. But the numbers and letters remained readable. Ralph Wayne Cooper. William Charles Swan. Lola skimmed past the names and fixed on the faces, the exuberant sideburns, the embarrassing teeth. "That's them. The ones I was supposed to meet." She knew the coincidence should have surprised her. It didn't.

"I know." The sheriff repeated his routine of checking his pockets. This time, he handed her something enclosed in a plastic baggie. Her own business card, blood smeared across its raised lettering. "This was in one of their pockets. I disremember which."

Lola thought of the angry scratch across Swanny's face. Maybe Judith had inflicted it. Maybe that had infuriated Swanny. Maybe Judith had fled into the frozen night, preferring the risk of an impersonal death in the snow than the certainty of one at his hands. Too many maybes. Now she'd never know for sure.

Lola gave Thor back the copies of the driver's licenses. He studied them. "Seems strange doesn't it, that they get killed on the very day they were supposed to meet you? And in one helluva bizarre accident. There's no way that wire line should've gotten away like that. It's almost like someone interfered with it. I might have a criminal investigation on my hands. If I were you, I'd watch your back. Good thing you're leaving in the morning."

Lola hadn't said she was leaving. "I'm not sure I am," she began. There was the matter of the other girls. Maylinn, she reminded herself. Annie. Carole. Nancy. All along she'd thought that maybe they'd followed Judith to the patch, drawn by the lure of easy money dancing. Of course there was the worse scenario, that none had gone willingly, and that they'd been pressed into far more unsavory service. But now, with so many deaths in such quick succession, the stakes had risen considerably. She'd relegated them to second-class status while she focused on Judith. But Judith was beyond help, and these girls were still alive. At least, she hoped they were. The tea burned acidic in her stomach.

"Of course you're going home," Thor said. "Everything happening here is going to keep me pretty busy for a while. I can't be of much help to you, and for sure it's not safe for you to be wandering around on your own."

Lupine, she thought. Her stomach lurched again, swift, insistent. "I think," she said, "I ate something bad at The Mint." She tried to remember what she'd eaten there. She'd never ordered a meal. "The butter on the rolls, maybe. It might have been rancid. Excuse me." She just made it to the tiny bathroom under the stairs before she threw up.

CHAPTER TWENTY-NINE

Once again, Lola sat wan on the sofa, wrapped in the afghan. "I'm never going to get out of Burnt Creek if I stay on this couch."

Charlotte patted her shoulder. "Best place for you. I don't wonder that you got sick. All of this stress, this violence. You're not used it. None of us are."

Actually, Lola thought, she was used to it, on a far larger scale and even more violent. But she couldn't explain to herself, let alone to Charlotte, why these deaths bothered her so much more than the routine butchery she'd witnessed in Afghanistan and other places during her years overseas. Certainly the fact that she'd had a passing acquaintance with Judith and DeeDee and Ralph and Swanny was part of it. And yet again she found herself silently protesting that life wasn't supposed to be so cheap in her own country.

"You must see your share of it at the clinic," Lola said. Maybe she and Charlotte had more in common than she'd first thought. But Charlotte shook her head. "Oh, no. Anyone hurt bad goes straight to the hospital at Williston. The clinic here is more a sore throat-and-sniffles sort of place. That, and STDs. Well, really," she said at the look on Lola's face. "What did you expect? All these men away from their wives and families. I hear the clinic hands out more condoms than aspirin these days. Doesn't seem like they're using them, though."

"What do you mean, you hear? Aren't you there?"

Charlotte lifted her chin and sniffed. "I stick with the sore throats and sniffles."

Lola wondered how anyone got through nursing school, let alone actual practice, with delicacy so firmly intact. She scolded herself for the thought. The upheaval the oil boom had brought to Burnt Creek was nearly akin to wartime, all the old rules turned on end, hardest on women and children, and Charlotte's job at the clinic had given her a ringside seat to its most unsavory aspects, whether she opted to deal directly with them or not. In fact, Lola wondered if she should have asked Charlotte about prostitution instead of Thor. She launched a clumsy attempt. "Where are they catching all those diseases? There's hardly any women in this town."

Charlotte turned away and fussed with the sofa cushions. "Williston, most likely. I hear anything and everything—and everyone—is for sale up there."

It hadn't occurred to Lola that Judith might have been working in Williston. It made sense. It was the biggest city in the patch. Maybe she'd gone there after leaving The Train. But no, Lola was sure that Swanny had mentioned Burnt Creek that morning at Nell's. Charlotte pushed something toward her. "You want to watch a little TV? Here's the remote."

The prospect of canned laughter and overpaid inanity amid the reality of recent and violent loss set Lola's stomach churning anew. "No, thanks." The girls, she thought. The girls. Thoughts of them pushed past her desultory chatter with Charlotte about the clinic, grabbing the forefront of her consciousness, holding tight. Lola slid her hands under the coverlet and tapped a text to Jan under the afghan as Charlotte moved restlessly about the room, rearranging the Hummels, blowing nonexistent dust from their chubby painted cheeks.

"Keep after anything you can get on those girls. People are dying out here." Her fingers hovered over the keys. "Maybe," she added, "it's time to call Charlie." He'd blow a gasket. But Lola could say, without having to widen her own eyes and stare deceit into his, that she'd gotten nothing of use when it came to Maylinn and Nancy and Carole and Annie. Hadn't even really made a concerted effort. She'd given Jan a hard time for not writing about them when they disappeared. But she hadn't been much better.

Charlotte laid the back of her wrist on Lola's forehead as she passed. "I think you might be coming down with something. You're a little warm. You're sure about the TV?"

"Positive."

"At least let me give you something to look at." Charlotte pulled aside the drapes that Lola had so carefully closed. "All those flares out by the rigs look kind of pretty, don't they? It's like having Christmas all winter long. Before, when you looked out this window, there was nothing but black."

Lola wasn't sure the rigs were much of an improvement. The flares were nice enough at night, but daylight revealed rigs surrounding Burnt Creek like a forest of skeletal trees. One of those flares wavered above the site of the day's gruesome deaths, she thought. Or maybe that particular rig was hidden beyond the swells of prairie. It might be five miles from town, or fifty. The man who'd accosted her outside her truck that first night—Dave, she remembered—had said the drive to his rig took at least an hour. She gnawed at a broken nail, trying to even out the ragged edges. Like Ralph and Swanny, he'd also mentioned a trailer. He'd said something else, too. "Anytime you're thirsty, you stop by the Grub Steak. Between work and sleep, that's where I live. Beers are on me." She looked at her watch. It was after nine.

Charlotte stood. "I know it's early, but we're turning in. After the last twenty-four hours, Thor and I both need to catch up on our sleep. And so do you. You've got an awful long drive ahead of you back to Magpie tomorrow."

Lola went through an elaborate yawn and stretch. "You're right. Think I'll go to bed, too. Besides, I need to pack." She'd seen the Grub Steak on her travels around town. It was only a few blocks away, a daunting distance in the cold, but manageable. She'd wait half an hour to make sure Charlotte and Thor were asleep, then she'd check it out. If she were lucky, he'd be there. And if something in Burnt Creek finally worked in her favor, she'd get him to help her find that trailer. Given that Thor seemed so determined to push her out of town, it was her last chance.

Lola hesitated at the top of the steps, boots in her hand, trying to think of a good reason for going out if she encountered anyone. She listened for a sigh, a snore, a creak of bedspring. Nothing. The home's deep-pile wall-to-wall carpet had seemed a throwback to another era when she'd first seen it. Now she blessed the way it muffled her footsteps as she crept down the stairs, and negotiated the rooms booby-trapped with their tiny, wobbly tables topped with those fragile china figurines. She turned sideways, trying to compensate for the parka's extra bulk. She turned the knob to the mudroom door in slow motion, stooped and put her hand to Bub's muzzle. He quivered beneath her touch. Lola knew there was no way to leave him behind. She inclined her head toward the back door. He shot to it. She pulled on her boots and eased through the door, Bub at her side. The snow squealed at each step, making her homesick yet again for the deep, hushed snowfalls of her childhood as opposed to this strange, protesting variety. Nighttime brought a new species of cold, different in ways that went beyond a simple drop in temperature. Her skin tightened. Her nostrils closed against it. But it burrowed into her lungs, grabbing at each breath, snatching it away in short gasps. She put her hand over her mouth, trying to keep her own warm breath close, almost expecting the motion to shatter the air around her like glass. She tiptoed, uselessly, for a few steps, then hastened down the darkened street toward the lights of the business district, Bub frolicking as though they were going for a summer stroll. Along the way, she listed the week's casualties.

"Judith—dead. My story—dead. DeeDee—dead. Ralph and Swanny—dead and dead. With my luck, Bub, we'll show up at the Grub Steak and this guy will be on the floor having a heart attack. That is, if he's there at all." And she continued to curse her luck along the entire frozen route to the Grub Steak.

CHAPTER THIRTY

Dave, as it turned out, was very much alive, sitting in a back booth, slouched over the remnants of a greyish burger and limp fries and the third beer of a lonely man. She slid into the booth beside him. The startled look he turned on her changed to puzzlement. "I know you. Don't I?"

"Not as well as you'd like." Lola reached over and picked up his bottle and took a sip. It was warm. He'd been there awhile. "We've met, sort of. I was in a truck. So were you. You made me an offer. I refused." She held the bottle before her face to hide her inadequate smile. This sort of banter never came easily to her. He didn't seem to notice.

His gaze focused. Briefly. "I remember. You were on your way to the trailer. Going after your sister. Something like that."

Lola finished off the beer, slid the empty bottle back to him and waved toward the waitress. "I'm thirsty. Here, let me buy another round." She left a tip sizable enough to guarantee they wouldn't be bothered for a good long time. "I never went to the trailer. I looked around some other places first."

Dave put his hand to his mouth to cover a belch. "Sorry." He'd been clean-shaven the first time she'd met him. Now stubble roughened his cheeks. Lola looked away. She wondered how much more time it would take in Burnt Creek before he bothered to try to hide a burp, or apologized for one, or stopped shaving altogether. He wiped his hand across the back of his mouth. Lola's pointed look at his napkin was lost on him. "Good. The trailer's a bad scene," he said.

"Why?"

"Why what?"

Maybe more beer hadn't been the best move, Lola thought. "Why is it a bad scene?"

Animation flickered in his face. "Those girls were young. Teenagers. I've got daughters that age."

Lola put both hands on the bench and pressed down hard to steady herself. *The girls.* "You notice anything else about them?"

"I got out of there before I could notice anything else."

Lola couldn't help herself. "Without doing anything?"

He tilted the bottle high and downed his beer in a single long swallow, Adam's apple bobbing like a tennis ball.

"Oh," said Lola. So he hadn't left.

"Just the one time. Besides." Again, his eyes found focus. He snorted at some memory.

At this rate, Lola thought, it would be midnight before she even got around to asking him how to find the trailer. "Besides what?"

"Girl didn't even know what she was doing. Just lay there. Hell, I can get that from my wife for free. I asked for my money back but they threw me out. Back when I was in business, I'd have been ashamed to charge people for a no-good product." He straightened and in that moment, Lola upgraded his former life from a cubicle to an office, put him behind a desk where he was the one handing out the pink slips until the day one came right back across the desk toward him.

Lola's beer was nearly untouched. She lifted it, wet her lips, and set it back down again, the memories of knocking back shots with Ralph still too fresh. "Thing is," she said, "I didn't find my sister anywhere else. So it's back to the trailer. But I don't remember how to get there. Maybe you could tell me?" She held her breath.

Dave picked up a couple of fries and jammed them into his mouth and chewed. "If you're really looking for your sister"—letting her know he wasn't going to make this easy—"you won't find her there. Let's just say she's the wrong complexion."

Lola wanted to leap from her seat, shout her triumph to the smoke-stained rafters. She'd cast the flimsiest line onto unpromising waters and actually had landed good information. She flexed her fingers, unlocked her jaw, and wished she'd attended that poker-face class that she was sure existed at the police academy. Or at least gotten Charlie to give her lessons. "But the girls there—they might be able to tell me where to find her. This sort of trailer, it can't be the only one in town. I'm looking for the other ones, too." Eyes-wide stare. "But I should probably start with this one."

"It's in the man camp," he said. He rasped the heel of his hand over his chin, seeming to notice for the first time that he needed a shave. "Not the old one east of town, but the big new one on the west end. You'll never get by the guard, though. Sometimes guys sneak women into the camp—I had a roommate did that—but you're going to have trouble on your own."

"How'd the girls get in?"

He looked at her as though she were not particularly bright. "They pay off the guards. Same way everything else works around here. Take those two guys who got killed today. You think the company'll own up to making a mistake? They'll just hand their families a wheelbarrow full of money and that'll be the end of it."

Lola wanted to hear about that, too, but she needed to hear more about the trailer first. "I can pay."

He shook his head. "Won't work. Those other girls, it was obvious why they wanted in. But you—a woman on your own and too old, besides. Only one reason you'd be heading into the camp, and that's to cause trouble."

Lola moved closer, let her leg fall against his. "I could pretend to be your girlfriend. You could be sneaking me in, just like that other guy."

He leaned against her. "Really? What's in it for me?"

She put a hand on his knee. Walked her fingers a couple of steps up his thigh. "Things that would make you holler."

He grabbed her hand, tried to pull it higher. "Show me."

The waitress caught Lola's eye, her look a clear signal: Take it someplace else. Lola gave her a little wave, fingers spread wide.

Five more minutes. She steeled herself. Lay her lips against her companion's ear. He tasted of sweat and petroleum. "I promise you won't have any complaints. But here's the thing. Tonight I've got to find my sister. I'll be back, though. I know where to find you. Found you tonight, didn't I?"

His sigh was mournful. His grip on her hand slackened.

Good, thought Lola. Too soon. Dave hadn't given up. "Show me anyway. In my truck. I'll get you into the camp for free afterward. C'mon, girl. It's been weeks. I'm dying here."

Lola tapped her foot against his. She wondered if he could even feel it through his heavy work boots. "Tomorrow."

He pulled back. "You're really not gonna do me tonight?"

Lola fell back on an old lie. "Can't. Wrong time of the month."

"Like that'd matter for a blowjob." His eyes were slits in that square face. "You're playing me."

Lola threw it back at him. "Could be."

"Maybe you're a cop."

Lola braced herself for a final humiliation, reasoning that lips to earlobe had been at least as intimate as what she was about to do. She begged forgiveness from the journalism gods for turning her back on all ethical principles, and leaned into him. Extended her hand. Lowered it to his crotch. Sure enough, beneath the layers of coveralls and long johns, he was hard. She forced herself to count to three before snatching her hand away.

"Cops don't touch," she said. "So you can rule that out right now."

The skin around his eyes relaxed. The muscles in his face shifted. Some sort of calculation being made. "I still can't figure you. But you're good. I'll give you that. So you want to go there? To the trailer that serves up all the goodies?"

"I do. I really do."

"Then we'd best get moving."

In her haste to gather her cap, her coat, her gloves, Lola knocked over her beer. The waitress smirked knowingly. Lola turned her head and spat the taste of him into her napkin and gave thanks that he hadn't called her bluff in exchange for taking her to the man camp.

CHAPTER THIRTY-ONE

Lola crouched beneath the tarp in the truck's half-size back seat as Dave tossed things atop it. An insulated coffee mug. Something soft and floppy: a sweatshirt, she guessed. A quick succession of harder objects, book-sized, but lighter. DVDs, maybe. Porn, probably. A lunchbox landed with a thud.

"Watch it!"

Dave grunted. She heard some sort of scuffle and a yelp before the truck's door opened and slammed shut. "The dog stays here," Dave said.

Lola flung the tarp aside and sat up. "No! He'll be quiet. If we leave him, he'll freeze."

"He's a dog. He'll figure it out." The truck began to roll.

"No!"

Bub ran beside the truck, leaping at it, toenails scraping the side. Lola leaned over Dave and reached for the door handle. He grabbed her wrist, bent it back and stomped on the accelerator. Bub raced behind the truck, body low to the snowy street. Lola watched him get smaller as the truck's speed increased. "Stop! Please. He doesn't know where he is."

Dave turned and straight-armed her. "Get down. Pull all that shit over you again. And shut up. We'll be there in a couple of minutes." Something different in his voice. He was the one in charge now. Within moments, the truck slowed. Lola heard the window's electric hum.

"Late night, Dave? Where'd you wind it up tonight? Sweet Crude? Or maybe"—a guffaw—"The Train?"

"You know me. Back at the Grub Steak, same as always."

The guard's footsteps crunched across the snow toward the truck, receded as he skirted the hood, grew louder as he circled toward the back. They stopped at the rear window. Lola's breath came so ragged she was afraid the guard would hear it above the country music blaring from Dave's radio. Her whole body shook. What if her fear dislodged the pile of junk atop her, sent it cascading to the floor? Did they arrest people for trying to sneak into the man camp? Would she have to face the sheriff? And if she did, what would she say? That she'd decided to celebrate her last night in Burnt Creek with a man she barely knew? By the time she realized the truck was moving again, it had already made a turn or two.

"Damn." She'd meant to keep track of its route in case she needed to find her way back.

"Problem?" Dave asked. "I thought it went pretty well myself."

Lola kicked at the tarp and sat up. "Oh, it did," she reassured him, pushing past her fear for herself, for Bub. The dog was smart, she reminded herself. With luck, he'd retrace his tracks to the sheriff's house and she'd find him sleeping on the back step when she returned. *If* she returned. Doubt flared as Dave turned, his face contorted. "Get the hell back down. We're not even close."

Lola pulled the tarp back over her. "Maylinn, Annie, Carole, Nancy," she chanted beneath her breath. Was it worth it to lose Bub over girls she'd never even met? But Bub, although he might be lost, was still alive. Judith—and of course DeeDee, and Ralph and Swanny, too—were dead. "Maylinn, Annie, Carole, Nancy." The tarp smelled of grease and dirt, normal, reassuring. Charlie had one just like it in the barn. He pulled it out every few weeks for the oil changes he insisted upon doing himself. She'd had a brief notion to call him earlier in the day, but had cast it aside. She wasn't sure how she'd ask him anything without blurting out the question at the forefront of her mind. Did he really have a child? And if so, who was the mother? And what sort of relationship did he have with either of them? Lola had made mental lists of the young women she'd met on the reservation, trying to remember how they'd looked at her when she walked into council meetings, powwows, school events. No one had been less than polite and quite a few had been more. At some point, she'd have to ask him. The truck stopped.

"Here you go," Dave said. "Get out. Now."

Lola kicked the tarp away a final time and crawled into the front seat and put her hand to the door, careful to keep her head low. Rows of long white prefab buildings stretched away on either side of her.

"Which one?"

"Back two rows. Take a left. It's midway down. You'll know it when you see it." He reached past her and opened the door, put a hand to her shoulder and shoved her into the snow.

Lola rolled fast to the side as the truck roared away. Floodlights laid shining carpets between the rows of modular units. She pressed herself against the side of one of the trailers and scanned the landscape to make sure no one was out and about. The wall behind her vibrated with the pounding bass of hip-hop. Lola put her hands to it and shoved herself off, sprinting to the shelter of the next row, then the next. Around her, the units throbbed with life. Washing machines thumped nearly as loud as bass lines. As she sidled along a building, snores were audible from one unit; from another, an argument about the merits of the Green Bay Packers. Televisions blared laugh tracks, game shows and yes, the feigned moans of porn. She counted windows. Ten. Presumably with counterparts on the other side. So, twenty men to a trailer, unless they doubled up in the rooms. Then, as many as forty. She rounded a corner and stepped into darkness. All the previous units had been floodlit, but the lights for the next unit were out. "The trailer," she breathed. It had to be. Lola wondered how much money it took to keep the lights off. She crept closer. The door swung open. Lola flattened herself against the closest modular unit. A man stood briefly on its step. He hitched his pants and fastened his coat and pushed a stockman hat low and tight on his head. Lola followed the hat's movement as he turned his head to one side, then the other. He hopped down from the unit's metal steps and set off around the corner. Lola heard an engine start. She waited until long after the sound had faded, until her toes were numb and her fingertips going quickly to agony, before daring a dash to the unit. She stood on tiptoe beneath a picture window, hoping for an opening in the curtains. But they were drawn tight. She stomped an unwise foot in the snow, then recoiled from the crunch. The door opened again. Lola pasted herself to the wall again and closed her eyes, falling back on a child's reasoning that if she couldn't see someone, the person couldn't see her. She eased her hand over her face, afraid that the clouds of her own condensed breath would give her away. A familiar scent, deeply out of place, slipped between her fingers. She started at the sound of heavy footsteps, then relaxed when she realized they were heading away from her. She opened her eyes. The departing man held a white paper bag in his gloved hand. Lola dropped her hand from her face and breathed in.

Fried chicken?

This particular customer was on foot. Lola waited until she heard a door slam farther down the row, then backed slowly away until she had a good view of the unit. She peered through the darkness and saw what she'd missed the first time. Suddenly, the burnt-out floodlight seemed less sinister. A lot less. Far from being furtive, the unit advertised itself with a homespun sign with the same sort of saucy come-ons about breasts and legs and thighs she'd seen at the same sorts of places around the country. All available at Mama's Fried Chicken.

"They've got everything in there," she remembered Thor saying about the man camp. "Even a fast-food place."

"You want the trailer that serves all the goodies?" Dave had asked. And that's exactly where he'd brought her, no doubt as a way to repay her in full for leading him on. "Son of a bitch," she muttered. She spent a bitterly pleasurable moment imagining tipping the waitress at the Grub Steak to spit in his beer, or serve up an Ex-Lax brownie for his dessert, before she turned her back on her final failure in Burnt Creek and began the long trudge back toward town.

By THE time Lola made her way back to the sheriff's house, she was pretty sure she was frostbitten someplace on her body. Maybe all over. She'd had to wait inside the camp until the guard had ambled away on a break—headed for the fried chicken stand, for all she knew—before daring a dash through the spotlight-flanked gates. Halfway back to the sheriff's house, she'd ducked into the first warm place she could find that was open in the middle of the night—a convenience store, where she lifted the lid on the crock pot of obscenely pale and bloated hot dogs and let the steam wafting from the greasy liquid thaw her face. She drank three cups of tepid coffee before the clerk's pointed glare finally drove her back into the cold, tottering along on feet she could barely feel. She passed The Train just as its door swung open, disgorging heat and drunken men. She thought, for just a moment, about going in. Then one of the men slipped his hand beneath her parka and she fled, cloaked in laughter and humiliation.

When she turned onto the Breviks' street, the darkness was incomplete. True dawn would not come for another three hours, but the blackness was lighter somehow, gathering itself for its too-brief withdrawal. Lola saw lights in a couple of the houses, early-rising rig workers lucky enough to have been born in Burnt Creek and thus have real homes, returning nights to their own beds warmed by their own grateful wives instead of making do with the sterile comfort of the man camps. She approached the house with deep apprehension, but it was dark and hushed and still. Too still. She'd hoped to see Bub rising stiffly from the back step to greet her, his tail making feathery sweeps in the deeper snow of the yard as he trotted toward her. She whistled, low and soft, hoping maybe he'd emerge from around a corner. Nothing. She stood on the back step, and pulled her boots from numb feet and let them fall behind her into the snow, and eased into the mudroom. She waited, listening to the silence. The narrow little bed upstairs, so strange two nights ago, exerted a newly powerful pull. She longed to sink into it, pull every one of the blankets over her, grab a few blessed hours of unconsciousness before deciding what to do about the dog and every other disaster that had occurred while she'd been in Burnt Creek.

She weaved through the living room, leaning this way and that as the Hummels grinned threats of crashing betrayal. By the time she got to the stairs, her feet had begun to thaw. Fire shot through them. She bit her lip against a gasp each time she ascended another step. She almost fell into the bedroom door, grasping at the knob for support.

Something rustled on the stairs.

"Bub!" She whirled.

Charlotte loomed behind her, all pink robe and fuzzy bunny slippers and butcher knife raised high in her manicured hand.

CHAPTER THIRTY-TWO

Footsteps pounded up the stairs. Thor rounded the landing, stark naked, his business flapping and bouncing as he took the steps two at a time. Lola's attention shifted to the service weapon he wielded. A scream died in her throat.

"What's going on here?" He swung in a semicircle, eyes darting to all corners of the narrow hallway outside the room. The gun moved with him. Lola flattened herself against the wall as the gun brushed past her. "Did somebody break in?"

Charlotte found her voice first. "Just Lola, apparently."

Thor lowered the gun. It dangled from his fingers, hanging at thigh level, drawing Lola's eyes in an unfortunate direction. Thor appeared to have awoken abruptly. She glanced away, only to realize Charlotte had caught her looking. "I didn't exactly break in," she began. "Look, we can talk about this downstairs? After you've had time to—"

"Time to what?" Charlotte's voice could have cut glass.

"Dress."

Charlotte squeezed past Lola, climbed to the stop of the steps, and kicked open the bathroom door. She grabbed a towel and tossed it to Thor. "Here. You appear to have embarrassed our guest. Or excited her. I'm not sure which."

Thor flipped the towel around his waist and held it loosely at his hip. It drooped, barely covering him. A trail of blond hairs curled toward it. "What do you mean, Lola broke in?"

Charlotte folded her arms across her chest, the knife blade winking with the motion. "I heard something. You were dead to the world and I knew—at least I thought I did—that it was way too early for Lola to be up. So I went to check. Grabbed the knife on my way through the kitchen."

Thor's face was all hard suspicion. "Why didn't you just wake me up?"

Charlotte's expression mirrored his own. "Because you've had such a terrible few days. You need all the sleep you can get. Besides, I was sure I was imagining things. Until I got up here and saw her in her hat and coat. Were you on your way in or out? And where were you heading, anyway? Or, where had you been?"

Lola had been thinking about the answer to that very question ever since Charlotte had appeared behind her—or at least, ever since Charlotte had lowered her knife and Thor his gun. "The dog," she said. Like his wife, Thor folded his arms. The towel fell to the floor. He kicked at it. Lola, her embarrassment relegated to secondary status, blurted out the only excuse she'd been able to come up with. "I couldn't sleep. So I went downstairs for a snack. I was going to share it with him. He's pretty spoiled."

"Yes," Charlotte agreed. "He is."

Lola tried to detect a softening in her words and settled on the fact that Charlotte had responded at all. "But when I let him out, he took off after something. I was scared. It's so cold. So I bundled up and went looking for him. But I can't find him." At least the hitch in her voice was real.

"Poor thing." Charlotte handed the knife to her husband and put her arm around Lola, who slumped into the welcome solace of her embrace. "Thor, either put some clothes on or go back to bed. I'm going to get Lola warmed up and fed, and then we're going to help her find her dog."

But when Thor came down to another of Charlotte's gargantuan breakfasts, dressed—to Lola's great relief—in his uniform, albeit one free of scorch marks, he advised against any such thing. "We'll find your dog. But best you stick to your plan to go straight home.

We've hit a rough patch here, what with that girl getting killed, and I don't see things getting better anytime soon."

"And those guys," Lola reminded him.

"What guys?"

"The ones killed on the rig."

Thor waved a bacon strip. "The way these things usually turn out, it'll be an accident. Thank the good Lord. I don't have time for another investigation right now. As to your dog—"

Lola leaned across the table. The sweetness of the syrup-drenched pancakes clashed with the salty tears at the back of her throat. "You have to understand. I just can't leave here without him. He was my best friend's dog." And now *he's* my best friend, she added silently.

Charlotte poured more coffee. "We'll find him, sweetheart. And we'll take good care of him until we can get him back to you. Do you two have enough food?"

"He's got a collar, right? Tags?" Thor said. "Is your number on it?"

"Of course." Charlie's number was on the tags, too, but Lola decided not to give Thor another opportunity to bring up her connection with Charlie.

"He won't be gone long. Someone will find him. Purebred border collie like that, they'll either call you, or let me know. When he turns up, we'll send him back to you with Dawg. He picks up extra money driving truck. Makes that Seattle run all the time. Say we find your dog today—the way Dawg drives, I'd lay odds he'd get him back to Magpie before you even get home."

Lola slid a piece of pancake through a puddle of syrup. "Are you sure?" She herself was not sure at all. But she didn't want to insult Charlotte and Thor.

"Positive." He turned what was likely his final smile upon her. Lola wondered how old she'd have to be before she developed some immunity to the charms of handsome men. She'd found reassurance in Charlie's homeliness, pushing away the notion that maybe she thought him more likely to stay with her solely through lack of options. Apparently, given that there might be a Charlie Junior out there somewhere, that wasn't the case at all.

Charlotte busied herself at the counter, assembling food in plastic containers. She wore an old-fashioned bib apron, triple-pocketed and ruffled, over her scrubs. "I don't want you eating road food. That stuff will kill you, or at least give you indigestion so bad you'll wish you were dead. I've got an apple and banana in here for your fruit"—Lola had not thought fruit existed in the Brevik household—"and a piece of spice cake. And I'll make you a chicken sandwich. White meat or dark?"

"Dark. Really, you don't have to make my lunch." Even to herself, Lola's protest sounded insincere. At least, she thought, she felt guilty about the way Charlotte tended to her, while Thor appeared entirely unaware of the effort his wife expended on his behalf.

Charlotte, ever attentive, reinforced that guilt. "You'll call us when you get there safe?"

"She won't need to do that," Thor said. "That sheriff of hers will call. Used to be I only talked with Charlie Laurendeau at those sheriffs' meetings we have once a year. I've heard from him more this week than I have in the whole time I've known him."

"He's not *my* sheriff—oh, never mind."

Charlotte put the lunch containers in a paper grocery sack and handed Lola the Thermos. "I just filled it. That looks like a good Thermos. It should get you through at least the first half of the trip." She stood on the back step, coatless, arms crossed, as Thor handed Lola her bags, and then unplugged the battery cord and tucked the plug into the truck's grille. Lola started toward the truck, and then stopped. She wondered what Charlotte's life would be like when she left. She felt around in her pockets until she found a business card. She gave Charlotte a quick hug, slipping the card into Charlotte's apron as she did so. She pressed her cheek to Charlotte's, inhaling for the last time the teasing scent she'd never been able to define. "You can call me anytime." Charlotte dropped her arms and stepped back. Lola wondered if she should have said anything at all.

Lola climbed into the truck. Thor joined Charlotte on the step. "Come back in the spring," Thor suggested.

"I know. Ireland. The lupine." She raised her hand in farewell and drove away from their house without looking back.

CHAPTER THIRTY-THREE

Lola headed east on Burnt Creek's main street, tailgating a triple-trailer semi, eager to put the town in her rear-view mirror and to floor it on the highway until mountains rose ahead.

The semi's lights flashed red, and Lola tapped her own brakes, impatient at the delay. A dog trotted across the street, weaving adeptly between the trucks. There was no mistaking it for Bub—it was brown, and loped easily on all four legs—but Lola's throat constricted with new tears. She yanked at the wheel, turning onto a side street, and then another, her eyes scanning the sidewalks, the narrow spaces between buildings, looking for a spot where a black-and-white dog might curl up in hopes of warmth, of food, of his owner come to retrieve him. She started with the north-south streets, driving from one border of Burnt Creek to the other, then repeated the tedious process with the east-west grid. The sun inched upward, teasing with its false prospect of warmth. She took a second pass at the main drag, but thought she saw Dawg's distinctive swagger heading down the street ahead of her, and hastily backed up and chose a different street. Thor and Charlotte believed her to be well on her way by now. It wouldn't do for them to think she didn't trust them enough to find the dog. Lola cruised Burnt Creek's neighborhoods, street after street of small frame houses, many porches stacked high with cordwood, that hinted at the quiet community Burnt Creek must have been when those homes sheltered normal families instead of renting out every spare bedroom and pullout sofa and even floor space—extra for carpeted—to roughnecks and greenhorns. Her phone sounded, interrupting her reverie. Lola looked at the number. Jan.

"I'm on my way back," she snapped into the phone. "I didn't get anything. I'm sure those girls are here, but I haven't got one good goddamned idea where. I busted my butt and ended up with squat and I've lost Bub besides." She pressed her lips together, too late. The admission of defeat had already escaped. But Jan didn't appear to have heard anything she said.

"Lola." Her voice sounded small, far away. "Lola."

Lola thought maybe the connection was bad. She shook her phone and checked the bars. They were full. She shouted into it anyway. "I'm right here."

"Tina's gone."

Lola turned back onto the main street, into the path of an oncoming tanker. Its horn blasted so loud she dropped the phone. She waved an apologetic hand and pulled to the side of the street and felt around on the floor for her phone. "Lola," Jan babbled from somewhere beneath the seat. "Did you hear me? She's gone."

Lola retrieved the phone and pressed it to her ear. Its surface was gritty. "I heard you. What do you mean, gone?"

"I mean she didn't show up at work yesterday. We thought she was out on an assignment, but then the person she was supposed to interview called the paper, wondering where she was. Finch took the call and told the person that Tina was probably just running on Indian time and forgot about it. He didn't think to tell either me or Jorkki about the call. So hours and hours went by before Jorkki got all twitchy about her missing her deadline and Finch finally said something, and by then her mother was calling—"

"God. Just like those other girls."

Jan's voice regained some of its old confidence. "Not just like them. Those girls had been in trouble for years. But this is Tina. Basketball star-honor-roll Tina. I doubt that girl has had as much as a sip of beer in her whole life. Charlie and all the tribal cops are shaking every tree and bush in the county, chatting up everyone who's ever so much as said hello to her, to see if anyone's seen her in the past day."

"The past *day*? Just how long has she been gone?" Lola tried to keep her own voice calm, despite her rising fear.

"Her interview was set for three thirty yesterday. She left school at three and seems to have just dropped off the face of the earth. She was safe enough on the reservation, but coming down here to Magpie to work, with all these strangers driving through here on their way to and from the patch—" Jan's voice trailed off.

Lola looked at her watch. Noon. She knew—and she knew that Jan did, too—that the first twenty-four hours after a person disappeared were crucial. After that, the chances of finding anyone alive plummeted. Tina had already been gone nearly that long. "I'm on my way back." She cleared her throat and tried to speak with assurance. "I'm positive that by the time I get back, you'll have found her. Maybe winter got to her. Maybe she just took off for Great Falls or Missoula, just to see some bright lights and people on the streets." Knowing even as she spoke that her words were preposterous. For all the reservation's problems, Tina loved the sheltering arms of extended family, of its leisurely rhythms, of being on sure footing within its borders. She had a lock on a full scholarship to the state university in Missoula four hours away, but had spoken often of her trepidation of dealing with an all-white world, and a crowded, bustling one at that.

Jan put Lola's thoughts into words. "You're an idiot. Just come on home."

"On my way," Lola repeated. "Wait—did you get my text about all these people dying out here? Not just dying, but getting killed? Did you ever talk to Charlie about it?"

"I tried. But I only got as far as saying 'I just got a text from Lola' and before I could say anything else, he gave me an earful about how he didn't want to hear your name again in polite company. What's with you two?"

"Never mind." Lola figured it wasn't the time to ask about Charlie's child. She rang off. But she didn't leave, not yet. The truck was parked across from the Grub Steak, the last place she'd seen Bub. She'd give it fifteen minutes more, she told herself. Given that she had a ten-hour drive, it wouldn't make an appreciable difference. Then she'd leave. Although, as happy as she was to flee Burnt Creek, the thought of returning was scant comfort under the circumstances. Tina gone, and not a single way to view that fact as anything but ominous. Bub missing. Her relationship with Charlie tenuous. And the reservation in turmoil with the loss of the first decent jobs people had seen in decades. She wondered, yet again, if it had been a mistake to walk away from the suburban assignment her newspaper in Baltimore had offered her as a sop to downsizing her from Kabul. Magpie was, and always had been, small, obscure, and hardscrabble. She supposed she could leave and come back fifty years later and, but for a new crop of faces with familial resemblance to the old ones, nothing much would have changed—and that went double for the reservation. Baltimore, at least, would have had energy and options. Bub could have adapted.

Her breath had fogged the windshield as she sat in the truck. She pulled her sleeve down over her hand and rubbed a clear circle and scanned the street for Bub. She checked her watch. Seven more minutes. The truck's cab smelled of the lunch Charlotte had packed her. She unfolded the top of the bag and extracted the sandwich from its plastic container and unwrapped the origami of waxed paper that enfolded it, and took a bite. It was, of course, slathered in mayonnaise. Still, it was delicious, the meat dark and moist. "I love dark meat," she said, speaking out of habit to a dog who wasn't there. She glanced around, even though she knew no one would have heard her, and took another bite. The words of the Sweet Crude's manager came back to her, hawking the appeal of the darker-skinned dancers. Most of the clientele was white. "Where else are they gonna taste dark meat? Makes me think there's a tanning booth in Double Derricks' future."

Lola had never heard the crude term before. Men had probably patronized Judith and possibly the other girls, too, solely because of the color of their skin, a thought that roiled Lola's stomach anew. Lola thought back to Judith's body in the snow, the way her brown skin had gone pale in death, making the ugly tattoo on her arm even more prominent. A slanted brand was called "running," Charlie had told her. Had the brand been used on a calf, it would have signified the Running Heart ranch. Lola unwrapped another sandwich and lifted the top piece of bread.

"More dark meat." Now that she knew the term's other meaning, it made her squeamish to say it aloud. And yet she did. "Dark meat." And again. "Dark meat. *God.*" No longer caring that she didn't even have the pretense of a dog to talk to.

"Not chicken. Girls. Mama's was exactly what Dave said it was. That place sells girls."

CHAPTER THIRTY-FOUR

She hit the gas so assertively that the truck's wheels spun in the snow before the studded tires caught, shooting her into the street, where she narrowly missed a Grub Steak patron, whose curses followed her down the street as she sped toward the sheriff's office. But when she got there, all she found was Dawg, feet propped up, lug sole boots dripping melted snow onto the desk, sliding a buck knife with precision beneath his fingernails.

"Where's the sheriff?"

"You're letting all the warm out again. He's not here."

Lola kicked the door open wider behind her. "I can see that. Where is he?"

Dawg held up the knife, inspected it, and blew something from its tip. He started on his other hand, working the blade beneath a yellowed and horny thumbnail. "Don't know. Working on some trouble you stirred up, no doubt."

Lola let go of the door. It slammed shut behind her. The room shrank. Dawg and his knife were three feet away. "What do you mean?"

"That girl from the titty bar. I saw you talking to her." He wiped the knife on his pants. The blade was a good six inches long. It caught the fluorescence from the ceiling light and flashed it around the room.

"So?"

"So now she's dead."

Deciding to ignore Dawg's unsettling comments, Lola reached for the doorknob. "I need to see Thor. Right away."

"You mean Sheriff Brevik. Whatever it is, you can tell me."

"I don't think so." Lola would just as soon have stood in the middle of Burnt Creek's main street and shouted her suspicions to strangers before saying a word to Dawg.

He held up his middle finger and shaved a sliver from the nail. "Might be he went home for lunch. Maybe a nooner with the missus. Woman like her can keep a man warm at night and in the daytime both." He put down the knife and retrieved something from beneath the desk. A paper bag. White, with grease smearing its red lettering. "Mama's." He pulled a drumstick from the bag and gnawed at it. His laugh followed her out the door. She stood a minute on the other side and flashed her own middle finger before heading back to the truck.

LOLA RAN up the back steps to the Breviks' house and pulled open the door, ever unlocked, and ran in without shedding her boots. Charlotte stood at the sink, up to her elbows in soapy water. Steam rose from its surface and her hair curled damply around her flushed face.

"Why, Lola. Whatever are you doing here? I thought you left hours ago. Did you find your dog? Honey, you're tracking snow."

Lola looked uncomprehendingly at the white patches melting across the floor. "I'm sorry. I need to talk to someone."

Charlotte lifted reddened arms from the water and dried them on a hand towel. "Sounds like you're in trouble. You'll want Thor. I think he's at the station."

"I just came from there." She followed Charlotte's glance toward her feet and belatedly pulled off her boots. Charlotte handed her a paper towel. She wiped up the floor and carried her boots to the mudroom and tossed the sopping paper towel in the small trashcan by the back door. She padded back across the damp floor in stocking feet and sat at the table and gave reluctant voice to the kernel of a suspicion that had sprouted into full flower the minute she'd seen Dawg with his bag of fried chicken.

"I'm not sure Thor is the right person. Charlotte—"

Charlotte twisted a knob on the stove until the gas caught beneath the teapot. "Yes, Lola?"

"I think Thor and Dawg might be involved in something. Something bad."

Charlotte opened a cupboard door and contemplated the boxes within. "Regular or herbal? I'm thinking herbal. You're upset. It'll calm you. Honey, I think you have a wrong idea in your head about Thor. I know you think he can seem hard on me. But, you're not married, are you?"

Lola shook her head.

"Maybe someday you will be." Lola took full note of the insult beneath the *maybe*. The same sort of dig Charlotte had aimed at her husband the previous day. "If that day comes, you'll understand how complicated marriage can be." She held up two teabags. "Which one?"

Lola pointed to the darker of the two. "This goes beyond however I might feel about Thor. If he and Dawg are mixed up in what I think they're in, it could mean trouble for you."

Charlotte put the teabag—the herbal one, Lola noticed, despite her choice—into a cup and poured boiling water over it. "Whatever it is, I think you'd better share it with me."

What the hell, Lola thought. Before she was halfway through her recitation, Charlotte's arms were around her. "What a terrible thing. And you were right there at that place. Are you sure, though? It seems awfully farfetched."

Lola let her head fall onto Charlotte's bosom. "I'm almost positive. That's why we need to talk to somebody. Somebody who isn't Thor."

Charlotte turned to the cookie jar. Lola jumped when it oinked. Charlotte sat the tea in front of her with a cookie on the saucer. "Losing that dog has hit you hard. You're all worked up. Things will turn out fine. You'll see."

Lola picked up the cookie and put it down without tasting it and sipped instead at her tea. Charlotte rose and stood behind her. She massaged Lola's neck with the sure, firm touch that Lola remembered from the first time they met, when Charlotte had examined the injuries inflicted by Lola's attacker. "Your back is like a board. It's no wonder. So many bad things have happened to you here. You're overwrought." She dug a fist into Lola's shoulder.

"That feels nice. Thank you." Something snagged at Lola's skin. "Ow!"

Charlotte's hands lifted away. Lola's muscles snapped back into quivering tautness. "I must have broken a nail," Charlotte said. "Sorry."

Lola rubbed at the spot on her neck. "It's fine. You're right. I'm jumpy." Charlotte sat down across from her. Lola blew on her tea and took another sip. "Do you think I'm crazy?" She *felt* crazy. Her tongue was fat in her mouth.

Charlotte's head moved back and forth in slow motion. "No, honey." The words came from far away.

Lola sat down her tea, very carefully, and watched the cup tilt onto its side. She tried to raise her hand and couldn't. The amber liquid beaded up on Charlotte's snowy tablecloth before sinking into it. "Oh, no," she tried to say, but couldn't form the words.

Charlotte's face swam before her, a cellphone pressed to her ear. "I think you need to come home right now. Our house guest is back and she's got some funny notions in her head."

Lola listed to the side and thought she was just like the teacup, falling and falling, with no way to catch herself. She blacked out before she hit the floor.

CHAPTER THIRTY-FIVE

Consciousness returned in a series of discrete details, none good.

She was cold.

Naked.

Bound.

Gagged.

Without opening her eyes, she blinked, feeling for the brush of cloth against her lashes. There was none. At least she wasn't blindfolded. She kept her eyes shut, unready and unwilling to face her new reality.

"Go ahead. Open 'em. I know you're awake."

Someone was with her. An accent. *Ah* know. So that someone was Dawg.

Lola jerked and screamed, forgetting the bindings, the gag. The cords around her wrists and ankles tightened. The scream died against the wad of cloth in her mouth. She sucked in air through her nose and blew it back out. And again. In. Out. Trying for something like calm before she opened her eyes. Oh, hell, she thought. Get it over with. Then wished she'd kept them shut a little longer.

Dawg loomed above her, shirtless. The tattoos on his chest and abdomen writhed when he laughed. "It's nice and warm in here. I don't even need my vest. Specially since I don't have to worry about you busting in and leaving the door open the way you always done at the sheriff's office."

Lola let her eyes roam, eager to look at anything but Dawg. She was in her room at the sheriff's house. The skylights leaked grey light. She wondered how long she'd been out. Half a day? Or a day and a half? She had a fierce need to pee. But something else was even more worrisome. Impossible not to imagine what Dawg might have in mind. She finally let herself look at him again. He regarded her with knowing eyes.

"You're pretty. But not as pretty as those other girls."

Lola nodded. Or maybe, she thought, she should shake her head. What was the best way to convey that no, she was not pretty at all, certainly not worth raping? But if it came to that, she thought as her discomfort increased by the moment, at least she'd have the satisfaction of peeing all over him. Maybe that would make him stop. Or maybe that would just make him mad. She whimpered.

"Shoot," said Dawg. He reached for a gun on the nightstand. Lola hadn't noticed it before. It was the one Charlie had given her. Largely useless except at close range, he'd said. It didn't get much closer than this, she thought.

"No," she screamed uselessly into the gag. "Don't shoot!"

Dawg frowned at the frantic, inarticulate sounds. "Mama said I was supposed to take you to the bathroom when you woke up. She didn't want you to mess up the bed. So I'm gonna untie you. Don't mess up. Or"—he waved the gun—"we're gonna have ourselves an even bigger mess."

By the time he had freed her wrists and ankles, Lola had abandoned all thoughts of escape. "Mmpph! Mmmpph!" she said, pointing to the bathroom. And rushed toward the door, ignoring the pressure of the revolver against the small of her back.

At least Dawg didn't accompany her into the bathroom. But he stood just outside the door, which he left slightly open, foiling her plan to search the medicine cabinet for something that could be used as a weapon. Which she had nowhere to conceal, anyway. Maybe it was wishful thinking, but it occurred to her that her nakedness might have been a precautionary tactic instead of a prelude to rape.

Dawg rapped at the door with the gun, shoving it open a few inches farther. "C'mon out of there, now. I know you're done. Unless you're poopin'. Are you poopin'?"

"Jesus," Lola muttered against the gag. She raised her voice. "Uh-uh," she shouted against it, hoping he got the gist. She stood from the toilet and flushed and pumped liquid soap onto her hands and ran water over them, eyeing the soap dispenser. Maybe she could remove the pump and jab him in the eye? But before the thought had time to gel, Dawg pushed open the door and took her by the arm and dragged her back to the room and threw her onto the bed.

"Now, you listen," he said. "I'm gonna leave you here. I can even take that gag out if you like."

Lola nodded so hard it hurt.

"Can't no one hear you scream in here, anyhow." Lola remembered what Charlotte had said, about how the insulation left the room practically soundproofed. Dawg reached for her. It took all her strength not to cringe away. He fumbled with the back of the gag until the binding loosened. Lola spat the wad of cloth from her mouth and sucked in air in great rasping breaths. "Thank you," she forced herself to say. And then, "What time is it?"

"About nine."

"What day?"

He told her she'd been out since the previous afternoon. Dawg picked up the cloth from the gag, and untied the ropes that had bound her to the bed, and tucked them into his vest pocket and put the vest on.

Damn, Lola thought. She had thought the cloth and rope might have proved useful in some way she had yet to figure out. Now she wouldn't have to. Dawg stood in the doorway. "You done good," he said. "Nice and quiet. Not all of them are so smart. That's when things get ugly. It's a shame. You just sit tight. Mama'll be lookin in on you in a bit."

Them, Lola thought? *Them?*

Which was nothing compared to the other thought short-circuiting the wiring in her brain, making her forget she was naked, that she was trapped, that it was well within the realm of possibility that she'd be killed. Twice within the last few minutes, Dawg had called Charlotte "mama."

Charlotte, with that indefinable spicy scent lingering beneath her powder and perfume, the one Lola had never been able to place because it didn't belong, the one she finally—too late, too late—recalled. Fried chicken. Charlotte was Mama. She threw back her head and screamed and screamed within the soundproofed room, hurling herself at the locked door until her bare skin was a mass of bruises and she fell back onto the floor, drained of breath, of strength, of all hope.

CHAPTER THIRTY-SIX

Incredibly, Lola slept.

Which gave her a blessed moment, upon awakening, of forgetting. She yawned. Lifted her arms above her head and stretched. Pain flooded her muscles, bringing memory with it. She fought the urge to leap from bed, to fling herself once more against the door's unforgiving surface. Instead, she sat up slowly. Took stock. She hit the light switch beside the bed and held out first one arm, then the other, inspecting the bruises along their sides, the raw circles where her wrists had been bound. She bent, forward and then back, to one side and the other. The muscles in her back rebuked her. She cursed herself for the useless assault on the door, which had only added new bruises atop the old ones. She'd need all her strength for whatever was to come.

She stood. On tiptoe, she could press her hands against the skylights' surface, no more yielding than the door. The light fixture was likewise impenetrable, a hard plastic cover screwed tight against the ceiling. Lola had thought to remove the lightbulb, shatter it, use the jagged remainder as a weapon. Somebody else apparently had thought of that first. She circled the room, running her hand over every surface, then knelt on the floor and did the same, seeking a loose board. None. The Raggedy Anns smirked their uselessness. She inspected the bed and end table, the only pieces of furniture. Maybe she could dismantle them, wield a leg as a club. But the pieces were fastened so tightly together that the screws were embedded in the wood. She wound the corner of the top sheet, worn and soft, around one hand and gave it a quick yank. It pulled free from the bed. She took an edge between her teeth and another between her hands and tore. Then again. In short order, she had a pile of neat strips of torn cloth. She braided them together until she had a passable rope. She tugged at the ends. It was strong, not too long—just long enough to wrap around someone's neck if, that is, she had the advantage of surprise. She made the bed and tucked her makeshift rope beneath the mattress, leaving one end dangling, concealed by the bedspread. Then she sat and thought awhile.

She considered lurking behind the door and jumping Dawg from behind when he came in, wrapping the braided sheet around his neck, pulling with all her strength. It could work. Maybe. She looked at her bruised arms, her battered legs. Dawg probably had close to eighty pounds on her. She imagined him shrugging her off with those massive shoulders, one of his lug sole boots coming down on her bare feet. She glanced down at her body, ruing the bruises anew. Dawg hadn't tried to rape her. But he'd looked at her naked body for a good long time. Maybe, when he returned, she could get him to look again. Rattle him by seeming willing. Distract him with soft words, her lips to his ear, her arm around his neck—and then, before he knew what was happening, the rope, too. She remembered Joshua telling her that his sister was named for the biblical Judith, for her courage in beheading Holofernes. Lola wondered if she'd have the same sort of strength. She considered the fact that she'd apparently stumbled across a lucrative and highly illegal side business run by the man who was supposed to represent law and order in Burnt Creek, and imagined the only fate possible under the circumstances. She'd need to have the strength—if only she didn't get herself killed in the process.

CHAPTER THIRTY-SEVEN

Footsteps sounded before Lola was ready.

She fell back onto the bed, seeking a languid pose, as though she were just waking. She turned on her side, bent one knee, crooked an arm beneath her neck. Her other hand crept beneath the blanket, along the side of the bed, and fastened to the tail of the braided length of torn sheet. She tried to still her breathing as she heard the tumblers clicking within the lock, watched the knob turn. "Back so soon?" she'd planned to say, her voice pitched low and husky. But it came out in a squeak.

"Charlotte?"

The Raggedy Anns smiled their witless grins.

" 'Fraid so, Cupcake." Charlotte could have been talking to her across the kitchen table, so casual was her tone.

Lola curled away from her, scooting into the far corner of the bed grabbing the quilt as she went, pulling it around her. She tightened her grip when Thor loomed behind his wife, stepping into the room and pulling the door shut behind them. Lola looked into Charlotte's—Mama's—eyes and wondered how she'd managed to miss their reptilian flatness. No wonder Thor and Charlotte had been so eager for her to leave. Or—fingers of dread crept along Lola's skin as she thought of Charlotte stealing up behind her, butcher knife in hand—to have people think she'd left. But something had saved Lola from a bloody, slashing end. Maybe Charlotte had never killed anyone before. But she'd been willing to try. Lola was going to need a plan, one that took that fact into consideration. Problem was, she had no idea what that plan would be.

Charlotte folded her arms across her chest and shook her head. "Lola, Lola, Lola. What are we going to do with you?"

"Give me my clothes back and let me go?" Lola showed her teeth in what she hoped was a grin. If she was out of ideas, the least she could do was try to unsettle them with feigned confidence.

"Not going to happen." Thor's lips barely moved as he spoke.

"One out of two? Under the circumstances, I'll take either one. Clothes in here or naked on the street. Come to think of it, I'd prefer the latter." She tried the smile again. Given the utter lack of reaction by either Charlotte or Thor, she wondered if her face had even moved.

"You'll get your clothes back. Maybe," Charlotte said. "We're going to have to keep you awhile."

Never had Lola invested a simple word like "awhile" with such hope. Charlotte's next words made her more hopeful still. "Unfortunately, we can't just kill you."

"Unfortunately is in the eye of the beholder," Lola said. "Out of curiosity, why can't you? Not that I don't think it's a fine decision." Somehow, the words came out exactly the way she'd intended them, relaxed, a little flippant, no shakiness at all. She wondered how long she could keep it up. A tremor ran through her legs. She wrapped her arms tighter still around them.

"Because we've already got too goddamn many dead people floating around," Charlotte snapped. She looked at Lola, but Lola got the feeling her words were directed at Thor. "Somebody thought it would be a good idea to send that idiot Dawg after that one girl when she ran. Which she wouldn't have been able to do in the first place if that lunkheaded fool hadn't fallen asleep on the job."

"She turned up dead all the way over in Montana. So she doesn't count," Thor said. Lola held her breath right along with him, awaiting Charlotte's comeback.

"Doesn't count? Well, let's think about who does count, starting with that slut of a stripper. For some reason it seemed like another stroke of genius to go after her, too, in case she started blabbing around about whatever she talked to Lola about."

"I didn't get a chance to talk to her about anything—"

Charlotte spoke past her. "At least Dawg didn't screw that one up. Besides, who misses a stripper?"

Thor's head jerked up and down in emphatic agreement. "You said it yourself. Who misses a stripper?"

Scarlet washed high and unhealthy across Charlotte's face. Lola thought of the blood pressure medicine she'd seen in the downstairs bathroom. "But then those two guys—that kind of put things over the top. Anybody else turns up dead, people are going to get all het up, wondering what the hell's going on out here in Homestead County. Next thing you know, we'll have folks from the attorney general's office up here sniffing around. But somebody didn't think about that, did he? Same way he didn't think to make sure this one had actually left town."

By the time Charlotte finished her diatribe, Thor's head was bowed, his shoulders hunched around his ears. Lola had barely adjusted to the fact that Charlotte was Mama. Now this. Lola wondered if the whole downtrodden wife business had been an act. Or, if Charlotte had been referring to this very same reversal of roles when she'd lectured Lola on the complications of marriage. Thor got to needle Charlotte about her weight in exchange for Charlotte running a whorehouse? Lola's head ached all out of proportion to the lingering effect of whatever drug they'd given her. She couldn't arrange her thoughts in any way that made sense of her current situation.

"She was supposed to be gone," Thor said. "She should have been well on her way to Magpie by now."

Lola sat up straight, forcing herself not to fling out her hands as though to catch the gift Thor unwittingly had tossed her.

"Yes, I should have. And that's a problem."

Charlotte swung back toward Lola. Thor raised his head. "How's that?"

"They were expecting me. They'll wonder where I am."

"Bullshit." Lola blinked. It was one thing for Charlotte to drug her, to strip her, to stuff her in a locked room. But the cursing? She hadn't thought Charlotte capable.

"It's true." Lola no longer had to feign the certainty in her voice. "Check my cellphone. The last call on there is from my friend, wondering if I'd left town."

Charlotte spoke to her husband without turning her head. "Get the goddamn phone."

The room fell silent as they waited for Thor. Lola worked at keeping her face blank as her thoughts raced. What could she say to Jan that would tip her off? Thor returned far too soon. He held out the phone to Charlotte. "She's right. There's the call."

"How do we know it's from her friend? What if it's from that sheriff?" Charlotte held the phone close to her face. "Who's PITA?"

"That's my nickname for my friend," Lola said. That part, at least, was true. She'd changed the name on Jan's listing in a fit of pique one day, deriving childish satisfaction from showing Jan her new designation.

"What's it mean?" Charlotte challenged.

"Pain in the Ass. Because she is."

Charlotte screwed up her face. Powder sifted from her pores. "Looks like you're no better at being a friend than you are at anything else."

Entirely possible, thought Lola, who'd spent the past few moments wishing that she'd worked harder, much harder, on her friendship with Jan.

Charlotte checked the phone again. "You've got a bunch of incoming calls from that number."

"No surprise. Like I said, I was supposed to be back by now. She's been working all kinds of overtime while I've been out here. I'll tell her I had car trouble. We can forget any of this ever happened." Lola made the impossible offer as though she had every expectation of seeing it accepted.

"Get your gun," Charlotte commanded Thor.

"Jesus. *No*!" Lola lost all pretense of calm.

Thor drew his service weapon and regarded it thoughtfully, then leveled it at Lola's head. Lola scooted backward across the bed. Charlotte laughed. "Where do you think you're going? If he decides to shoot you, you're stuck in this room. You'll just end up with more holes than necessary, and I'll end up with a big mess to clean up."

If. She'd said if. Lola unwound by degrees from her fetal position. Charlotte held out the phone. "Take it. Call your friend. Tell her that story about the truck. And make her believe it. Or—" She glanced toward her husband. He obligingly waggled the gun. "Or," he said, "big damn mess, just like Mother said."

Lola reached for the phone, beyond caring that her hands were visibly shaking. Thor pressed the pistol to her forehead. The cold steel warmed slowly.

"That had better be your friend's number," Charlotte said. "If a man answers—"

Lola beat her to the punch. "I know. Big damn mess." The gun dug into her skin. She hit the number. The tone sounded. *Answer. Answer, dammit*, she prayed. It sounded again. *For God's sake. Answer.*

"Lola? It's about time. Where the hell are you?"

Lola held up her hand as though Jan could see her. "Wait—" She couldn't risk Jan mentioning Tina.

Jan's voice rocketed through the phone. "Just because Jorkki fired you when you didn't show up doesn't mean you get to quit right away. We need you more than ever now that—"

"Wait," Lola said again. "Shut the fuck up, Mary Alice." She spoke fast into the second of stunned silence. "I'm still out here in Burnt Creek. The truck broke down. Besides, the story got bigger. Mary Alice, I'm finding out all kinds of things about Judith. He won't want to fire me when he hears what I've got. And Sheriff and Mama Brevik are being nice enough to let me stay at their place—"

Charlotte took a step toward her. Thor racked the Sig Sauer's slide. Lola gasped and spoke faster still. "Anyhow, that's the deal, Mary Alice. Sorry to screw up your plans. Gotta go." Charlotte snatched the phone from her hand before she'd finished talking. She jammed her thumb against the off button and gave the phone to Thor. He sat it on the end table and smashed the butt of the gun against it until it shattered. They stood before her, faces contorted.

"Sheriff and Mama Brevik? *Mama*?"

"I'm sorry. I'm sorry. He keeps calling you Mother and I was nervous—I mean, my God. You've got that gun right on me. But there's no way she could know about Mama's. It was just a slip. A stupid, stupid slip." Lola figured she was about to find out just exactly how stupid she'd been. Charlotte seemed happy to tell her.

"And you let her know you were staying here."

"Half the town knows I'm staying here. If anyone comes looking for me, that'd be the first thing they'd find out. But they won't. I'm fired. Didn't you hear? Nobody's going to come." Lola's voice caught, her incipient tears real.

Thor lowered the gun. "Well, if anyone does, they're not going to find you here," Charlotte said. "Get up. I was going to give you back your clothes, but that little stunt shows me you're not ready for privileges. Here." She reached for the corner of the quilt and in a single sharp move, yanked it from beneath Lola's body. Lola tumbled to the floor. Charlotte stared at the bed. Lola scrambled to her feet and followed her gaze, trying to see what Charlotte saw. Thor voiced Lola's thoughts.

"What's wrong, Mother?"

"Something. Not sure what." Charlotte bent and ran her hands over the sheet, then around the sides of the mattress. Her hand stopped at the inch of fabric protruding between the mattress and box spring. "Ah. Here's what's wrong." She tugged on the fabric, drawing Lola's makeshift rope inch by inch from its hiding place.

"Miss Lola here destroyed a perfectly good top sheet. Lord only knows what she planned to do with this." She ran the rope through her hands. "But I know what I'm going to do with it. Thor, her hands."

Before Lola could react, Thor had laid down his gun and grabbed both of her wrists. Charlotte ran the rope around and between them, tying it off in a knot that was cruelly tight.

"Give me the gun." Thor handed it to her.

For a big woman, Charlotte moved fast. The Sig Sauer's flat barrel caught Lola's left cheek, then the right side of her jaw as she tried to twist away, no match whatsoever for Thor's grip and Charlotte's ferocious dexterity with her husband's service weapon. Lola collapsed onto the floor, arms wrenching against Thor's hold, noting a spatter of blood on the floor beside her, and tried to focus on the fact that at least the damn mess she was creating wasn't lethal.

CHAPTER THIRTY-EIGHT

In the end, Lola got her clothes back—minus, of course, the reassuring weight of the gun in the pocket of her parka. And she returned to the man camp the same way she went the first time, in the back of a truck, beneath a tarp.

Before, she'd been worried about losing Bub. Now she was worried about losing her life. In fact, until she realized they'd brought her back to the man camp, she feared they were driving her to the edge of town and beyond, some remote place where they'd position her at the edge of a ravine, put a bullet in her brain and watch her tumble over the edge, certain of the snows to come that would hide her body for so many months that its eventual discovery would barely cause a stir. It could so easily be blamed on roughnecks who'd passed through the patch months ago. So sure was she of this scenario that the glimpse of the fried chicken stand, as Charlotte and Thor rushed her from the truck and up the metal steps into the trailer, provided the first sliver of real hope she'd allowed herself. They won't kill me here, she thought, even as they moved single file down a hallway, the tarp still over her head. They stopped. A door opened. A hand struck her back. She stumbled forward, her shins striking a bedframe. As she fell onto the mattress, someone rolled away from her.

"You should feel right at home here." Charlotte closed the door behind her. Lola wanted to tear off the tarp, run to the door and test it; if it opened, to dash down the hall in a futile rush past Thor with his gun and Charlotte with her iron will. She forced herself to lie still instead, to slow her own breathing until she could hear the sobbing gasps of the other person on the bed. The mattress creaked. Soft hands patted at her back. Lola moaned and the hands fell away, tugging instead at the tarp. Lola blinked in the room's harsh light. Her eyes widened. A hand fell across her mouth, suppressing sound. There before her, lines of adult worry gouged across a face that still bore a childish roundness, was Tina Kicking Woman.

TINA WRAPPED her in a grip so tight that Lola could barely breathe. Lola let Tina's head rest on her shoulder for a moment or two, no more. Then she shoved Tina away with a hard shake. "We don't have time for this," she mouthed, the words barely audible. For all she knew, Charlotte was on the other side of the door. Tina's mouth hung slack, trembling. Her broken nails dug into Lola's hands. Her hair hung dull and tangled around a tear-streaked face. The skin around her mouth was red and raw. Lola wondered if she'd been gagged. Her words came in a stuttering plea.

"Helpmehelpmehelpme."

Lola's own fear took a step back in the face of the sixteen-year-old's terror. "That's why I'm here. To help."

Tina's gaze kept sliding away from Lola's face. Her teeth rattled against one another. Lola lifted her hand to her own jaw, her cheekbone, gauging the heat and swelling there. She tried to infuse her voice with the confidence that her appearance would not have inspired.

"We're going to get out of here. I've already sent a message for help." Guilt stabbed Lola at the trust in Tina's eyes. She prayed Tina never asked the details of that message, never realized that her call to Jan was the weakest, most bobbling Hail Mary ever lofted heavenward. "But I need all the information you've got. What are we dealing with here?"

Tina told Lola what she already knew. "This. It's a whorehouse. This room is where I'm supposed to work. Charlotte called it the deluxe room. It's because the bed is so big. You know for—" she stuttered anew "—for, for, well, for threesomes."

“Not threesomes,” Lola snapped. “Threesomes are consensual. Rapes.” The bed nearly filled the room. The spread was satin, tiger-striped, the colors vaguely reminiscent of the star quilts at Charlie’s house that Lola had found so comforting. Gold shag carpet covered the floor. Lola wondered what warehouse had held onto that carpet for forty years, or if there were businesses that catered specifically to modern-day bordellos. A single folding chair squeezed between the bed and the fake pine-paneled wall. Maybe, Lola thought, so the clients could sit down and pull their boots on afterward. If they even took them off. Two narrow doors stood open in one wall, one revealing an empty closet, the other a claustrophobic bathroom. Lola leaned forward to get a better view. “Where’s the shower curtain?”

“I asked the same thing. That Dawg guy, the one with all the tattoos, told me they took them all away after a girl tried to hang herself with one.”

Tina forgot to lower her voice. The door flew open. Dawg squeezed himself into the room, a rat shouldering through a mouse hole. “Somebody call me?” He shut the door behind him and crossed the room in a single step and lowered himself onto the inadequate folding chair. He crossed his arms and showed his metal-capped incisor in a grin.

“You wanted to know what we’re dealing with here?” Tina’s voice trembled so that she could barely force the words. “That. We’re dealing with that.”

Dawg was happy to explain, telling Lola far more than she’d demanded to know.

“Are you here to guard us?” she asked him. “Because that just seems stupid. It’s not like we can get away from here. Even if we could get out of the trailer, we’d never get out of the camp.” Trying to goad him into at least moving into the next room. She desperately wanted time alone with Tina—if she could calm her down enough, at least—to glean more information from the girl who now curled shrimplike, whimpering into a fist shoved against her teeth. "MommyMommyMommy." Lola thought of Brenda Kicking Woman's towering fury were she to see her daughter in such a state. Imagined a confrontation between Brenda and Dawg. Her money would be on Brenda.

"Y'all would think nobody could get out of here," Dawg agreed, ever amiable. "But that one girl did. Ever since, Sheriff and Mama like me to stay around here whenever one of them can't be here."

"That one girl," said Lola. "You must mean Judith."

"The pretty one." Dawg's voice turned wistful.

Lola wanted to slap the sentiment out of him. "Not so pretty that you didn't kill her."

His little eyes widened. "No. I didn't. She run off with some trucker. I was supposed to bring her back, but I never found her. But then Sheriff told me she died anyway."

Every time Lola saw Judith in the snow, she seemed a little smaller, a little farther away, the eagle feather in her hand harder to see. She remembered Charlie's weariness that day. He'd been up all night because of the truck accident, but it went deeper than that, a blow to his very spirit, yet another young tribal member lost to drugs. Her drifting thoughts snagged on a detail. The truck accident. "She ran off with a trucker?" she asked Dawg. "Did you go after him, too?"

Dawg's teeth flashed. Lola wished he wouldn't smile. "He died." *Dahd.* He turned his renewed cheer upon Tina. "Don't you cry. You'll be fine. You're pretty, too. I sure wish I could help you."

"You can help her," Lola snapped. "You could get her out of here. Keep me." The words were out of her mouth before she could recall them. She wasn't sure she'd meant them. In fact, she was pretty sure she hadn't.

Dawg continued unperturbed, oblivious to her inner turmoil. "Naw. I mean *help* her."

Lola kept one hand firmly on Tina's back, smoothing circles onto her shirt, trying to calm her or at least reassure her with friendly contact. The other she raised, palm-upward, an unspoken question to Dawg.

"Whenever Sheriff and Mama get a new girl, they keep her up to the house a few days. You know, in that room you was in. Some of them girls are pretty rough. They need to dry 'em out, get 'em cleaned up. And then I go and help them, get them ready to start work over here."

Cold washed over Lola. She had to ask. "Help them how?"

He actually blushed. Lola tried to hold onto that, to tell herself that the hulking caricature before her actually possessed some humanity. "You know. I do the things the mens do to them. To get them ready."

The light in the room went patchy. Lola rubbed her eyes, trying to clear the cloud across her vision. Or maybe to draw it tighter, to blot out the image of Dawg assaulting girl after girl, letting each one know that no matter how onerous the task of servicing untold numbers of greasy, stinking roughnecks night after night, something far worse awaited if a girl balked. Somehow Lola managed to lean over, so that she puked on the floor instead of the bed.

CHAPTER THIRTY-NINE

"Don't you move," Dawg commanded. "I'll get something to clean that up with."

Lola couldn't even look at Tina. The idea that the girl had been forced to submit to hideous carnalities with Dawg would become far too real if she did. Tina seemed to understand. "He hasn't touched me."

Lola dragged her sleeve across her mouth and met Tina's eyes. "He hasn't? Are you sure?" Lola brushed Tina's hair away from her neck, looking for a telltale pinprick, thinking that Charlotte could just as easily have drugged Tina, too. In fact, Lola wondered if she drugged all the girls as a way of keeping them compliant.

Tina's lips, dried and cracked, twisted in a sort of sarcasm that was a relief from her panic of minutes earlier. "They're saving me for someone. Someone who's paying big money." Lola watched the fear return to her eyes as she imagined what lay in store.

"Who?"

"I don't know. He's driving over—they didn't say from where. Just that he should be here t-t-tomorrow." She pushed the words past fresh sobs.

"It takes a day to get here from just about anywhere. Even Magpie," Lola said. Magpie. On the border of the reservation that had seen so many girls go missing over the last year. Lola couldn't imagine that, no matter how much money was involved, and no matter how badly drug-addled the girls, they'd willingly jump at the chance to prostitute themselves—especially not so far from home. Turning the occasional trick with a Glacier-bound frat boy was one thing. But an army of roughnecks, day and night, was another matter entirely. Lola thought it unlikely that their addictions were so far gone as to make the prospect palatable. They were too young. Somebody had to be directing them there. Or luring them. Or—her stomach clenched at the thought—kidnapping them and forcing them. "Tina. How'd you end up here?"

"I don't know," Tina wailed. Lola put her finger to her lips.

Tina gulped for air. Lola thought of film and TV scenes of people hyperventilating, of women in childbirth. "Blow out," she said. "Like this." Puff. Puff. Puff.

Tina dutifully puffed, fast at first, then more slowly. Finally, she drew a single long breath. "Better."

Lola cast an eye toward the door. The scent of fried chicken wafted into the room. In the kitchen, grease sizzled in a pan. Voices rose above the sound—Dawg and Charlotte. The latter sounded distinctly unhappy. "Make her clean it up herself," Charlotte said.

"Tina," Lola urged.

"I was on an assignment for the paper. They sent me out to interview somebody at a ranch. But when I got there, nobody was home. I knocked and knocked on the door and all of a sudden somebody pulled it open and put something over my mouth. I passed out."

"Chloroform," said Lola. "Or some facsimile. I'm pretty sure you just can't walk into a drugstore to buy it, but I think it's one of those things that's easy enough to mix up. How long were you out?"

"Not long, I think. The next thing I knew, I was all tied up in the back of a car. Then they put me in what felt like a semi cab. When he used the horn, it sounded like—"

"I know what a semi horn sounds like," Lola said. Tina needed to move it along.

"Anyhow, I ended up here."

"What ranch?" With beef prices so low, ranching was such a losing proposition that Lola thought it wasn't out of the realm of possibility that a hard-luck rancher might try and get himself in on the girl trade.

"Old Man Sullivan's."

Lola thought aloud. "That doesn't make sense. His kids have been fighting over it ever since he died last year. Nobody's worked it since."

Something clanked outside the door. Dawg pushed his way in, preceded by the smell of bleach. He handed Lola a ratty towel and sat a galvanized bucket on the floor. Frothy water slopped over its top. "Mama says to clean up your own mess before it soaks too far into that good carpet."

"I heard her. You'll have to move. I can't clean this up with you standing there."

"I'm supposed to watch you."

Lola tilted the bucket and let the water flow onto the rug. Dawg took a hasty step away. "Just stand outside until we get this done. Where the hell are we going to go? Out there?" She flapped the rag at the room's single oblong window, high on the wall. Dawg recoiled as droplets hit his uniform. "Look at that thing," Lola said. "It's too small for even Tina to squeeze out of it."

He remained stubbornly in place. "Mama says hurry up. The mens are coming soon and she doesn't want the place smelling all barfy."

"Lunchtime break," Tina mouthed.

Lola waved the rag again. "Go on. Get."

To her surprise, Dawg got. "I still don't get it," Lola said, returning to their earlier conversation. "Why in the world would Jorkki send you to an abandoned ranch?"

"Something about somebody looking at it for a conservation easement. It was a *news* story. Not another stupid fluff feature." Pride briefly trumped fear. Tina's shoulders straightened, her chin lifted. "Besides, Jorkki didn't send me. Finch did. He thought it would be a good way to show Jorkki I could handle more responsibility."

"Finch?" The rag stilled in Lola's hands. In all the months she'd worked at the *Daily Express*, she'd never seen Finch go beyond his regular assignments of the obituaries, the wedding and engagement announcements, the police blotter. "The blotter," she said.

"What about it?"

The blotter, with its endless list of local crimes and the names of those charged. The girls' names wouldn't have been on it, of course—they were juveniles—but it wouldn't have been hard for Finch to figure out which families routinely strayed from the law, who struggled with nascent addictions, whose parents were less than vigilant. Who could go missing with only a resigned, "It was only a matter of time."

Finch. His mysterious disappearances took on new meaning. Lola imagined him sailing across the Hi-Line in his Caddy, sweaty hands slipping on the steering wheel as he ferried a girl to some halfway point between Magpie and Burnt Creek where he could hand her off to Dawg.

"That bastard," Lola nearly shrieked. "I'll punch his fat face in!"

The outburst brought both Dawg and Charlotte into a brief scuffle at the door, each trying to shove past the other into the room. Dawg had height and hard muscle but Charlotte, as Lola had only belatedly begun to realize, had sheer meanness on her side. She burst first into the room, brandishing a syringe.

"Do I have to calm you down? Do I have to?"

Lola tried to flatten herself against the wall behind the bed. She couldn't. Tina had gotten there first. She felt the girl's shuddering breaths against her back.

"Now, listen." Twin infernos burned in Charlotte's eyes. "Lunchtime's coming. It's about to get busy in here. I can't have any trouble from you two." She jabbed the needle toward Lola, who slammed backward, ignoring an "oof" from Tina. "Something tells me it would be smarter to give you this. But we're looking at a busy night and we're still short a girl and Princess here is on reserve for a special order. We might need you, and the customers don't like girls who just lie there. You catch my drift?"

Tina began her whispered mantra again. "MommyMommy Mommy."

Charlotte folded her arms across her chest. The needle's tip glinted. "Do we understand one another?"

Lola couldn't believe she was capable of speech. But the word floated into the room. "Completely."

The door closed, almost, behind them. Lola eased away from the wall. Tina fell to the mattress, incapable of forming even the single word. "M-m-m," she stammered. Lola took her by the shoulders, eased her upright. Put her hands to either side of Tina's face, her thumbs beneath Tina's slack jaw, and pushed until Tina's lips were mashed together. Held it until Tina's teeth stopped chattering.

"I talked to Jan earlier today," she whispered. She watched the notion swim past Tina's dull gaze, noted the slight jerk as the idea took hold. "Jan," she said again, trying to force Tina's thoughts away from her unthinkable present back to that other world. She gave Tina another second or two to recollect Jan, the newspaper, her whole previous life. She checked an impulse to slap the girl. The shock might bring her back. But if things didn't work out, there'd be more than enough slaps and worse in Tina's future. And—she pushed the thought away—her own. She lowered her face to Tina's and forced the girl to look into her eyes.

"You need to focus. We don't have much time."

"Much time for what?" Tina asked. Good question, thought Lola. If only she had an answer. The one she came up with surprised her almost as much as Tina's accepting nod.

"Until we figure out how to get the hell out of here. Because that's what we're going to do."

CHAPTER FORTY

"Lunchtime, shift changes, any time the men are off—those are the worst." Lola had asked Tina to tell her the trailer's routine, mostly as a way to help Tina refocus, and to give herself time to think. In her brief time in the trailer before Lola's own unplanned arrival, Tina had managed a quick conversation with one of the other girls from the rez, Josephine's niece. "Nancy. She played basketball with me for a while. She wasn't as far gone into drugs as the others. I guess that makes it worse for her."

"Why?"

"Mama keeps them drugged up, just high enough not to really care." Lola remembered Dave's description of a girl who lay passive, unmoving. She already had assumed the girl was unwilling. Drugs added an ominous extra layer of the inability to protest.

"So how come we aren't?"

"Maybe she thinks she got you good enough to keep you in line." Tina pointed with her lips to the goose eggs from Charlotte's pistol-whipping. "And me"—her eyes went dark and flat—"the special customer wants me wide awake."

"We're going to be long gone by the time that damn special customer gets here." And if they weren't, Lola vowed, she'd find some way, no matter how unlikely the chance, to put a hurt on the special customer. She'd heard tales overseas about men paying a premium to have sex with a virgin. It made her sick then. Thinking about that being applied to Tina took her beyond sick to murderous. But it was also distracting. Lola gave herself the same advice she'd given Tina: *Focus*. "What about the other girls?"

"Nancy, she was trying to get clean when they snatched her. She tells Mama she doesn't need the stuff, pretends she doesn't mind the men. That's what Judith did. She'd worked so hard to get clean, and then they drugged her. She was so scared of getting hooked again. She told them she, um, worked better without it." Lola recalled the inflamed scratch across Swanny's face, his lewd appraisal of Judith's performance. "And it worked. She stayed clearheaded and got away. Nancy was hoping to do the same thing. But now there's somebody by the door all the time. And they leave the bedroom doors cracked even when the men come. Nancy says if they hear talking instead of"—the next word came out in a whisper—"fucking, Dawg or Mama will bust in, make sure nobody's plotting anything."

"Nobody's plotting anything now, that's for sure."

Around them, the trailer heaved and creaked like a ship at sea, buffeted by the wind without and the primal surges within. The men, at least, were quick. This bunch, Tina had explained, comprised day workers around town on their lunch breaks. Every few minutes a groan would sound, followed by relative silence. Then, the rustle of clothing being donned, the creak of a door, and heavy footsteps passing one another in the hall as the next man hurried toward his own brief assignation. From the direction of what Lola assumed was the living room or kitchen, Lola heard voices.

"C'mon, Mama. When you getting more girls? You promised."

"If she does get 'em, I get first crack. Right, Mama?"

Charlotte's voice was full, flirty. "Only because you paid. And not first crack. Somebody paid a lot more than you for that particular privilege." Lola wondered how many personalities the woman had. Prim housewife, fiendish madam, and now this new sultry version. All combined, she supposed, to make Charlotte a particularly astute businesswoman in her unsavory line of work.

"Har," another man chimed in. "Sloppy seconds for you, Larry."

Plates rattled. "Here," said Charlotte. "Eat your chicken while you're waiting. You don't want it cold. Although it's good that way, too."

"Indeed it is. Some days out on the rig, I don't know what I look forward to more. Your dark meat or theirs." General hilarity.

Lola turned to Tina. "So the fried chicken stand is a real thing?"

"They make money on the food and the girls, both. Nancy said that sometimes the guys don't even bother to wipe off their hands after they eat. The girls end up covered in chicken grease."

"Huh." Lola roamed the room as they spoke. She picked up the lamp, put it down. It was plastic, with no more heft than a toy. She checked the bulb. Charlotte must have squirreled away the old incandescent variety, or maybe the new curly ones simply hadn't made their way to Burnt Creek yet. Even if Lola shattered the bulb, the jagged edge of the eggshell glass would break at the first stab, allowing her to hurt someone only just enough to piss him off. She cast a glance over her shoulder through the just-open door, then pulled the folding chair beneath the window and stood on it. No matter how long, or from what angle, she studied the window, it was far too narrow to allow her, or even Tina, to squeeze through. The window gave a view of row upon row of trailers, with the endless prairie beyond. Despair gouged Lola's heart. "A wasteland," she'd called the prairie. Now its promise of space and freedom seemed wondrous. What if she never saw prairie again? Something flitted across the corner of her field of vision. She blinked hard. Sure enough, there was the motion again, a flash of black and white.

A dog. Nosing among the trailers. Listing on three legs.

Lola cranked at the window mechanism until it opened a crack, wet her lips, pursed them, and managed a quick whistle. Bub's head whipped around, ears at attention. Lola whistled again and he streaked toward the trailer. "Bub! Oh, Bub!" she gasped.

"What's going on?" Tina got up from the bed.

Lola turned, heedless of the tears washing her cheeks. "My dog. He's here! He can help us."

Tina clambered onto the chair and squeezed beside her, clinging to the narrow window frame for balance. "How?"

On any other topic, Lola would have welcomed the sudden skepticism in her voice. The girl needed to toughen up, and fast.

But this was about Bub. "We could write a note," she said. "Throw it from the window." Ignoring the foolish optimism in her own voice, the deeper foolishness of her words.

Tina showed no such inclination. "Did you see a pen anywhere in here? Paper?"

"Blood."

"What?"

Somehow, Tina had gotten the upper hand. Lola wanted it back. She raised her left arm to her face, tore at the soft skin of her inner arm with her teeth. Blood welled from the ragged cut. Lola lowered her arm, licked her teeth free of the coppery taste. The blood trickled toward her hand. "We'll write with this," she said. "We can use a scrap of sheet, or a shirt; hell, even our underwear, and throw it to him."

Tina's lips twitched in an almost-smile. "He's a dog. Throw him woman-smelling panties with blood on them and he's just going to eat them. Besides, even if he didn't, what's he going to do? He's not one of those TV dogs my gran'mother talks about, the ones who always came to somebody's rescue."

"Lassie," Lola said. "Rin Tin Tin."

"Whatever. Even if he were, who would he bring it to? Someone in the man camp? You think they'd help any of us? Mama's is the best thing that ever happened to them."

Lola knew Tina was right. "But," she said. Bub was her last link to home, to safety. Without him, she and Tina were alone, lacking—despite her brave talk—a single way out. She couldn't see the dog anymore. She called through the open window. "Bub! Bub!"

Tina gave a yelp. A hard hand clamped around Lola's neck. Dawg lifted her bodily from the chair with one hand, Tina with the other. "What do we have here? Trying to get somebody's attention?" He threw Tina onto the bed first, then Lola, and stuck his head out the door.

"Mama? Would you mind coming on down here for a second? We've got ourselves a situation."

CHAPTER FORTY-ONE

For the first time, Lola saw the other girls.

Charlotte waited until the last man in the trailer had finished his business, sending him on his way without so much as a cold drumstick, then slapped a "Closed" sign on the door. She gathered the girls on couches in what appeared to have been designed as a central rec room for the modular unit but must have served as a waiting room for the men, not to mention a place where she could serve up chicken platters. Three round white plastic tables and matching chairs sat in the center of the room; there were more seats still at the counter that served as a kitchen divider. Charlotte stationed Dawg with the girls, and waited in the kitchen with Tina and Lola after summoning Thor by cellphone.

"You need to get on over here. Dawg caught our new guests hollering out the window. And that's not the half of it. Wait 'til you see what I found." She waited in glowering silence. Lola sneaked peeks at the other girls. She wanted to throw a blanket over them. They wore cheap nylon negligees, lace gone grimy, nipples showing dark through the translucent stuff. In her jeans and heavy sweater, Lola felt overdressed. She forced her gaze to their schoolgirl faces, noted the telltale dullness in their eyes. She reminded herself that, at least according to what she'd heard, most of these girls were known users. Maybe three squares, a warm, dry place to sleep, and a regular supply of junk without any hassle from parents or police was all it took to enslave a teenage addict. Lola looked at Charlotte and hated her a little more, something that until that moment, she hadn't thought possible. Charlotte smirked, dimples digging craters in her cheeks. Lola imagined that her unspoken dialogue with Charlotte consisted of a single word on each side: "Die."

"I have to know something." Lola kept her voice low so the girls wouldn't hear their conversation. "How'd you get into this line of work? I thought you were a nurse."

"You know what they pay nurses over in the clinic?"

"I do, actually." Lola thought back to the budget document, the obvious discontent of the county clerk and the librarian. She'd been right about the tension over old salaries versus new money.

"I did keep on nursing a while. But then Thor took note of all these man camps and suggested the fried chicken stand. Turns out Thor had been sharing his lunches with Dawg, who told him he was a fool to give away chicken that good for free. Pretty soon, I could afford to quit nursing. I still work a spare shift once in awhile so I can get the drug samples. But mostly now I spend my days frying up chicken. Everyone tells me my chicken makes the colonel's taste like dogshit." Charlotte puffed up like a pigeon at the remembered compliment.

"I'm still not seeing my way from frying chicken to running girls."

"Oh, that," Charlotte said, as casually as though she were talking about selling crafts at a church fund-raiser. "Dawg was all the time telling me how he used to work for a guy who ran girls, back where they didn't have half the market as the patch. He knew there was extra room in the trailer. And then there was this one guy Dawg met over at The Train and started bringing to the camp for his meals." Dawg's head turned at the sound of his name. "Somehow, he got wind of how Dawg was pushing us to do this."

It was Dawg's turn to go all prideful. He stepped to the counter at the sound of his name, keeping an eye on the girls. "I used to see him down at The Train, mooning over an Indian girl who worked there. She wouldn't have nothing to do with him. But he got me to thinking about how many mens like their meat dark."

"Let me guess," said Lola. "Fat little guy. Glasses. Sweaty."

"The very one," said Charlotte. "Smart, too. He said he could get girls. And he did. Not just any girls. Indian girls. Young, or at least young-looking. Seems the patch attracts a particular brand of pervert. Anyhow, you need to specialize, have a niche. That's where the money lies."

Spoken like a true entrepreneur, Lola thought. She wondered what it was about Charlotte that had made Dawg comfortable with floating the idea—to the wife of an officer of the law, no less—of running girls. Maybe it was a gut thing. The same way Charlie had said he could sniff out liars, maybe Dawg could detect folks willing to bend the rules, had divined the greedy, grasping thing within Charlotte that Thor foolishly left unfulfilled.

"We had the location, right in the man camp," Charlotte said. "We had the cover—the chicken stand. And we had the space. I'd been thinking to knock out the walls between the bedrooms, turn this place into a real restaurant instead of a takeout stand. But it turns out they're way more profitable as bedrooms."

Lola let her babble on. Her mind returned to something Dawg had said. "What happened to that girl you saw dancing at The Train? The one the little guy liked?"

Neither Dawg nor Charlotte answered for a moment. "She was the first one came worked for us," Dawg said finally.

Lola looked into the waiting room at Maylinn-Carole-Annie-Nancy. "Which one is she?"

Dawg opened his mouth to reply. "She quit," Charlotte said.

Judith, Lola thought.

There was one thing Lola still couldn't understand. "How'd you get Thor to go along?"

Those ghastly dimples again. "We started small, just the one girl. I told Thor she was a runaway I'd met at the clinic who needed a safe place to crash." Lola wondered how they'd lured Judith to the trailer. Tried to imagine at what point Judith had realized it was best to pretend to go along, to submit with an eye to eventual escape. Jan had called Judith's brand a running heart. Grotesque as the brand was, it had epitomized Judith in the end. That big heart of hers had run straight home to her people. Despite everything, she'd hung on to that eagle feather, and she'd died free.

Charlotte nattered on. "By the time Thor realized what was going on, she'd been turning tricks for weeks. Then it was just a matter of pointing out a couple of facts to him."

"Those being?"

"The only way for him to stop it would be to arrest his own wife."

Implicating himself in the process, Lola thought. Charlotte didn't even have to point out the unlikelihood of Thor convincing anyone he hadn't known about the operation from the start. "You said there were two things," Lola asked. "What's the other one?"

Charlotte dipped a hand into her apron pocket and came out with her fingers wrapped around a wad of cash. "This."

Lola saw lots of bills with multiple zeroes. Before she could estimate the considerable amount, a knock sounded at the door. Charlotte tucked the money away.

"It's me," Thor called. Dawg lifted a curtain and nodded to Charlotte. She hustled Lola and Tina to the couches with the other girls as the door opened. The room had been warm and, just like that, it was cold. Lola noticed that none of the underdressed girls so much as flinched. Whatever Charlotte was giving them was powerful stuff.

"What's going on? Why are we closed? Do you know how much money we lose every hour we're shut down?" Thor shed his coat, his cap, and his clown-size puffy gloves as he spoke. His face was red with cold. His nose dripped. He pulled a handkerchief from his back pocket and blew. He was not, Lola decided, nearly as handsome as she'd thought when she'd first met him.

"You've only yourself to blame." Charlotte's voice dripped acid.

Thor walked to the counter that divided the room from the kitchen, studied a platter heaped with pieces of chicken and chose a thigh. He settled himself at one of the tables in the lounge and tore at it with his teeth. A long strip of skin pulled away with it and hung from his mouth. He sucked it in. "How do you figure?"

"You took this one on." Charlotte pointed at Tina. Lola had worked on the reservation just long enough to find it rude when people pointed with their fingers, instead of discreetly with their lips or chin. "This . . . this . . . Miss Priss." Charlotte fairly spat the words. Tina edged closer to Lola. "Those other ones. Nobody was surprised when they went missing. Nobody cared. But this one. Here. I printed this out at home. Take a look." She slapped a piece of paper onto the table. Lola craned her neck. It was a story from the *Missoulian,* the largest newspaper in the western part of the state. "Missing," read the headline over a three-column photo of Tina holding the basketball team's championship trophy. "Near as I can tell, this photo ran in every single newspaper in the state."

"So?" Thor lifted a shoulder. He took another bite. Chewed for a long time. "Needs more salt. No one knows she's here. It's not like she's done any work yet. I don't see the problem."

"That's because you're an idiot."

There it was again, Lola thought. The inevitable resentment of the girl who married the best-looking boy in the class, only to watch herself go to bloat over the years while he stayed fine as ever. It had to have nagged at Charlotte, especially when she considered the fact that she'd gotten them both into a business where no doubt Thor sampled the goods.

"She's not going to be able to do any work. Not now, not ever. We can't risk anybody seeing her."

By the way Tina stiffened beside her, Lola could tell that she'd grasped the deadly significance of Charlotte's words.

"What about the special customer? He paid in advance," Thor said. "Real money."

The hope leaping within Tina was practically palpable. Thor had found the only way, Lola thought, of making the prospect of the special customer seem, if not actually desirable, at least tolerable. Considering the alternative.

Thor's hand flicked. The thigh bone sailed over the counter and landed in the sink. He licked his fingers and wiped them on the uniform Charlotte had laundered and ironed with such care. The skin around Charlotte's eyes tightened. "It's not like he's going to tell anybody," Thor added.

Charlotte hesitated. “Fine,” she said. “But after that—we can’t risk any more of their little escape tricks. We got lucky with that other one who got away.” The air went out of Tina.

“That’s not the only problem,” Charlotte said. “These two were calling out for help. Dawg caught them both at the window and Lola here was trying to talk to someone. She needs to be taught a lesson. Let her know she’s no better than the others. You know what I mean. Do it.”

Thor pushed his chair back, stood, and hooked his fingers through his belt loops. He went into the kitchen and turned one of the knobs on the stove. There was the smell of gas. It whispered and caught. Thor cranked the knob until the flame burned high. He extracted something long and straight from the tight space between the refrigerator and the wall. Tina gasped. Lola looked to her for an explanation, but Tina stared at the object in Thor’s hand. He held a metal rod with an oval handle at one end. He poked the other end into the fire, turning it this way and that, until the metal turned scarlet then glowed orange. He turned to Lola.

“It’s . . . it’s—” Tina’s whisper defined terror.

Her mouth opened and closed, fishlike.

“It’s—”

She tried again.

“It’s a branding iron.”

CHAPTER FORTY-TWO

Dawg grabbed Lola from the couch and wrestled her into a straight chair, twisting one arm behind her back and extending the other before her. Thor approached. He slid up her sleeve, exposing the tender flesh of her forearm. The brand hovered a few inches above it, so close Lola could feel the glow, though not yet close enough to carry the blistering heat of her nightly candle-snuffing. She forced herself to look away, into Thor's face. He smiled, open-mouthed. Lupine, she thought.

Thor turned the iron to display the white-hot heart shape. He moved it closer.

Lola willed herself still, even as her skin began to warm. *One thousand one*, she counted silently. *One thousand two.* "This is just stupid," she said.

"How so?"

"That's how you marked Judith."

"So?"

"Whatever you do with me, someday I'm going to be found. And unless it's years and years from now—and maybe even then—that brand's going to be on my arm, the same as it was on Judith's. Except that, unlike with Judith, a lot of people will know that I'd been staying with you and Charlotte. Put that heart on my arm and you might as well tie a tag to my toe that says 'Thor Brevik did it.'"

"She's right."

I am? Lola bit back the words. The speaker was the girl who'd taken Tina in her arms when Dawg snatched Lola away. Lola put her at sixteen, maybe younger. Lola wondered if she were

Josephine's niece. This girl's voice, when she spoke yet again, held the same fine contempt Lola had heard Josephine turn on tribal council members who dared to present her with budgets whose details did not meet her exacting standards.

"Goddammit." Thor looked at the iron. "It's cooling off."

Dawg's grip loosened. So did Lola's gut, so suddenly she feared she'd be sick again. She choked back bile. But it rose insistently as Charlotte fiddled with the stove knob until the burner caught again. "Forget the heart and lay the rod up against her, Thor. I don't care what you do. Just mark her. She needs to learn her lesson."

Thor crossed the room. The brand went back into the flame with a hiss. Thor held it immobile, then withdrew it. The glowing heart preceded him as he walked back toward Lola. Dawg squeezed Lola's arms tighter. She heard his panting breaths behind her.

Which were drowned out by a pounding on the door that shook the entire trailer, along with the most welcome words Lola thought she had ever heard.

"Open up!"

"Charlie!" Lola screamed his name.

"Shut the fuck up." Dawg loosed his grip. Thor's backhand knocked her from the chair. She lay on the floor, watching blood soak into the carpet. She probed at her nose, just a second's touch, enough to confirm it was broken. It didn't matter, she thought. Charlie had come. Their ordeal was almost over. She pulled her sleeve down over her arm and held it beneath her nose to stanch the blood.

The pounding resumed. It hurt her head. Everyone else in the room seemed frozen.

Bang.

Bang.

Bang.

"Goddammit, open up. I know you're in there. We've got fifteen guys here heading out on an extended shift." Lola swallowed blood. Whoever was out there, it wasn't Charlie.

Thor dropped the branding iron. The acrid scent of singed carpet filled the air. Thor looked to Charlotte. She nodded. Thor reached for the door and opened it a crack. Lola rolled to one side. She could just see through the opening. A man stood on the steps, bundled mightily against the cold, wool watch cap pulled down low over his brow, a scarf wrapping the lower part of his face. Maybe, she thought crazily. Maybe. But even though her eyes had swollen almost shut and her head spun with every motion, she could tell the man there was too short to be Charlie. Behind him, a van idled.

"Come on, man." The man's voice took on a wheedling tone. "We're talking three weeks out there with no trips to town. This is our last chance. Unless Mama starts doing take-out!" A laugh leaked through the scarf. "We'll pay extra."

Again, the glance to Charlotte, the nod in response.

"Fine," said Thor. Charlotte held up both hands and spread her fingers. Closed them, spread them again. "Twenty percent extra," said Thor.

"Hell," said the man. "We'd have paid twenty-five. Lemme tell the boys."

"Give us a few minutes," said Thor. "The girls were taking a break. They'll need to get themselves set up."

The man paused on his way back to the van. "They don't need to be settin' up. We'll take 'em lying down."

Thor closed the door and pointed to Lola and Tina. "Get them out of here," he told Dawg. Charlotte swept into the room with a wet rag and attacked the blood on the floor. "Girls," she said, scrubbing hard at the rug. "You know what to do. Thor, pop some of that chicken in the oven and heat it up. The ones waiting will be hungry."

"Shouldn't I nuke it?"

"The microwave takes all the crispiness out. Ruins it, in my opinion." She stood, the bloody rag in her hand. "Hurry up, before they change their minds. Lola, don't you drip more blood on my clean floor."

Dawg wrestled her and Tina into their bedroom with a final warning. "Now you know what can happen. No trouble. And stay away from that goddamn window." He slammed the door.

Lola lowered her arm.

"Sweet Jesus!" Tina's eyes went wide.

"That bad? I don't think I've ever heard so much as a damn from you."

Tina steered her to the bathroom mirror. Lola steeled herself. Looked. Her eyes were purple and puffy, the bruises running into ones from the pistol-whipping, her nose swollen and skewed to one side. Blood sluiced over her lips and down her chin. Tina pulled wads of toilet paper from the roll and held them beneath the faucet. "Here."

Lola dabbed at her face until the toilet paper came away clean. It wasn't much of an improvement. "I thought it was Charlie. But it wasn't."

"I did, too. I thought I recognized the voice." Tina squeezed past Lola out of the bathroom. Lola heard the chair creak as Tina climbed up on it. "Come here. Quick, before he catches us."

Lola joined her, pressing her face to the window. Exhaust wrapped the waiting van, nearly obscuring it. Still, there was something familiar about it. "Is that—?" She looked at Tina, then back to the van. Its door opened. One man after another emerged, waddling in layers of clothing. The driver came last, carrying something.

A drum.

The others lined out along the trailer's length. Shed their coats, their hats. Shook out long, long hair, let down voluminous skirts sewn with hundreds of tiny tin bells. The air came alive with color, with sound. With women. The only man among them, Roy deRoche, reached back into the van and came out with a folding stool and a tarp. Shook out the tarp on the snow. Placed the drum upon it. Settled himself upon the stool. Took up the stick made of a flexible section of fiberglass fishing pole and tapped the drum's surface. Made an adjustment. Tapped again. Nodded, satisfied. Struck the drum again, four real beats this time. Threw his head back and let loose with the falsetto quaver that began the song.

Feet moved. Bells jingled in the glassy frozen air as the women of the Blackfeet Nation began the dance of life to save their daughters.

CHAPTER FORTY-THREE

"Mommy! Mommy!" Tina worked at the window crank, turning it the wrong way in her confusion. "Mommy! I'm here!"

Lola turned, expecting Dawg to burst into the room. But the only explosion of activity was beyond the door—Thor shouting, Charlotte yelling back, while up and down the hallway, a chorus of voices joined Tina's, young women turned little girls again. "Mommy! Mommy!"

"Hell with it," Lola said. "Let's get out of here." She took Tina's hand and jumped down from the chair, the landing sending a fresh gush of blood from her nose. They ran from the room and crashed into the other girls, a collective headlong rush of flesh and chiffon toward the trailer door.

Where Thor stood facing them, gun drawn.

"I don't know where you girls think you're going, but nobody leaves this trailer." Beside him, Dawg crossed his arms over the mound of his muscled chest. The girls moved as one toward the window. Pulled back the drapes. Men emerged from the rows of prefabs, phones held high, videoing the spectacle of women doing a jingle dance in the snow. The women stepped high in dresses of turquoise, gold, jade green, royal blue. Bright beaded leggings flashed beneath the skirts, moccasins trod the snow. The women held heads high and cocked one hand on their hips; with the other, they raised eagle-feather fans in time with the drum's beats.

Josephine's niece hammered at the window with the heel of her hand, the other girls crowding around her. Thor swung his gun toward them. "Knock that shit off."

Lola pulled Nancy's hand from the glass. "It's okay. She knows you're here. They know we're all here. We're going to be all right."

"How?" Tina spoke up. "He's got a gun."

Lola swiped a hand beneath her nose and studied the bloody smear on her fingers. She rubbed her hand on her pants. "So? What's he going to do? Shoot us? Shoot them? All that would do is make a big mess. We know Charlotte doesn't like that. They have to let us go now."

"Like hell we do." Charlotte emerged from the kitchen, breathing hard.

Lola pointed toward the window. "But you're busted."

Charlotte actually smiled. She dug in her pocket and came out with a tube of lip gloss and ran it across her mouth. Thor had his gun. Charlotte girded herself for battle in her own way. She pressed her lips together, parting them with an audible smack. "I don't think so."

Lola's head throbbed, confusion adding to the pain of Thor's blow. "Yes, you are. There's a dozen women out there who know who you are. Who know what this is."

Charlotte's smile, appropriately outlined now, widened. "Who are they going to tell? The sheriff?" Even as she spoke, Thor's cellphone buzzed. He took it from its case on his belt and hit a key.

"I'm on it," he said. "Some sort of demonstration. Looks like environmentalists protesting the oil patch. Same old, same old. This bunch isn't any too bright. You'd think they'd wait 'til summer. Nothing to worry about." He clicked off the phone and gestured with his gun. "I'm the only law in a hundred miles. If I say there's no problem here, there's no problem."

The watching men began to filter back into their warm trailers. The women danced on, circling the unit. Lola noted their blueing skin, their slowing, stiffening movements.

"They can dance until they turn into popsicles for all I care," Thor said. "They're going away empty-handed."

"But," said Lola. Surely it wasn't that simple. "They can call someone else. Another sheriff." *Charlie*, she thought. Was it remotely possible the women had come without contacting him?

Thor seemed to have read her thoughts. He opened the door. The women and Roy were alone outside the trailer, the only ones to hear the words he shouted. "I've got your daughters. By the time your sheriff—or anyone else you think you might want to call—gets here, each and every one of these girls can be dead. Is it worth it?"

"Best y'all go on home," Dawg called over his shoulder. Thor stepped aside and Dawg took his place, his massive frame filling the doorway. Thickets of golden hair raised up on his goose-pimpled arms.

The women lifted their left feet. Tapped the ground twice, lightly, with their moccasins. Slid a step sideways.

"He's right," said Thor. "Forget you ever came here."

The right feet went up. Tap, tap. Sideways slide.

"What would you rather have? Your daughters dead? Because that's what's going to happen if you don't get the hell out of here and pretend you never came. Or would you rather have them whoring, but alive?"

The compelling drumbeat grew louder. *One*-two, *two*-two, *three*-two, *four*-two. The sound pierced the air and bumped against a sky heavy and low with snow. Roy raised his voice, his song lifting above Thor's pitiless words. The tune pierced Lola's heart with its mixture of purpose and hopelessness. She thought she had never seen anything so brave as these mothers dancing for daughters they apparently were not going to be able to reclaim. She wished she could understand the words to Roy's song. His haunting falsetto rose and fell, not unlike the wail of a siren, signaling danger, promising rescue.

Lola frowned. It wasn't just that she couldn't understand the words. She couldn't hear them anymore. She looked at Roy. His hand hovered motionless over the drum. He craned his neck, looking at something beyond her field of vision. The women, too, paused, frozen as though the cold had caught them in midstep. But the sound continued, rising and falling, a real siren this time, growing louder as Charlie's cruiser rounded the corner and slid sideways to a stop amid a backwash of flashing lights and snow.

CHAPTER FORTY-FOUR

Dawg was in the doorway and then he wasn't, caught in the crush of the girls who simply shoved in a single mass past him. Lola took a step after them and collapsed onto her knees, felled by an attack of vertigo. The branding iron lay nearby, a heart shape scorched into the carpet. She grabbed it and used it to lever herself to her feet. She leaned on it, swaying, watching through the window as the girls rushed headlong through the snow in their fluttery lingerie, seeking the warmth of their mothers' arms. Shrieks dissolved into sobs. Women hugged their daughters close, pulled back to stare hard and ensure the vision was real, before once again crushing the girls to their breasts. Dawg picked himself up out of the snowbank where he'd landed and shook himself off, looking to the sheriff as though for instructions. Bub appeared from somewhere and circled him, stiff-legged, growling. Charlie stepped from the cruiser, gun raised. Bub dashed to him, touched nose to pant leg, and then raced back to resume his patrol of Dawg. Lola's cheeks burned, some new torment atop her injuries. She touched a hand to her face and felt tears. She ducked her head, wiped her face, and cleared her throat. "Charlie," she called, "you're just in time."

"Maybe not." Despair tightened his voice. Lola followed his gaze to the group of women. One stood alone, arms dangling empty at her sides, her face a mask of anguish. Tina's mother.

A woman emerged from the van. Until that moment, Lola had thought it empty. "Where's Tina?" asked Jan.

"Jan! You came!"

"Mary Alice, you mean." So Lola's phone call had worked. "Slick move," Jan said. She tried a grin. It wobbled and disappeared entirely. "Where's Tina?"

Thor's voice rang out. "You mean Princess? She's right here."

A BOOT thudded against Lola's shin. She stumbled and would have fallen again but for the support of the branding iron. Thor moved past, down onto the trailer's steps, Tina in a chokehold, his forearm like a vise across her neck. He raised the other hand as if to emphasize the gun it held, then pressed the barrel once again to Tina's temple.

Charlie's own gun twitched in his hand.

Thor dug the barrel of his gun into Tina's flesh. She sagged back against him. Her lips parted, a single word escaping, the one she'd said so prayerfully during her ordeal and now, just at the moment it seemed she might have been saved, mouthed again as a sort of farewell.

"Mommy."

TRAILER DOORS opened anew. Men, faces alight with curiosity, took in the scene, the weeping women, the inadequately clad girls, one sheriff immobilized with his gun drawn, the other facing him with a gun to a girl's head.

The onlookers read it wrong. "About time somebody cleaned up that nest of sin." Heads swiveled. The man who'd spoken was older than many of the others. He'd stepped coatless from his unit. Strands of fine grey hair blew about his face. He had the hooded eyes and elongated mournful countenance of a Castilian noble who'd awoken one morning to find himself in the wrong century and the wrong place. A gold cross dangled from a chain around his neck. It caught the weak sunshine and held it.

“Well, listen to the preacher.” Another man stepped forward. Lola took in the Oakleys, the angled toothpick, and recognized a man who’d approached her at The Mint that first night in Burnt Creek. He’d added a leather bomber jacket, jaunty but entirely impractical for the weather. Men slapped his back. Probably the trailer’s best customers, Lola thought. But others moved to stand with the first speaker, faces set. Lola recognized Dave, the man who’d smuggled her into the camp and dropped her at Mama’s, before she’d realized what it was. He hovered between the groups before joining the one clustered around the older man.

“Somebody call 9-1-1,” Charlie said. “Tell them to get some backup out here.” Several men tapped at their cellphones.

Thor ground the gun deeper against Tina’s head. Her face went ashy except for the reddening circle where the barrel scraped her skin. “Make all the phone calls you want. 9-1-1’s just going to go to my office. He doesn’t have jurisdiction here. Can’t none of you stop me.”

“They can,” said Charlie. He pursed his lips, pointing with them toward the women. “And them.” He lifted his chin toward the man wearing the cross, and the others around him. He started, looking beyond them. His face lightened. “And them.”

A knot of men jogged around the corner toward the trailer—the uncles and Joshua, too, sprinting ahead. “We got here as fast as we could, once we found out where the women were headed,” he called to Charlie.

Lola had a good idea how he’d figured that out. Jan must have phoned him from the road to let him know. She wondered if Jan had called Charlie, too.

Joshua took in the crowds of men, the girls and the aunties—and the raised guns. He held up his hand. The uncles stopped behind him. The man camp went silent. Even the wind held its breath. Thor’s voice emerged relaxed and confident.

“You all have got some wrong ideas in your head. This girl was trying to escape custody,” he announced to the crowd. “She’s under arrest. Just like these others. Move along now, unless you want to join them. Last I checked, prostitution is a crime in North Dakota. I think more than a few of you know these girls.” Up and down the rows of trailers, doors slammed behind men who subscribed to the eminent good sense of Thor's argument.

"Go on, now," Thor said to the rest of the onlookers. "Get on out of here. The missus and myself, and this girl, too, have a trip to take."

"What about me?" Dawg's voice rose in a high whine. Bub circled him, growling, easily dodging a ponderous kick.

"You're driving."

Dawg rubbed his hands along his bare arms and smiled.

"You're not going anywhere," Charlie said.

"Go ahead," Thor challenged, lowering his voice so that only those closest could hear. "Try and stop me. First person who takes a single step my way and this girl is nothing more than a big damn mess of red on all that pretty white snow."

"And the next step you take after that will be the one that gets you caught," Charlie said. "Then you'll be facing a homicide charge in addition to all the other ways you're in trouble for whatever this little operation of yours is here. It's not worth it."

"It's not? Goddammit, stand up straight. You're killing my arm." Thor jerked his elbow upward.

Tina's feet scrabbled for purchase on the trailer's slick metal doorstep. Her mother sank to her knees in the snow. "Please," Brenda Kicking Woman moaned.

"Talk to your Sheriff Laurendeau," Thor told her. "He's the one can make this easy. Here's how it's going to go. Dawg brings the truck around. The missus and myself and this one here"—Tina made a choking noise—"get in. And we leave. It's that simple."

Charlie gestured with his gun. "There's nothing simple about it. No, I take it back. There's one simple thing. You'll be caught in a New York minute."

Thor's laugh seemed entirely genuine. "But we're not in New York. This is Dakota. I'm the nearest law in two hours. By the time any of 'em get here, we're long gone."

Charlie shook his head. "But I'm right here. What's to stop me from tailing you? And even if I didn't, they'd get you at the border."

"I'll tell you what to stop either of those things." The voice was Charlotte's. She moved from the kitchen past Lola to stand in the doorway behind her husband. Lola's head still throbbed, but had cleared considerably.

"This girl here," Charlotte said. "She'll stop them. Thor. Make her quit sniveling."

Thor lifted the gun and rapped Tina's head before jamming it back against her temple.

"Please!" Tina's mother screamed.

"Pay attention." Charlotte again. She shoved her hands into her apron pockets and rounded her shoulders against the cold. "If you follow us," she said to Charlie, "this one dies. We get stopped at the border, this one dies. We get stopped ten miles inside Canada, this one dies. We get stopped as we're boarding an airplane, any airplane going any place—you get the picture."

Charlie's knuckles were white against the dull black of his service weapon. "You can't keep her forever."

"We can keep her long enough. You'll get a phone call from her. That's when you'll know we're gone and you can come pick her up."

Tina's mother fell, hands clawing at the snow as though somewhere beneath it lay the answer to an impossible situation. Charlie's voice was very tired. "How do we know that you just won't kill her anyway?"

Charlotte chortled. "You don't." She moved closer still to her husband, slid one hand from her apron pocket and rested it on Thor's shoulder in wifely support. "But what's the alternative? Come after us and she dies for sure." She kneaded her fist into her husband's shoulder. "Honey," she said. "You're so tense. Relax. Everything's going to be fine."

Lola held her breath throughout the exchange. Everyone seemed to have forgotten about her. Charlotte adjusted her chubby hand yet again, just below Thor's shoulder, largely out of sight from the people standing frozen in place in front of the trailer. Something poked from Charlotte's fist, something small and round and silver. Popguns, Charlie had derided them. Ladies like them, he'd told Lola, because they're small. Cute. It's the only gun his mother would carry. But you've got to be entirely too close to do any damage, he'd told her, and you'd better shoot straight because accuracy isn't their strong suit.

Charlotte's hand wormed around, getting the best aim on Charlie, who stood only ten paces away. Maybe fifteen. Close enough, Lola thought, even for the Saturday night special that Charlotte had retrieved from Lola's coat. Charlotte's hand stopped moving. She'd found her sight line.

Lola lunged, swinging as she stood, pouring all her strength into a single fluid motion, the branding iron splitting the back of Charlotte's head, the shot meant for Charlie soaring wild into the winter sky.

CHAPTER FORTY-FIVE

Lola hung in the trailer's doorway, clutching at the jamb for support, looking out over a crime scene that consisted of a dead woman in the bloody snow, a suspect whose wrists were so large Charlie abandoned his metal cuffs in favor of a triple wrapping of the plastic ones, and a traditionally cuffed sheriff—who'd lost his grip on his own gun when his wife's body slammed into him—cursing in the back of Charlie's cruiser. Not to mention a half-dozen hysterical girls and the aunties and uncles, and onlookers forming a crowd that grew deeper and closer by the moment. Lola eased down the trailer steps and stood at their base, Bub plastered against her legs, and let Charlie sort it out.

He spoke first to Alice Kicking Woman, as was proper. "It'd be best if you and these young ladies and their mothers could please wait in the van." He pointed to the coats the woman had shed into the snow when they began their dance. "The girls need those coats more than you do right now. Roy can turn up the heat in the van on high. I'd grab some blankets from the trailer, too, but it's a crime scene now."

Nancy deRoche fairly spat the words at him: "I wouldn't go back into that trailer if I was frostbitten from my head to my ass."

Charlie almost smiled. "I can appreciate that." He stepped back and held out his arm to help Alice up the van's steps. "The van, then."

Even though Nancy and the other girls were the most lightly clad, they stood back and waited as Alice and then their mothers clambered into the van's lifesaving warmth, centuries of tribal politesse trumping the modern insults of the moment. The uncles milled around outside, casting dark looks whose intent left nothing to the imagination toward Thor and Dawg. Each time Dawg made as though to move, Charlie swung his gun toward him.

"These women need hot food. I need you all to go find some—coffee, soup, whatever you can—and bring it back to them," Charlie suggested. No one moved. "*Now*. Your wives and daughters need your attention more than these pieces of nothing." Joshua stood rooted, but the others moved off muttering toward their assigned task. Charlie raised his voice so that the lookie lous, who had swarmed again from their units at the sound of the shot, could hear. "I'll need you all to step back and give us some room. We may need to collect some evidence from this area. And I'll need to take statements from anyone who watched this go down. All of you who took any photos or videos on your cellphones, don't even think about deleting them. But if any of you have some coats or blankets you could share with these young ladies and their mothers—" He looked stone-eyed at men who no doubt had availed themselves of the girls' forced services. Finally, a few ducked their heads and shuffled their feet in the snow and then returned to their own trailers, emerging with arms full of warm clothing. Charlie handed the heap into the van except for one thin blanket, which he used to conceal the mess that was Charlotte's head. Next he turned his attention to Dawg, sitting in the snow, straining unsuccessfully against the plastic binding his wrists behind him. Lola watched his gaze move from Dawg to the cruiser and back again. Dawg's lips and fingers had gone beyond blue to a blackish-purple. It would be dangerous, Lola knew, for him to spend much more time in the snow. But Charlie didn't dare put him in the cruiser with Thor. Charlie's gaze swept the crowd, alighting on Joshua. "I'm deputizing you. That okay?"

Joshua snapped to attention. Lola thought he might salute. Charlie unlocked the cruiser's trunk, removed a rifle and handed it to Joshua. "Take him to the guard shack and keep him there," he told Joshua. "If he tries to run—and I mean if he so much as eyeballs you funny—take him down."

Joshua turned the gun over twice in his hands. Then he waved it in Dawg's direction. "You heard him." Dawg struggled to his feet and found his balance, quickly ahead of Joshua, his boots leaving triangle-studded tracks in the snow.

Lola knelt and buried her hands in Bub's fur. Charlie turned.

"Lola."

"Hey, Charlie."

And then, to her horror, the world went aslant. If only she hadn't dropped the branding iron, she thought. It could have kept her upright. But the branding iron was gone and she was falling, fast, too fast to even put her arms out to keep her face from bashing into the polished granite surface of the snow.

Lola came to in the van, stretched out across the long seat in the back. She heard a commotion and tried to lift her head. Pain wiggled its knife between her eyes.

"Put your head back down." Jan stood over her with a handful of snow. She packed it onto Lola's forehead. The girls and aunties crowded close behind. "Don't move."

"Oh," Lola moaned. "That feels good. Good being relative at this point."

"Don't talk, either." Jan glared down at her through tears. "Don't you think you've caused enough trouble?"

At the sight of the tears, something coiled within Lola loosened. She and Jan were going to be all right. "How'd you find this place?" she murmured.

Josephine pushed her way past the others to stand next to Jan. "A menu for Mama's was in Judith's pocket. Charlie showed it around last night, asked if it meant anything to anyone. It didn't take a rocket scientist to figure it out, especially given that Jan had told us you were staying with 'Mama' Brevik. Only problem was, we didn't put it all together until late. It took awhile to round up everyone. We left about four this morning."

It took me long enough to put it together, Lola thought. But then, no one had hurled "dark meat" epithets her way for half her life. She pushed away the thought and tried to take satisfaction in the fact that Charlie had taken Judith and the missing girls seriously after all. He just hadn't wanted her to know it. But why had the women preceded Charlie to Mama's? She wondered as much aloud.

"He didn't know we were coming," Jan volunteered when no one else said anything. "The aunties decided on their own to see if the girls were there, and to bring them home. They thought it would be easier on everyone if the whole thing were on the down low. The idea was that the dance would shame whoever had them into letting them leave."

It might have worked, Lola thought, if they'd been dealing with people who had even a shred of shame. Which Thor and Charlotte didn't.

"And you just happened to be with them?"

Jan's response was oblique. "I heard they were going."

From Joshua no doubt, Lola thought. She ventured a guess. "So you just showed up and hitched a ride with them." Taking advantage of the fact that the aunties would never have been rude enough to turn her away. That, and they probably wouldn't consider that even though they'd all known Jan from childhood, her determination to be on that bus likely stemmed at least as much from her pursuit of a story than those lifelong friendships. Melting snow trickled down Lola's temples. Her head felt better. She started to sit up again. This time, her stomach rebelled. She turned on her side, retching toward the floor. "Sorry," she gasped when the spasms ended. "I think I picked up a bug while I was here."

Josephine put her hands to Lola's shoulders and gently pushed her back down. "You just rest. And don't worry. It goes away after a couple of months."

"A couple of *months*?" Lola tried once again to sit up. Josephine increased the pressure on her shoulders. Smiles flitted among the women.

"Oh, dear child," Josephine said. "Don't you know you're pregnant?"

CHAPTER FORTY-SIX

Five miles passed. Ten. Twenty. Lola sat small beneath the weight of the silence within the cruiser, the only sounds the roar and fade of passing trucks, the whomp of snow against the side of the car followed by the thunk of wiper blades to clean the cruiser's begrimed windshield. The horizon fled before them, level as a chalked string snapped against the sky. Lola sneaked an occasional sidelong glance at Charlie. But his jaw remained set, hands clenched around the wheel, gaze drilling straight ahead. It had taken more than two hours for a contingent of highway patrolmen and federal agents and sheriffs from neighboring counties to make their way to Burnt Creek and take Thor and Dawg into custody. The women and their daughters were long gone by that point.

"You can't leave," Charlie had protested as they prepared to go. "Someone will need to take their statements. And the girls should be checked out at the clinic here."

"We have our own clinic on the reservation. After what they've been through, another day isn't going to make a bit of difference." Josephine moved aside so Alice could come forward. Smart move, Lola thought. Charlie would never dare disagree with an elder.

Alice's lips worked soundlessly while she gathered enough breath to force the words. "We're taking our girls home. They can give their statements there—if they feel like it."

"I'll ride home with them," Jan said into the hush. Lola wondered how long it would take Jan to pull out her notebook.

"Me, too," Lola said.

"No, you won't," Charlie said. "You're coming with me."

Jan raised her eyebrows and whistled soundlessly. "Good luck," she mouthed to Lola. She grabbed the handle on the side of the van and swung herself inside just before the door closed. Charlie hadn't spoken to Lola since.

Bub lay across Lola's lap, sleeping so deeply that even his legs, which usually paddled ceaselessly during his dreams, were still. At some point, a man from one of the trailers had emerged with a paper plate of roast beef. "That dog's been hanging around for a couple of days," he said, in the elongated syllables of the bayou. "Might be it's a bit peaked." He returned with a second plate, heaped higher still, when he saw how quickly Bub inhaled the first. Lola drummed her fingers lightly against Bub's distended belly. "Who told you?" she said, as though she and Charlie had been chatting all along.

"What do you mean?" Each word distinct, bitten off. Not so much as a glance her way.

"Jan?" It would be just like Jan, she thought. Give the women enough of a head start toward Burnt Creek, then make a surreptitious call to Charlie, maybe while they made a rest stop. Jan would have wanted the law on hand to deal with the two hundred ways the women's plan might have gone awry, not to mention the fact that Charlie's presence would mean maximum drama, and an even better story.

"Nobody told me." Lola flinched at Charlie's harsh tone. Bub quivered, opened a single sleepy eye, then breathed deeply and fell back asleep.

"Then how did you know to come here?"

"Bub."

The dog groaned and raised his head, his displeasure clear at being forced to pay attention yet again. Lola stroked him back toward slumber. "What about Bub?"

"I got a call. From a security guard, actually. He said the dog had been hanging around the man camp and he finally caught him. He called you first and then, when he couldn't raise you, called me."

That part, at least, made sense, Lola thought. Both their phone numbers were on Bub's tags.

"So I came out here to pick him up. I knew that if you weren't with him, something was wrong." The ice in his voice cracked, betraying the hours of tension.

"But." Lola struggled to fit the pieces together. "You knew to come to the trailer."

"I didn't." He slammed a fist into the dash. The cruiser swerved. A semi blared its bullfrog horn. Bub was barking before he was fully awake, wobbling on his three legs before finding his balance in Lola's lap. She steadied him as Charlie straightened the car. She counted to ten—she peeked at Charlie—then to twenty before venturing another question, softening it to a statement just before she spoke.

"You had the siren going when you pulled up. I thought—" She left it to him to fill in the blanks.

The quiver in Charlie's voice spread to the corners of his mouth. Bub kept a wary eye on him. "It was because of the dog again. When the security guard handed him over to me, he bolted. Ran right through the man camp. I jumped in the car to follow him and put the siren on when he turned a corner. Didn't want to run over some poor roughneck out for a stroll. Imagine my surprise when I saw Josephine and the rest of them."

Lola imagined. Chasing a dog through a foreign landscape one minute, coming upon his own people the next. Tiny Alice Kicking Woman moving her frozen feet in intricate dance steps. The long-gone girls, tacitly acknowledged as dead, pouring alive from the trailer. Thor at the door with a gun to Tina's head. His girlfriend's voice calling to him from within.

She reached for him. He shuddered away. She dropped her hand.

"We shouldn't talk until we get back and somebody can take your statement." He'd regained control of his voice.

Lola matched her own to its flatness. "Fine." She tried to relax against the seat. It probably wasn't the best time, she decided, to ask him about the child Charlotte had alluded to, let alone to say anything about Josephine's impromptu diagnosis of her nausea. She closed her eyes and slid her hand inside her sweater and felt the flatness of her belly and did math in her head. Until she'd started getting sick to her stomach, she'd had none of the usual signs. Josephine was flat wrong, she told herself. There was no way she could be pregnant.

CHAPTER FORTY-SEVEN

Lola sat on the edge of the tub in Jan's apartment and stared at mocking blue plus signs, a half-dozen of them. The previous day, she'd driven to all the towns within a fifty-mile radius and bought a pregnancy test from every drugstore or grocery store clerk she didn't recognize. She'd waited until Jan called an entirely too cheerful good-bye to the neighbor who rented the other half of the bungalow, and then spent hours drinking water and peeing and watching as one "positive" sign after another emerged. Then she simply sat and cursed under her breath.

"Holy shit." This time, the cursing wasn't in her head. Jan stood in the doorway of a bathroom so small it was possible to stand in the tub and touch all four walls. Lola grabbed the trash-can and swept the sticks into it. Too late. Jan's eyebrows climbed high. "Why'd you go and waste all that money on tests? Josephine already called it."

Lola tried going on the offensive. "What are you doing here?"

"Take it easy. For starters, I live here. Besides, I brought you lunch." Jan held up a paper bag that wafted scents of grease and burnt meat. With her other hand, she waggled a cup. "Milkshake, too. Figured you needed a calcium boost. Under the circumstances."

But for a too-lengthy visit to the local clinic to get her broken nose examined and reset, and then her circumnavigation of the county in search of pregnancy tests, Lola had been at Jan's ever since her return to Burnt Creek two days earlier. Charlie didn't give her a choice. "Whatever problems you two have, work it out," he'd said over her protests when he'd pulled up outside Jan's place. "I can't have you staying with me until this investigation's done."

Now Lola reached for the distraction of food. "I'm starving," she said around a mouthful of cheeseburger. The next minute found her heaving over the toilet.

"Dammit. I spent good money on that food. Hate to see it go to waste." Jan reached over Lola and flushed, then took Lola's place on the edge of the tub and picked up the burger and took a bite. Lola turned away and groaned.

"Do you have to eat that in front of me?"

Jan took another bite. "At least the room's got the right color scheme." Jan's bathroom was from a bygone era, its fixtures powder blue, the tiles pale pink. "Maybe I can hold a baby shower for you in here."

Lola scooted on her bottom until she was in the hallway, putting a little distance between herself and the smell of food. "I can't be pregnant."

Jan nudged the trashcan with her foot. The test sticks rattled within. "All evidence to the contrary."

"But we always took precautions."

Jan licked a bit of ketchup from her finger. She crossed her legs and jiggled a cowboy boot. "Always? Every single time?"

"Well. When we needed to."

Jan pointed a french fry at Lola. "There you have it. Half the girls in my high school class ended up pregnant because they thought they were safe that week. I thought you were smarter than that."

Lola took a deep breath. In the space of a single split second, her stomach traded queasy for ravenous. "Hand over that milkshake." She slurped her way to the bottom of the cup. "Did you eat all of the fries?"

"Yes."

Lola took the bag and ran her finger around the bottom, feeling for fragments. "Were you ever going to tell me about Charlie's kid?"

Jan nearly lost her balance on the edge of the tub. "What are you talking about?"

Lola wondered how long she'd have to live in Magpie before people stopped treating her like an idiot. "I know about him. Or her. Which is it, anyway? Charlotte told me while I was in Burnt Creek. I can't believe Charlie never said anything to me."

Jan wadded up the empty food bag and threw it into the trashcan. "You two need to work on your communication, along with your birth control. But maybe the reason he never said anything is that there is no other kid."

Lola pushed herself up from the floor and splashed cold water on her face, taking care to avoid the unwieldy bandaging on her nose. She brushed her teeth and considered the possibility that Jan was telling the truth. "Why would Charlotte say that?"

"Possibly because, at least from what you've told me, the woman was a stone lying bitch. But maybe Thor ran into Charlie at one of those sheriff's conventions when Charlie was taking care of his niece. His brother's girlfriend had a baby awhile back and then ran off and left him and the baby, too. Navajo girl. Don't know what she was doing all the way up here. Anyhow, Charlie took the baby in for a while when his brother went down to Arizona to try and patch things up. Must have worked out because they're there still, the baby, too. Although I guess she's not a baby anymore."

"Stop saying baby." Lola kicked the trashcan. Her stomach performed an ominous, slow-motion revolution. "I need air." She rushed to the porch. But the bracing gulps of subzero air she expected eluded her. Slush sprayed from a passing car. Water dripped from the porch eaves. A soft breeze slid past. Lola lifted her face to it and slitted her eyes against a sun that had emerged full strength from wherever it had been hiding for weeks on end. "What's going on? Everything's melting. It's so warm."

"I know." Jan followed her out onto the porch, straddled the railing, grabbed one of the supports and leaned far over the melting yard to catch the sun. Bub lay on the newly bare sidewalk a few feet away, sprawled to soak up maximum warmth. "It was ten degrees this morning. I'll bet it's sixty now. Warmer, maybe. It's a Chinook."

Lola braced her hands on the railing and leaned out beside her. "Whatever a Chinook is, I like it. I can't remember the last time I was really warm. Does this mean it's spring?"

"Hah. We've got weeks and weeks of winter left. It'll get cold again. But not as cold, and not for as long. We'll get a warm day here, a warm day there. One day we'll wake up and the snow will be gone and the whole prairie will have gone green—"

"—as Ireland. So I've been told. But I don't believe it."

Jan held out her hand to catch the droplets of melting snow from the porch roof. She touched her tongue to her palm. "I wonder if I should be doing this. Used to be snow water was the sweetest. But now with the crap spewing into the air from the patch, there's probably all sorts of pollutants in this. What are you going to do?"

Lola rocked forward, leaning farther still over the yard. "About pollution?"

"Don't be coy. You know what about. And be careful. If you fall and hurt yourself, you might not have anything to be coy about." Lola straightened and stood. Her hand went, seemingly of its own volition, to her stomach. "Huh," said Jan. "There's a telling move. Are you going to keep it?"

Lola snorted. She touched the bandage that felt as though it covered half her face. Her nose hurt. "That would be crazy. I'm not exactly the maternal type. I don't even know if Charlie and I are together anymore. I can barely take care of myself and Bub, let alone a baby. Besides, there's probably something wrong with it. I got beat up. And Charlotte gave me some sort of drug."

"Babies are tough. My mom rodeoed while she was pregnant with me and my sister, right about 'til when we popped. Besides, Indian people aren't big believers in abortion. There aren't enough of them. Did you know there aren't even twenty thousand Blackfeet?"

"I'm not an Indian." Lola pointed out the obvious. She clasped her hands behind her back, to keep them from straying again to her abdomen.

"But that baby is. Or at least, a descendant."

"It's not a baby. It's just a blob. What's a descendant?"

Jan's pocket buzzed. She pulled out her phone. "Damn. Jorkki's on me to write a story about the Chinook. And he wants to know when you're coming back to work. Want me to tell him you're still too traumatized?"

"Descendants," Lola reminded her.

Jan tapped a text into the phone. "Why don't they make an emoticon that looks like a middle finger? Anyhow, a descendant is anyone who's less than twenty-five percent Blackfeet. Some people want descendants admitted to the tribe. Some don't. The blood quantum people will figure out which your baby is. They've got it down to a science."

Lola smacked a porch support. "Stop calling it a baby. And stop acting as though anybody has a say in this other than me."

Jan swung back down onto the porch, her boots clattering against the boards. "At least one person does."

A cloud scooted across the sun. The temperature took a nosedive. Lola crossed her arms over her chest. "Charlie."

Jan gnawed at the end of her braid. "When do you think you might get around to telling him?"

The cloud kept moving, the Chinook triumphing. But Lola was still cold.

"Now," she said. "I'm going to tell him now."

CHAPTER FORTY-EIGHT

When Lola had first moved to Montana, she'd wondered at the way houses sat hard by the roads, entirely too close for her taste to the admittedly sparse traffic. Once the snows started, daily layering driveways, she understood. Charlie's place was an anomaly, well off the road at the end of a curving lane. In addition to his cruiser, he kept a geriatric pickup that seemed largely held together by Bondo, but that served its sole purpose of pushing a snow blade. Lola parked her car next to the truck, its raised blade gleaming in the sun, and looked around for Charlie.

She saw the Appaloosa first, tied up outside the corral, the winter's accumulation of grit brushed from his coat. Despite his winter shagginess, Spot looked newly sleek, stamping a forefoot in anticipation of the ride, the first one in months, that apparently awaited. Bub soared from the truck and ran to him. Spot lowered his head and they touched noses, the horse nickering in the back of his throat, Bub's body a wriggling blur.

Charlie came out of the shed, a bridle in his hand. He stopped when he saw Lola. "I was going to call you."

Lola liked the sound of that. "I need to talk to you, too. What's going on?"

"I thought I'd take advantage of the Chinook, take Spot for a ride. He could use the exercise." But he draped the bridle over the fence, and turned toward the house. A deep porch wrapped it on three sides, populated by fast-dwindling stacks of firewood—and, on this day, a pyramid of taped and dated cardboard boxes. Lola recognized them. She'd packed them herself, when she'd decided to leave the newspaper in Baltimore and take a chance on a new life in Magpie. She didn't recognize one of the boxes. He'd have assembled that one himself, she guessed, filling it with the contents of her single dresser drawer, the few pieces of clothing she'd hung in the closet, the handful of things from her side of the medicine cabinet.

Her mouth went cottony. "What's this?"

Charlie's hands hung by his side. Lola wanted to go to him, take those hands, wrap his arms around her. She'd always felt safe, protected, in his embrace. She'd never wanted to admit to that, not to herself and definitely not to Charlie. She took a step toward him. His eyes warned her away.

"Charlie?"

"Lola. You saved my life back there in Burnt Creek. Don't think I'm not grateful. But you don't base a relationship on gratitude. We both know this wasn't working. It hit me after you left. Your being gone wasn't a whole lot different than your being here. Look at your things—you hardly unpacked anything from home, and the few things you did barely filled a whole box. You have no concept of relationships, of family." He fussed with the bridle, arranging the reins so they wouldn't fall into the snow. He had to know about the baby, Lola thought; almost certainly had amassed quite the collection of voicemails and texts and e-mails from people vying to be the first to let him know his girlfriend was pregnant.

Lola had practiced casual, confident phrases on the drive over from Jan's. *Don't worry. I'll take care of it.* Or, maybe, *I've made an appointment at the clinic in Missoula.* She hadn't. But she would. Now those phrases fled. "You know why I'm here."

He shook his head. "I don't. I told you to stay at Jan's, not to contact me. But you didn't listen. Again." He leaned over the fence and slapped Spot on the flank. "Go on. Git. There's not going to be any ride for a while." Spot sulked away, ears pinned back against his head, Bub gamboling beside him.

Fine, Lola thought. If he wanted to pretend he didn't know, she'd go along. She fell back on work. "Has Jan set up an interview with you yet?"

"You know I can't talk to you about this. Either of you."

Lola wasn't surprised. "Doesn't matter, really," she said. "Jan and I can get your part from the court documents."

"What documents are you talking about?"

In her work, Lola frequently played dumb. She didn't appreciate it when someone turned the tables on her. "Oh, come on. The incident reports, the complaints, the affidavits. Even if you strip them down to the bare minimum, the charging documents will be a gold mine."

"What charges?" Charlie stood with his back to the bright sun, his face in shadow. Lola couldn't see his eyes.

"I figure rape, at a minimum. Aggravated assault. Drug possession—even if Charlotte came by that stuff legally, it wasn't supposed to leave the clinic—and trafficking. Kidnapping, for sure. And taking the girls across state lines, that's federal."

A muscle jumped in Charlie's jaw. "And negligent homicide. Don't forget that."

Lola struggled to remain impassive. He must have decided Judith had been murdered after all. "Dawg, right?" she said. "How did he do it? Was it a deliberate drug overdose? Or did he just beat her the way he did DeeDee? Because I'm sure he killed her, too. Was Judith dead before she ended up in that snowbank? Have you told Joshua yet?" She stopped. She couldn't pinpoint the expression on Charlie's face; knew only that somehow she was on the wrong track.

"Not Dawg," he said. "You."

The world stopped. Lola couldn't hear her own question. But she heard Charlie's answer.

"For killing Charlotte."

For once Lola wished she could throw up. It would have provided a distraction. As it was, she stood staring at Charlie, waiting for him to tell her he was joking. Which, after a pause that lasted entirely too long, he did. Sort of.

"It's something that had to be considered," he said. "They took my word that it was self-defense."

Lola took two steps and latched onto a corral post for support. "Of course it was."

He lifted a shoulder. "All scenarios had to be considered."

"What about Thor and Dawg? And Finch, too? What are they being charged with?"

"Well." Charlie rubbed his toe across the melting snow, revealing the sparse, frozen grass beneath. "That's a problem. Finch, especially. His part's pretty nebulous. Pretty sure he's the courier and the special customer, too, but none of the girls saw who took them from the reservation. And for sure nobody's identifying him as the special customer, although it makes sense. Maybe Dawg or Thor will dime him out, but I don't have much hope. Dawg's easier. He's on the run from charges in about a half-dozen states. They're all fighting, each trying to push him off the other, because nobody wants the cost of jailing him and prosecuting him. We might be able to go after him for that poor trucker. The boot prints match, for starters. Although other states have stronger cases." He moved his foot in a circle, uncovering more grass.

"And Thor?"

"That's problematic, too." He sounded so tired, so uncharacteristically embittered, that most of Lola's fear and anger drained away. "But I'll let you find out for yourself why. Come on. Let's get this stuff into the truck."

Lola, numb, walked behind him in the strip of grass. He led her to the porch and handed her a box. He stacked another box atop a third and lifted them both. It took less time to load them than she'd thought. Charlie stood by, a hand on the pickup's hood. He had to know, she thought. He'd just been bluffing.

"You're wrong," Lola said. Her voice wobbled. She cleared her throat. "What you said awhile ago about family. I do have a concept of family. More than just a concept." There. She'd given him an opening.

He slapped the hood. "You take care of yourself, Lola. You and—"

She held her breath. So he did know. Which meant there was no way he'd let her drive away. As long as he stopped her, she could forgive him the bluff. He cleared his throat. "You and Bub," he said. "I'll miss him." He whistled. Bub, fur soaked and paws muddy, streaked beneath the corral fence and jumped into the truck, leaving tracks across the seat. Lola brushed at them, succeeding only in smearing dirt into the upholstery. She climbed in after Bub. Started the engine. Headed down the lane. The phrases she'd practiced on the way to Charlie's came back to her. *Don't worry. I'll take care of it. The clinic in Missoula . . .* She rested her hand on Bub's back until she stopped shaking. She tried out her voice. It, too, had lost its quiver. Good, she thought.

"Let's go back to Jan's and pack. How do you feel about a couple of days in the big city, Bub? Looks like we're headed to Missoula."

CHAPTER FORTY-NINE

Lola didn't recognize the car parked outside Jan's house. She assessed it—the sagging profile resulting from shocks defeated by too many years on too many gravel roads—and decided Jan's visitors were from the reservation. She hurried into the house, Bub at her heels, and confronted the lineup on Jan's futon.

Alice Kicking Woman sat in the middle, flanked by Tina and her mother, and Josephine and her niece, Nancy. In their regalia, slowly circling the trailer in the man camp, the women had been regal, powerful. Now, sleeplessness scribbled their faces. Distress bent their spines. Brenda and Josephine twined their girls' hands in their own, as though to release them would be to see Tina and Nancy disappear again.

Jan rose from a chair across the room, her face a warning. "Here's Lola now. We'll get coffee for everyone."

"What's going on?" Lola hissed as soon as they were in the kitchen. "Did you set up an interview without telling me? Are you trying to cut me out of this?"

"Don't go all preggo emo on me," Jan said. "They just showed up."

Lola thought of what Charlie had said. That the case was problematic. And that he'd let her discover how. She figured she was about to find out.

"Shit."

"What?" Jan paused with a cutting board that she'd pressed into service as a makeshift tray, mismatched coffee mugs balanced upon it.

"I've got a bad feeling. Let's get this coffee ready." She and Jan worked wordlessly, Lola making the coffee while Jan opened and shut cupboard doors, finally emerging with a package of Oreos. "You had Oreos?" Lola whispered. Jan wiped dust from the package with a paper towel before opening it and arranging the fossilized contents on a plate. Lola turned the wrapper over to check the sell-by date, but Jan shook her head. "Doesn't matter. They're all I've got."

Both Lola and Jan took their coffee black. Lola took a quart of milk from the back of the refrigerator, opened it, sniffed, then shoved it even farther back into the fridge. Jan scrabbled around the same cupboard that had yielded the cookies until she found a can of condensed milk. She shoved a sugar canister toward Lola, who chipped at the crystallized surface, digging through to the soft stuff beneath, shoveling it into a soup bowl. Lola thought of the times she'd showed up unannounced at Josephine's house, at the way home-baked rhubarb bread or steaming bowls of stew, thick with chunks of beef or venison, miraculously appeared. Lola procrastinated in the kitchen, lingering over the thought that for all the difficulties of the women's lives—husbands away for weeks in the oil patch, girls gone missing, the unrelenting grind of reservation poverty—they somehow managed orderly households. Whereas she and Jan, with their adequate incomes and no one else to care for but themselves, seemed stuck in some sort of slipshod dorm room time warp. Lola had looked through Jan's underpopulated cupboards and seen the packets of ramen noodles there. She knew they had more to do with ease than thrift. Since moving in with Charlie, who apparently cooked himself dinner every night and simply doubled the amount to include her, she'd gained weight. Or at least, she thought, rubbing her abdomen, she'd assumed that's why she'd gained weight.

Lola carried the cutting board into the living room and sat it on the carton of printer paper that served as Jan's end table. Jan followed with a clutch of spoons and a roll of paper towels. Lola went back into the kitchen and returned with the soup bowl of sugar and another mug full of the condensed milk. "I couldn't find a pitcher," she apologized.

Jan dragged another chair in from the kitchen. She and Lola sat facing the women. Sunlight spilled through the windows, highlighting the dust that furred the room's surfaces. The women doctored their coffee, the condensed milk running down the sides of the mugs as they poured it, splattering onto the printer-paper carton, raising damp blisters. They stirred in sugar with great solemnity. No one spoke. Alice raised her mug to her withered lips, blew across the coffee, and took a sip. Everyone else followed suit.

"Please," said Jan. "Have a cookie."

Alice picked up one of the Oreos and gummed it. She sat it back down on the edge of the plate. It showed no appreciable damage. Josephine, who had reached for one, withdrew her hand. Lola wondered if it would be rude if she took one—or three—for herself. Her stomach rumbled audibly.

"Why don't you tell Lola what you started to tell me?" Jan said to the women.

Josephine looked to Alice, who nodded permission. "You two are planning to do a story," Josephine began.

Lola spoke quickly into the pause. Best to halt Josephine's objections before they started. "Naturally. What happened here—people kidnapping these girls, using them the way they did while the law not only looked the other way but actively participated—it's outrageous." She'd hoped for a murmur of assent, but the women sat still and silent. Her stomach, so recently emptied, issued another demand for food. She grabbed a cookie and bit into it, then ran her tongue across her teeth to see if she'd chipped one. She submerged the cookie in her coffee and tried again. It was better, just. She chewed and chewed.

Josephine put a hand to her forehead and patted a stray hair back into place. Lola doubted Josephine had had a full night's sleep since boarding the van for the man camp days earlier. Yet her beehive towered as stately as ever, and she'd drawn on her eyeliner and applied her lipstick with a steady, sure hand. Josephine was singlehandedly credited with bringing years of slipshod, even felonious, tribal bookkeeping back into legality because, it was said, even the most corrupt tribal officer feared her wrath far more than any penalty the IRS might impose. Now she turned that wrath—contained, but only just—upon Lola.

"There will not be any story about our girls."

CHAPTER FIFTY

Lola sprayed cookie crumbs and coffee. Jan tore a paper towel from the roll. Lola took it and blotted her mouth and chin and dabbed at the front of her sweater. "Why not?"

"These girls." Tina's mother spoke this time, her voice shaking with strain. "What they went through. You know what people say about them already. And that's without even knowing the details."

Lola didn't have to ask what she meant. The *Daily Express*, like so many newspapers, provided a place on its website for people to comment on stories, a feature that, as far as Lola could tell, attracted nothing but bottom-feeders. She envisioned armies of brooding resentful men, bedeviled by dandruff and ear wax, skin like damp dough lapped over on itself in multiple layers, hunched in white cotton underwear gone grey, typing vileness into the night. No sooner had the story about Tina's disappearance gone online than the comments had begun. "Sl*t probably ran off with a white guy," was one of the few that actually made it past the profanity filters by dint of its sneaky asterisk. "I'm sorry about the comments," she said. "Try not to read them. I keep asking Jorkki to take them down, but the marketing guy says we have to do it."

Brenda Kicking Woman waved her hand. "It's not just that. Our daughters need to heal. It's going to be hard enough without this being in the public eye. You helped get them out of there. You know what they went through. Do you want to be responsible for even more damage to them? Do you know what people are calling them? Oil patch pussy." Despite eyes filling with tears, she fixed Lola with a look. Tales of her red pen abounded. Mrs. Kicking Ass, her students called her behind her back.

Lola put down her coffee and leaned forward. "Don't you see? It's only by exposing it that we put a stop to things like this, save other girls from the same ordeal." That old line.

Brenda Kicking Woman's left eyebrow arched high. "Really? A story in the *Daily Express* is going to put a stop to prostitution in boomtowns? Do you know what Charlie told me?"

Lola was afraid to ask. Brenda told her anyway. "That what was going on in Burnt Creek is the least of it. That up in Williston, they've got big-time cartels moving in, bringing in drugs and girls from all over the country, even from out of the country. The local cops and the feds both are running themselves ragged trying to deal with it. How much time do you think they're going to invest in one penny-ante operation? That sheriff out there might never get half of what's coming to him."

"Which makes it even more important that the story be told. Burnt Creek is like the tip of the iceberg. The canary in the coal mine." Lola bit her tongue before another cliché could escape. "That's why you have to talk to us."

"We don't have to do a goddamn thing," Nancy broke in. "Sorry," she muttered before Josephine could rebuke her for impermissible rudeness. Nancy's voice was strong, her eyes clear. She'd be all right, Lola thought. With a good rehab program and a few years beyond that, she'd be every bit as formidable as her aunt.

"I don't appreciate the way she phrased it, but Nancy's right," Josephine said. "Those cops filling in at Burnt Creek, now that the sheriff's gone, they've got better things to do with their time than to keep browbeating people who won't say a word."

"But what happens to Thor? He needs to be held accountable."

Josephine's laugh raised the hairs on the back of Lola's neck. "Oh, my dear." Josephine wiped her eyes. "Do you know what happens to white men who rape Indian girls?"

Lola thought back to the statistics she'd reviewed. "I do, unfortunately. Nothing."

Josephine slammed her empty coffee mug onto the cutting board with such force Lola wondered the cup didn't shatter. "That's right. Nothing."

Jan spoke into the corrosive silence. "He might never face a single charge in connection with this. But believe you me, everybody knows what he did. That's the thing about small towns." Lola thought of the way news zipped around the reservation and figured things weren't much different in Burnt Creek. "He'll never work in law enforcement again," Jan said. "And he won't be able to get back in the sex trade, either. Word gets around there, too. He'd be viewed as too much of a liability. I wouldn't be surprised if he ended up as a roustabout. That's its own punishment."

Taking away a person's livelihood, especially when the line of work was as much an identity as a means of support, was indeed punishment, Lola thought. Like taking away a story. She had one last hope. "Tina?"

The girl had been leaning against her mother, face pressed into Brenda's shoulder. She pulled herself upright.

"You want to be a journalist," Lola said. "All that talk about sunlight in dark places—this is it. What you went through, that's about as dark as a place gets."

Brenda started to speak. Tina squeezed her hand to stop her. "Please, Mom. I understand why you want to do it," she said to Lola and Jan. "And if it were just me, I might say go ahead. But it's not just me. It's my elders, my mother, my aunties, my cousins. My family. My people. I can't hurt them beyond how they've already been hurt."

Lola dropped the appeal to civic duty. "Fine. You don't have to talk. But we were there. I saw it from the inside. Jan rode over with all of you. She can write what she saw. I can, too. We can write the story without having to talk to you at all. We won't name any of you, of course. We never name sexual assault victims. But we can still tell the story. Whether anybody gets prosecuted or not, there'll still be documents. They're public record. And there were plenty of witnesses. We can interview them. This is a story with national implications. We have to write it."

Lola elbowed Jan. "She's right," Jan said, none too convincingly. "Lola likes her national stories. *International.*" Jan's tone was mild, but Lola felt the sting of her words. Jan rarely missed an opportunity to tweak Lola about her former status as a foreign correspondent as compared to her job at the *Express*, especially on days when Jorkki would throw an agricultural story Lola's way. "My, oh, my," Jan would say. "I see coyote depredations are up again. How does fifteen chomped-on sheep compare to a suicide bombing?"

Tina raised her head. Looked Lola in the eye. "You'd do that? Write it even when we've asked you not to?"

Lola stared back and thought of everything the girl had seen in the last few days. Worse, of the things she'd imagined. Of the things she'd believed, with every reason, would happen to her. "There's no shame in it," Lola said. "Nothing happened to you. And the others, they were forced. There's no shame in it for anyone."

Alice's voice floated into the fray, a tiny croaking bird. "But people will say there is."

"Yes," Lola said. Stupid to pretend it was any other way.

"Don't you think our people have been shamed enough?" Alice asked. She hoisted her bent frame from the sofa and hobbled to Lola and put her hand on Lola's stomach. "Our people—and now, your people, too. You would do this to your own?" She pressed hard, as though feeling for the knot of cells relentlessly dividing within. "Would you?"

Lola took Alice's hand, meaning to remove it, but Alice grabbed hers tight and pressed it back against her belly.

"How does it feel," she asked Lola, "to be on the other side of the story?"

CHAPTER FIFTY-ONE

There were two routes to Missoula. One, the fastest and in winter, the safest, followed two-lane roads to the interstate, where state snowplow crews worked round the clock to keep a single lane in each direction free of drifts. The snow was different farther west, heavier, resistant to the wind that blew the powdery stuff around on the plains wherever it pleased. The other road, its treachery as breathtaking as its beauty, unspooled along the southern boundary of Glacier National Park—or Not-Glacier, as some people had taken to calling it, in a nod to the climate change quickly overriding the eponymous designation. Lola took the latter.

Safer in a way, she reasoned, to negotiate a road that demanded maximum attention, rather than one that would allow her to cruise along focusing on her own thoughts, which were darker than the patches of black ice on the pavement, more punishing than the north wind that sliced the Chinook into fragments of memory. Roadside signs warned of avalanches, falling rocks, unwary wildlife. Still, Lola's pitiless thoughts intruded. The past several days had amounted to little more than a litany of failure, she thought, with ever more additions to the list: Job questionable. Charlie gone. Story dead.

"Oh, and you, too." She tapped her stomach. She'd taken to talking to it, in much the same way she spoke to Bub. "Biggest fuckup of all. At least I can do something about you." It would be the first step in retrieving mastery over her life, she told herself. Then she lost control of the wheel.

One moment it was steady in her hand, the next it spun without regard for her attempts to wrestle it into submission. Someone intoned "Oh, no. Oh, no." She recognized the voice as hers. The truck tilted and righted itself and kept moving. A postcard vista of snow-capped lodgepole pines slid past, then whipped away as the truck rotated in the middle of the road. And then . . . stopped.

Bub scrambled from the floor and sniffed her up and down. Lola leaned against the seatbelt that had pinned her hard in place. It gave reluctantly. "I'm fine," Lola assured Bub, as well as herself. "I'm alive. We're all alive." And shocked herself by bursting into laughter, and then tears.

WITHOUT ITS lights, the black and white cruiser blended into the landscape. Lola thought maybe she'd been mistaken. But the apparition grew larger, definitively resolving itself into Charlie's car. Slowing. Pulling up beside her. Stopping.

The window slid down. "Lola." Charlie's voice shook.

Her own went steady in response. She lowered her window and repeated her mantra of moments before. "Charlie. It's okay. We're fine. We're all fine."

"All of you?"

"Yes."

"You—"

"Yes."

"Bub—"

"Yes."

"And?" The single word turned two-syllable as it escaped on a fearful sigh.

Lola thought her smile would crack her face. "You do know!"

Charlie's head fell forward onto the steering wheel, his voice muffled as he spoke into his heavy coat. "Only just now. I dropped off a load of firewood for Alice. Sometimes the propane truck is late getting out to her place. In weather like this, I wanted to make sure she had backup. She congratulated me." He raised his head.

Lola could just imagine it, the sly smile, the delicious telling, the savoring of being first with the news. Alice might be old, but she was far from saintly, taking mischievous enjoyment in besting those decades her junior.

"How'd you find me?"

"I ran into Jan on my way out to Alice's. She said you were going to Missoula for the day. Somehow I had a feeling you'd take the bad road. Wish I'd been wrong. But I'm glad I found you. What's taking you there on a day like this? Couldn't you wait for spring?"

Lola didn't have to tell him the truth. There were all kinds of perfectly good reasons to visit Missoula—to shop in an actual department store, catch an art film, eat in a tablecloth restaurant, drink an expertly shaken martini—and every last one of them justified the three-hundred-mile round-trip, especially in the stir-crazy days of winter. But she didn't have a chance to fashion a lie. He figured it out before she opened her mouth.

"The clinic. It's in Missoula. You were going to the clinic."

The movies, the restaurants! Lola tried to form her protest. Charlie held up his hand. "It's time for us to be straight with each other."

Lola thought that if she were honest with herself, let alone Charlie, it was long past time. "You didn't say anything when I stopped by. You didn't try to stop me from leaving. So I thought—"

"I didn't try to stop you because I don't play games. And I didn't know about the—" A reluctant delicacy kept him from saying the word.

Lola supplied it. Finally. "The baby."

"If you're calling it a baby, you're not going to Missoula." He waited for her to confirm it.

Wind gusted through the lodgepole pines, carrying snow from branches to ground, flakes sparkling as they sifted downward. A creek ran beside the road, its waters inky against the snow, hurrying over the rocks too fast to freeze. Beside it, an elk raised its head and calmly studied the truck and cruiser. A bit of black moss, dubbed witches' hair by the locals, fluttered from its many-branched antlers.

"No," Lola said. "Probably not."

"Why is there any probably to this?"

"Some guy—it had to be Dawg—beat me up in Burnt Creek. Kicked me in the stomach, among other places. And Charlotte injected me with some sort of drug. The baby might not be okay."

"That's what doctors are for. And these are decisions we'll make together. Because that's what families do."

Bub crawled across the seat into Lola's lap and stuck his head out the window. His tail brushed her face, back and forth.

"See?" said Charlie. "Bub knows I'm talking sense."

"Then we should go home," said Lola. Thrilling to the final word of the sentence. "All my boxes are still in the back of the truck."

"Figures," said Charlie. "This time we'll unpack them. All of them. Speaking of the truck, how is it?"

Lola pressed her toe to the accelerator. The engine purred.

"Sounds good," Charlie said. "I'll follow you back, just in case."

Lola gave the truck some more gas and turned the wheel. The truck moved sedately back into its lane. The cruiser moved behind her, albeit at a respectful distance. Charlie, looking out for his family. She wondered if they would marry. Then thought of Thor and Charlotte, of the sort of grotesquerie that marriage could become. That cloud-across-the-sky feeling came over her. But the sun still hung incandescent overhead, teasing its promise of springtime warmth. The roiling black clouds were within.

Glittering icy peaks etched their profiles against the hard blue sky like diamonds cutting glass. The mountains had nourished Charlie's people in the old days, provided the fat elk and mule deer that fed them through cruel winters, bestowed the snowmelt that replenished the rivers and creeks, and housed sacred spirits whose significance Lola didn't fully understand, even as she half-way accepted their existence. Her hand crept again to her belly.

"See those mountains? And beyond them, too—north of here, there's a tall flat one that stands all by itself. That's Chief Mountain, Ninahstako, the most sacred of all. Sinopah's over there with the others. Some people say she's the prettiest. She stands over Two Medicine Lake. And when you get big enough, I'll take you to

Pitamakan Falls. Pitamakan means Running Eagle. She was a warrior woman. Fierce and good. You'll need to be like her if you're a girl. And somehow I think you are. You're going to learn all about Pitamakan and Sinopah and everyone else, especially your own people, the Niitsitapi. I think that's how you say it. I don't know where your dad is going to fit into this equation yet, but you'll have him, along with lots of aunties and cousins and elders to show you the way. You—you and I—we've got more family than we're going to know what to do with. You're going to be just fine.

"And you know what? As long as you're fine, I'm going to be fine, too."